Book 1 in the Christmas Town series

Sometimes it takes a village to fall in love.

Eccentric, reclusive, socially awkward project designer Evan Myles doesn't date. Paying for sex with professionals is so much more efficient and suits his needs well enough. But when he's on assignment in rural Logan, Minnesota, for the Christmas Town project and a handsome stranger at the bar catches his attention, Evan decides it's time to break his rule. It doesn't matter that he's never so much as flirted before. It can't be that hard, can it?

Davidson Incorporated lead architect Terry Reid hasn't been hit on so clumsily in his life. Terry's the first to admit he's a neurotic Prince Charming, and he's kissed his share of frogs of both genders, but he's never met anyone quite like Evan Myles. Evan calls Terry by the wrong name, mistakes Terry for a simple construction worker, and picks apart his work as an architect. Despite this rough start, Terry is lured by the brilliance of Evan's ideas, his quirky personality, and once they're alone in Evan's cabin, the man's mad skills in bed. Yet Terry knows it takes more than a single night of passion to make a relationship work, and after so many failures, he's just not ready to try again.

Evan and Terry's path is strewn with stones neither of them can dislodge. Fortunately, they're not alone on the road to romance. They're in Christmas Town, home to matchmakers, meddlers, and more "fairy godfathers" than they could possibly know what to do with.

Most importantly, in Logan, Minnesota, happy ever after is guaranteed.

Heidi Cullinan, POB 425, Ames, Iowa 50010

Copyright © 2017 by Heidi Cullinan
Print ISBN: 978-1-945116-28-5
Edited by Sasha Knight
Cover by Kanaxa
Proofing by Lillie's Literary Services
Formatting by BB eBooks

www.heidicullinan.com

The Christmas Fling

Heidi Cullinan

for Abby

I was going to write you a cute holiday romance just the way you like, but it got a little kinky.

Story of my life.

Acknowledgments

Thanks to Sara, as always, for being my WhatsApp sounding board, but also for loving Levi with me and helping invent twin brother George. Thanks to Dan and Anna Cullinan for surviving this fall with me and for putting up with the hermit who lives in that office off the hall on the first floor of your house. Someday she'll come out and join the family again.

Thank you always, forever, from the bottom of my heart to my patrons for lighting candles, loving me, supporting me, and cheering me on, carrying me bodily over this finish line, especially Pamela Bartual, Rosie M, Tiffany Miller, Marie, Marie, Sarah Plunkett, and Sarah M.

Chapter One

EVAN MYLES REALLY should have included an escort clause in his employment contract.

When he said as much to his assistant Charlotte as they sat drinking together in his Northwoods cabin one Saturday evening, she laughed. "Okay, I'll bite. Why would you need an escort clause?"

"For the obvious reason, of course." Evan grabbed the bottle of wine in front of him and took a swig. "I haven't gone this long without sex since I entered puberty and learned what to do with my dick in the first place. This assignment isn't difficult, but it's endless. It's not fair I have to learn how to arrange for sexual companionship in such an environment on top of everything else."

"To be fair, *I* arrange for all your needs except personal hygiene." Charlotte cupped her chin thoughtfully, resting her elbow on the tabletop. She had a glass of wine in front of her, but she sipped it slowly, as usual. "Though I hadn't thought of the problem of your personal life. I mean, I knew you had escorts in Minneapolis, but I didn't realize you *only* had escorts."

"I wouldn't have the first idea how to arrange for a sexual relationship in any other manner." He glared at the label of the wine bottle. "I tried to use apps here to find men. It didn't work. I don't think there are very many gay people in Logan, Minnesota."

"Please. The place is swimming in gay, proportionally. They aren't even a thousand people in town and yet they have not one, not two, but *three* married gay couples, plus whatever it is you want to call Dale and his librarian. There's also the lesbian veterinarian who moved in earlier this summer, plus that bisexual farmer. Dale has that Rainbow group too, and it's getting so big they're talking about building a center. This place is so queer it generates its own rainbow."

Dale Davidson was the owner of Davidson Incorporated, the company in charge of the construction and promotion of Christmas Town in Logan. Evan liked Dale, and he understood Logan was important to his employer. That didn't mean Evan cared for the place, especially when it was causing him so much frustration. "The point is there are no gay men for me to *sleep with*." Evan stared balefully at the countertop. "It's been over two weeks now. I've never gone this long without having sex. I'm starting to be convinced I might die."

Charlotte gave him a long-suffering look.

Evan relented. "Very well, I understand I won't perish without sex. However, my creative performance has absolutely suffered, stuck up here all this time."

"You've put out some of your best work while you've been in Logan. Try again. I mean, it's okay to simply say you're horny and be done with it. I'm not going to judge. We can buzz down to the Cities for a weekend pass, get you laid, and be back by Monday. Dale's busy with Gabriel at the moment, but I'll leave him a message, tell him it was an Evan emergency."

"You're missing the point. I don't want to go to Minneapolis and get laid."

Raising her eyebrows, Charlotte tilted her head at him. "You're right, I did miss the point. Tell me again, and I'll listen harder."

Most people would say something like that and they'd be teasing Evan, but Charlotte never made fun of him. She was as refreshing as always. "Escorts aren't only sex workers. They provide companionship for me. Yes, I pay them for it, but it's a tidy arrangement, and it suits me. I miss that more than the sex. I don't think I can find that kind of situation up here."

"You didn't say that, though. You told me how you'd never gone this long without having sex."

Evan drank more wine. "Well, I was embarrassed."

Charlotte winked as she rubbed his arm. "You know, if you were a woman, I'd have seduced you a long time ago and made you mine."

"It wouldn't have worked. I prefer men, and we're both too dominant in bed." He frowned. "I assume you're dominant."

"Oh, I am. It also wouldn't matter that you prefer men. If I wanted you, I could win you."

Pushing the wine bottle away, Evan threw up his hands. "*How?* How can you be so good at seducing people you can win them over even if they aren't interested in you? I can't believe that's true."

"Believe it. I've dined like a *queen* in Christmas Town. All the so-called straight girls *loved* having one-night lesbian stands with the wicked lady from Minneapolis, especially when they heard what I could do with my tongue."

Evan considered this. "So I should let the straight men know I give incredible blow jobs?" He tried to imagine himself walking up to men in Logan and shuddered. "I couldn't do it. I haven't even left the cabin once since I got here. I hide in the basement when the cleaning people come, or whoever it is bringing the food."

"That would be Frankie Blackburn, one of Dale's good friends. He's a hair stylist formerly from the Cities who owns a salon on Main Street, but he's also married to a local lawyer, Marcus Gardner."

The sea of names and titles had leaked out of Evan's ears, with the wine to sail away on. "The point is I don't speak to regular strangers, let alone strangers I'd like to sleep with regularly."

"Strangers you'd like to sleep with are easier than regular strangers. That's Charlotte's hot tip number one."

Somehow Evan found this claim suspicious, but he wanted to believe. "How are they easier?"

"It's not much different than your escorts, to be honest, except you're not paying them. The exchange is that you promise them a good time instead of money."

Already Evan wasn't fond of this. "See, I've had a few escorts who admitted they'd see me for free, which sounded like dating. I told them it would lead to complications and declined."

"You're one in a million, Ev. I take it this means you give your escorts a good time either in bed or out of it?"

"They usually tell me I take some getting used to because I'm so blunt, but I'm a generous lover."

"See? All we need to do is give you a bit of polish and set you loose on Logan."

Evan was nervous simply thinking about it. "I don't know about that."

"I do." Charlotte clinked his bottle with her glass. "Drink a little more wine, and we'll head into town and people-watch at the bar. If you see someone you like, you can go in for a dry run. If you don't, we get you an emergency session with an escort for tomorrow and try again with the locals next week."

The idea of *trying with the locals* at all was so terrifying Evan wanted to skip to the emergency session here and now. Except he *did* need to set something up in Logan. He'd be here for several more weeks at least, and he'd be back up again at some point for another phase of the project. Even if he could bring up an escort, he could only bring one, and in his experience relying on one escort made things awkward.

Charlotte patted his leg. "Don't worry, honey. I'm going to be with you every step of the way. Well, up until you bring your catch of the day back to your luxury cabin and decide to show him your shower attachments. Okay?"

Evan nodded. "Okay."

"Right. Class is in session, genius boy. I'm going to teach you how to get laid no matter where you are. Ready to get schooled?"

"I'm ready," Evan said, though he wasn't confident in this plan in the slightest. Somehow he was sure what worked for Charlotte wouldn't come as easily to him.

TERRY REID HAD earned the pitcher of beer in front of him.

He toasted his friend and team leader working with him on the Christmas Town project, Levi Daniels. "To the successful completion of Christmas Town phase one. May we live to survive phase two."

Levi met his toast and tipped his glass an extra inch before adding, "And to going the hell back to the Twin Cities."

Terry frowned and almost made a comment about how he'd been in Logan ten weeks to Levi's five days, but then he caught a glimpse of yet another bar patron casting nervous side-eye at Levi's tall black body, and Terry drank instead. He also made a mental note to tell Dale to step up his cultural sensitivity training with the locals before he brought more tourists up here.

Terry's brain, already groaning under mental notes, shot a crack of pain from his left eye down the back of his skull. He pressed his palm to the eye socket and rested his elbow on the bar. "I wish I could say I'm going to sleep for a week when I get back, but there's no way. We have to start getting cozy with the design team before the end of the month, and I don't know how to tell you the depths to which I'm not ready."

Levi's low voice was full of concern. "I'm going to have words with Dale about working you this hard."

"It's not Dale. I work this hard by choice."

"Then I'm having words with *you* about how hard you're pushing yourself. This is nuts even by your workaholic standards. Your voice is scrubbed raw, and I barely recognized you when I first saw you. I mean, what is up with that beard?" He tugged at the lapel of Terry's shirt. "Also, who's Kevin?"

Terry glanced down at the sewn-on name tag. He hadn't realized it was there. "I have no idea. I was running through too many clothes and didn't have time for laundry, plus half of them were destroyed when I set some concrete last week. So I went to a secondhand store and grabbed everything in size large I thought would survive the job."

"And you figured your thrift store clothes made

good club wear as well?"

Terry wrinkled his nose and cast a dubious gaze around him. "You have some weird standards if you're calling this hole-in-the-wall a *club*. Besides, I'm only having a drink with you before going back to Marcus and Frankie's house, passing out for six or seven hours, then packing up and heading back to my condo."

"Take more than six or seven hours. You're not twenty anymore. You can't run yourself like a maniac. Stay up here an extra day. *Relax*, Reid."

Terry ran his index finger through the condensation collecting on his cork coaster. "There's a lot of work to do, I know. Not just building the structures. I like designing Christmas Town. It feels hopeful, with all the other despair in the world. I like shutting off the news and working in this quiet place." He frowned and rubbed his throat. "I did overdo it a bit, you're right. Shouted too much on the site and scraped my vocal cords. I sound like I've picked up a pack-a-day habit."

"You have *got* to slow down. You have to stop moving for five minutes and breathe."

The very idea of slowing down made Terry feel queasier than the cheap beer. "You know I don't do well without a project."

"I know you need a life. Why don't you try dating again?"

Terry laughed.

Levi didn't. "Look, I get things didn't work out with Jessica. Why don't you find somebody else?

Someone to tell you to take it easy and not kill your-self?"

Terry grimaced. "That's what ended things with Jessica. She didn't like how often I worked."

"Case in point, man."

No way was Terry jumping back in that mess again. Every time he tried to date someone, he only ended up running away from the relationship and causing every-one heartbreak. "My career is enough for me. Dating someone is too much hassle."

"I'm going to tell that to my wife and let her lecture you." When this made Terry shudder, Levi laughed and clapped Terry on the shoulder. "Seriously, though. You're not healthy when you're in work-only mode. I get you don't want to do relationships. What if you only hook up with someone for sex on the side? Find someone for an occasional fling. Someone to tell you to fucking shave at least. You look like you escaped from ZZ Top."

Wounded, Terry stroked his beard. "Hipster beards are in."

"They were in a few years ago, on twenty-year-olds, and for the record they looked like shit the whole time. I can't believe the hair stylist you're staying with hasn't tied you down and chopped this mop off."

Terry sighed. "I didn't mean to grow it. I forgot my beard trimmer, is all, and then I got too busy to get somewhere to buy a new one or place an Amazon order. And yes, Frankie has been after me to let him give me a trim, but there hasn't been time. I could barely work in sleep and food, let alone luxuries like showers and haircuts."

"Hack the bush off as soon as you get back, and once you're trimmed up and no longer caveman, come over to the house. Laurel and the kids want to see you. I'll grill ribs, and we can all sit in the backyard and get eaten alive by mosquitos. Come back to civilization. Say the word, and I'll invite over a nice lady too. Or guy." He rubbed his chin thoughtfully. "Too bad George isn't around."

Terry held up a hand. "I *really* don't want to date right now, especially your brother, but thank you. I will take you up on the barbecue though."

"I'll hold you to it." Levi slapped a bill on the counter and rose, putting a hand on Terry's shoulder. "You going to be okay to get back to your place?"

Terry nodded and held up his beer. "This is going to be my one and only. Then I'm heading to bed."

"All right. You call me when you get back, you hear?"

Terry saluted him. "Will do. Safe travels home."

"Same to you."

Terry watched Levi go, then hunched over the bar and shut his eyes, soaking in the moment of silence. Well, relative silence—Whiskey River wasn't exactly known for its dignified atmosphere. The Friday night bar din swelled around him, men and women chatting, pool balls cracking against one another while men groaned their disappointment or cheered. Other shouts accompanied the broadcast of a game on the TVs mounted on the sides of the room, fighting against the country music piped behind the long bar where Terry sat.

The bartender cast Terry a curious glance, indicating his glass, but Terry only shook his head and added another bill to Levi's, leaving not only enough to cover his tab but also a generous tip. The beer here was pretty terrible, but the prices were rock-bottom, and it was easy to pay a little extra to keep the locals thinking highly of the annoying construction crews from the Cities who kept invading their territory. So far, Terry had done well in Logan. He made eye contact with and gave a smile and a nod to several men he'd worked with on different sites, people he'd encountered around town.

No, he didn't want to move to Logan. He wouldn't mind coming back, though. Not at all.

He was about to push off his stool when a shadow fell over him. Turning, he saw a tall, dark-haired man standing at his elbow, regarding him with an odd, intense expression through a thick pair of glasses. He looked to be in his early thirties.

Not sure who this man was or what was going on, Terry smiled and stood, gesturing to his stool. "Please, have a seat. I was just about to leave."

He was shocked when the man not only didn't reply, he nudged Terry back into his stool with grim, determination. "I came over to talk to you. You can't leave yet."

Terry glanced around covertly, hoping someone with this man would show up and corral him. He was lean, but he looked like he might have muscle on him, and he was taller than Terry by a few inches. "Is there something I can help you with?"

The man collapsed onto the seat Levi had been occupying, but he kept one lanky leg out, blocking Terry's exit. "I'm Evan Myles. I'm here with Davidson Incorporated. I'm head of design for Christmas Town."

Oh. Evan Myles. Terry had heard about this guy. This was the crazy genius Dale had found out in L.A. and brought back to Minneapolis and paid more in weird favors and gifts than money. This was also the guy Terry was going to start working with soon.

Alas, if only this guy had been a local. Terry could have extricated himself more gracefully from a Logan native son.

Evan squinted at Terry's lapel, adjusting his glasses. They were thick for plastic lenses.

"Kevin." Evan lifted his gaze to Terry's, sliding up the length of his beard, pausing to double back and take in the width of Terry's shoulders. "Tell me, Kevin. What do you do here in Logan?"

"I supervise construction." The construction of the buildings he'd designed, but he didn't have to share that detail just yet. Neither did it seem important to explain how Evan had gotten the wrong idea about

Terry's name, either. In fact, that misdirect might come in quite handy.

Evan brightened. "Construction? Oh, that's nice. What a small world." He put a hand on Terry's on the bar. "You'll end up building my designs someday."

I'm the fucking architect. You'll be adding bows and tinsel to my designs, more like. Initially Terry had planned to shave the beard as soon as he'd returned to Minneapolis, but now he vowed to retain it until the first planning meeting so he could watch this idiot's jaw hit the floor.

For now, Terry kept his smile in place. "Wow."

He did pull his hand back, however.

Evan shifted on the stool so his knee touched Terry's thigh. God, but his stare was almost unblinking. "I haven't had much influence over anything you've seen yet, but I will soon. I have a scale model of the next phase of construction in the cabin where I'm staying, with my designs added to modify the architect's. You should come over and see them."

Terry's smile slipped. *Modified?* This guy had modified Terry's designs? Did Dale know about these changes? Terry cleared his throat. "I wish I could see them." *You jerk.*

This time when Evan's hand closed over Terry's, it traveled up his forearm. "You can. Let's leave this dump and head over there."

Delightful as storming over to this guy's place and tearing up those modifications would be, that would definitely be a bridge too far. "You seem like you've had too much to drink for company."

Evan drew back, indignant. "What? I'm perfectly sober."

Terry raised an eyebrow. "No way."

Gesturing vaguely in the direction of a pale woman with short raven hair who toasted them with what appeared to be a glass of soda, Evan shook his head. "Charlotte's been pouring nothing but water into me for the past two hours. Plus it takes a lot for me to get drunk in the first place. I mostly get blurred vision and bloodshot eyes right up until my blood alcohol content is too high, and then I pass out. I have a weird metabolism."

The guy was weird on a lot of levels. Terry weighed his options. Possibly it would be better for Terry to approach Dale in the morning before he went back to Minneapolis, ask him about whatever this weirdo had planned. Going to this oddball's cabin at midnight when the man was drunk wasn't exactly Terry's most brilliant plan to date.

Evan pressed his knee more firmly into Terry's leg. "You're a handsome man."

Christ. It was time for Terry to leave. "Thanks. Hey, I've got a long drive ahead of me tomorrow, so—"

"When you smiled at your friend earlier, your whole face lit up, and you pulled me across the room to you."

It was a terrible pickup line, but the way Evan said it... There was something about this guy. He was so blunt, so odd, but he had no artifice at all. So when he said things like that, it was as if he…actually meant it. Terry swayed in his seat.

A hand slid around Terry's back, a subtle touch that made him shiver. "Come to my place, Kevin. Don't you want to see the magic behind the buildings you put up all the time?"

The soft bubble Evan's earlier words had cast burst. Shifting to extricate himself from Evan's touch, Terry smiled, though the gesture didn't reach his eyes. "I think that would be best, yes."

Evan winked at him and caught Terry's hand, drawing him out of his seat. "You're going to be impressed, I promise. It's a very nice place, designed by the same project architect. The only way it could be better would be if I'd been involved."

Terry followed him out of the bar, and by some miracle, he didn't punch Evan in the face.

Chapter Two

E VAN HAD LIED to Kevin. He was a little tipsy, and while he didn't get drunk like most people, he did experience judgment impairment like everyone else, and he wasn't sure if taking a total stranger back to his place alone was a good idea. He hadn't meant to take anyone home tonight, but what he'd said to Kevin was true. Evan had seen the man from across the room and felt as if he'd been pulled in by a tractor beam.

Charlotte had approved of the plan. She hadn't known who Kevin was, but she knew the man with him and said if they were together, that made Kevin okay. She'd coached Evan on what to say, patted him on the back, and sent him on his way. When Evan had left with Kevin to go back to the cabin, he'd deliberately walked past her in case she had something to say to him, but all she did was wink and toast him with her glass of diet soda.

Which was fine, but now that they were outside of the bar, alone, Evan didn't have anyone to confirm whether Kevin was what Evan hoped he was: a friend-ly, fuckable lumberjack. What if Evan was wrong and Kevin was in fact a homicidal-maniac lumberjack? Evan was terrible with people. He ran background checks on all his escorts and made them submit several letters of reference. He knew nothing about this man. How was this a good plan?

He was handsome, though, even with the messy beard. His eyes were soft and sweet.

Charlotte had said he should talk to get to know his date. So Evan would talk.

"It's such a nice night. Let's walk to my cabin."

Kevin tucked his hands in the pockets of his jeans and gazed up at the late-July night sky. "It's a gorgeous evening. I swear that's all Logan gets."

Evan cast a glance at the stars, but he didn't look up too high because it made him dizzy while he was trying to walk. It would have when he was sober too. Stupid equilibrium. "You can see so many more con-stellations here than in the city. When I get stuck while I'm working, I like to lie on the deck and stargaze to clear my head. But if they send me up here again, I'm bringing a mosquito net. I've had bites in places you shouldn't have to think about getting bitten."

"They can get aggressive, it's true." Kevin had a nice smile poking through that huge bush of a beard. Evan wanted to thread his fingers through it. "If you wear things with snug collars and cuffs, it helps. Then add a little repellent to your face and hands, and they stay away. I always forget to put it on, though."

"Well, I stargaze naked, so that would mean a lot of repellent."

Kevin gawked at Evan. "You…stargaze naked."

"Why not? I hate clothes in general. I think best naked, so I usually work that way. It's one of the reasons I came to work for Davidson Incorporated, because my employer lets me work from home as much as possible and has given me all kinds of software upgrades so I can stay home even more. Plus he's always giving me spa gift certificates. I *love* massages. Whether or not they have a happy ending." When Evan realized Kevin was too quiet, he turned to look at him, and then he tripped. And swore.

"Are you sure you're sober?"

More so by the second. Evan grimaced and massaged his right temple. "I have trouble focusing on things. My equilibrium isn't very good, and if I shift my vision too quickly, especially in the dark, I fall. I'm not legally allowed to drive. It's tough to walk and focus, but when I turn my head, it's all over."

Kevin frowned. "That has to suck."

Evan shrugged. "All my senses are overdeveloped. That bar stank like a sewer, in case you were wondering. It was too loud in there, and a woman laughing at the table next to me had too shrill of a laugh. But I don't mind, because I can also see color brighter than other people, and it's as if design patterns leap out at me, ready to be fine-tuned. Touch, though…"

"Easy to overstimulate you, is it?"

"God, no. I can't get enough." He made a face. "Not lovey-dovey touch or hugs. I can't stand it when strangers hug me. But things rubbing against my skin. Massages. Having my hair washed. Facials. Manicures. Pedicures." He indulged in a slow blink as a shiver overtook him. "And sex. I absolutely love sex."

Kevin laughed softly—was that in surprise? Awkwardness? Both? "You certainly are blunt, I'll give you that."

"Too blunt?"

"Mmm…no." That was definitely surprise. "I guess you're not what I thought."

Now *Evan* was surprised. "What did you think I was?"

"I don't know, really."

They were passing the road that led to the cabins where most of the Davidson Incorporated staff were staying, and some of the lights were still on. Evan gestured to the buildings. "I wish I'd been involved in the design for these cabins. I know Dale says they're simple tourist cabins and he wants my skills used elsewhere, but every time I look at them, all I can see is what they should have looked like."

Why did Kevin look affronted? "How would you fix them, then?"

Where to start? Evan considered his options. "The inside, or the outside?"

"Both. Let's hear the outside first."

"Well, the outside is too plain. I know Dale says they don't matter, but they do. They aren't going to draw people in as much as they could. They look like fishermen cabins."

"Isn't that what they are?"

"It's not all they're going to be. Not in the peak season."

Kevin shook his head. "They're building that hotel—"

"Which is going to overflow immediately, and they'll use these cabins."

Kevin stopped walking. His eyes were wide. "I'll be damned. I never thought of that."

Evan had no idea why a construction worker would, but whatever. Though that wasn't exactly fair. Maybe he would, but his superiors wouldn't listen to him. Certainly not the damn architect. "What kills me is the structural design for the cabins is excellent. It's just…why *not* add flair? Is there some law that says fishermen don't want good design too?"

"They don't want overly fancy, I know that."

He was bristly again. What was with this guy? "Yes, but it's a spectrum, isn't it? And the best design is so subtle you don't realize it, you simply feel it." He waved a hand, tired of trying to explain. "I have a mockup in the cabin. I'll show you."

"You mocked up a design for cabins already finished? Why? You think they'll actually go back and remodel them?"

"Oh, heavens no. I couldn't sleep one night, though, and I thought maybe if I got it out of my head, it would help."

They started walking once more. "Did it?"

"No. A blow job would have been better."

Kevin stumbled.

Evan glanced sideways at him, and he tripped too. "Goddamn it."

Kevin put a hand on Evan's biceps to steady him. "Stop doing that. One of these times you're going to fall and hurt yourself."

"Then *you* stop acting weird all the time."

"In my defense, you keep saying the damnedest things."

"What, that I want a blow job? How is that a damned thing? Don't you want a blow job?"

Kevin looked skyward. "You are *so blunt*."

"Is this a straight-guy thing? Because normally the guys I hook up with don't have a problem with the way I talk." Though granted, usually Evan paid them, and usually they didn't talk much beyond how the sex was going to happen.

Oh hell, Kevin was bristling again. "I'm not straight."

Evan's shoulders sagged. "Here I was thinking I had amazing straight-man seducing skills."

Kevin laughed, and Evan couldn't tell if he should be offended or not. "If it makes you feel better, I'm bisexual."

Evan brightened. "It does. Thank you." He considered some more and frowned. "Wait. No, that doesn't make me feel any better, because you still had the same odds of being attracted to me as a gay man."

Somehow this made Kevin *un*bristle, as if Evan had passed a kind of test. What a complicated man.

Evan didn't care what the man's orientation was, so long as he was interested in curing Evan's dry spell. "You do like blow jobs, yes?"

Now Kevin laughed. "Yes. I do. Though I haven't had one in quite some time."

The way he said *quite some time* was worrying. "Would you care to be more specific?"

"No, I would not."

"You do know you're aggravating, yes?"

Kevin snorted.

They were at the road leading to Evan's cabin now, the lake and the roof of the house visible beyond a line of trees. The cabin where Evan was staying was isolated, though by the time construction was finished, the lake would be dotted with luxury cabins. The two of them walked toward Evan's place in companionable silence until Kevin broke it with a question.

"Tell me what you think of the cabin."

Evan decided he didn't care why Kevin was so interested in the design of the project buildings. He simply welcomed a kindred spirit, and the idea that one had bloomed amidst the Logan locals only added to the charm. "It's the best-designed building of all the ones for the project so far, of the original construction projects. Anything renovated too."

This seemed to please Kevin, but he prodded Evan cautiously. "Why do you say that?"

"How technical do you want me to get? I have a lot to say. Charlotte tells me I get boring."

"I want you to get incredibly technical."

He said that in such a sexy way. *Kevin, you animal.* "Since you insist, then. To start, the cabin excited me. It was designed by the head architect working on the project now, the same one who designed the fishermen cabins, and the cabin told me the architect had real talent. I knew Dale had switched architects from the start of the project because the renovation style changed halfway through, but I could tell simply by looking at them the same person who did the fishermen cabins did this one."

Tension again. "You can tell the difference in the renovations?"

"Oh, I'm sure it's only me. I told you, I'm overly sensitive to design."

"Well, that's good." He sounded more relaxed, but he fidgeted. "So you think the second architect is good?"

"They're excellent. Like I said, at first I thought they were too uninspired, but then I saw my cabin, and I knew they had the spark. I should have known better, really. Dale only hires the best." He shook his head, being careful to shut his eyes first so he didn't trip. "I just don't understand why they did such a dull job on the first cabins. I wish Dale would have had me on board then."

"Maybe he's literal. Maybe he was told to make the cabins simple, so he did."

Evan waved a finger at him. "Don't assume the architect is male."

Why was the man so bristly? "I happen to know he is."

"Oh?" Evan stopped walking so he could turn to look at Kevin, interest piqued. "Do you know him personally?"

What an odd expression Kevin was making. "Rather, yes."

"So what you're saying is he *is* literal and he *did* make the cabins simple because he was told to do so." *So, so* defensive. The architect must be a good friend. "That's excellent. I'll take that to mean he accepts direction well, and when I ask for modifications to his designs, he'll adjust them without issue."

"I don't know about *that*."

Evan patted Kevin on the shoulder and started walking again. "It's not only the talent potential I like about the cabin. The unit itself is highly pleasing. You can tell he took great care with this design. I wouldn't be surprised to hear he'd dreamed of building a designer cabin for years. There are so many tiny details inside and out that make it stand out, but there's more. It's perfect as a rental cabin too, because there are elements for different types of guests, all of them accessible to people with disabilities." Evan gestured to the cabin itself, which was now visible in full before them. "Look how perfectly it's integrated into the landscape. It looks as if it grew out of the ground, not interrupting the view. Can you imagine being someone who rented this and driving up to stay? If their hearts don't race, there's something wrong with them."

Kevin was rubbing the back of his neck, and when he spoke, his voice was gruff. "It did turn out nice."

"Nice is an insulting understatement. The cabin is brilliant. I told Dale if he doesn't submit it for every architectural award it's eligible for, I'm quitting."

Kevin put his hands in his jean pockets, looking embarrassed for some reason. "Well, I'm glad you like it."

"It's the only thing about living up here I'll miss. I don't think I want to live in a house, but if I did, I'd have this man design it." Evan stretched. "We'll work together a great deal, Dale tells me, in the next phase of the project. Normally I dislike cooperative ventures, but this might not be too bad."

"You might be right."

They were at the cabin, passing through the cluster of evergreen bushes marking the opening of the drive and the half fencing that gave it just the right kind of accent. The driveway curved elegantly toward a double garage tucked around to the side, carefully designed to not detract from the visual of the front of the cabin. It wasn't precisely an A-frame, but it gave the illusion of being one, with the way the roof was shaped.

"The porches are one of my favorite features." Evan gestured to them as they approached. "There's one on every side, on the lower and upper levels. Out front, out back. A huge one lakeside, but there are little observatory decks everywhere, and they don't detract or make anything awkward. They invite you to go outside, reminding you that you came to the cabin to be part of nature." Evan smiled. "My favorite feature, though, are the lights. Logan is Christmas Town, so this cabin is decked out with subtle, permanent nods to Christmas—and it manages not to be tacky at all. I'd have done a few things differently, but I love what he did. I only wish he'd done the same thing with the fishermen cabins. That's what I did with the mockup models."

"I'd like to see those."

He would? Evan shrugged. "Sure. Come inside, and I'll show you."

Evan wanted to keep giving the tour, explaining how the wood they'd chosen for the stair rail was perfect, not only local to the area but one of the best hardwoods, one that would wear well, and they'd echoed the use of it throughout the house. Kevin seemed fixated on seeing the models, so Evan reluctantly forewent the tour and took his guest straight to the basement of the cabin, which wasn't exactly the basement, more the lower level that opened to the underside of the deck and the barbecue area. It was meant to be a media room, but it was where Evan kept his models, set up on tables Dale had sent over for him.

Kevin stood in the center of the room, staring, his mouth hanging open. "This...this is incredible."

Evan glanced around at the cluttered groups of mockups, feeling proud. "Thank you. They're my hobbies, some of them, though the more organized area on the right is what I'm going to propose for Christmas Town phase two, the downtown renovations. The fishermen cabins are in the middle, on the other side of the lake."

Kevin seemed rooted to the place where he stood. "You have the whole town here, and the surrounding area. What's *that*, though?"

"The hotel? I know that's several phases ahead and hasn't been designed by the architect yet, but I've been working on a mockup. I've put together three or four already, in fact. It's just for fun. I have insomnia a lot."

Now Kevin moved, picking up the hotel model carefully. "Do you have architectural plans for this?"

"Heavens, no. I don't have that training. I can only see how something should look. The fine details of putting it together isn't something I can do. Which is why I'm so glad to hear the architect is receptive. Sometimes they can be full of ego."

"They do a great deal of work."

"Yes, but they're no good if they won't take constructive criticism." Evan brought a fishermen cabin to Kevin. "These are the cabins. See how I added the same lights? I don't think any fisherman would object to them. They don't have to turn them on, but they can if they like. Plus I echoed the design elements the architect had already put in place. Well, and I tweaked them."

Kevin turned the fishermen cabin over in his hand. Evan had made the bottom open so his interior changes could be more visible, and Kevin stared at them intently. "These are good. They wouldn't be hard to add in renovations. Have you told Dale?"

Oh, Evan *liked* this man. "I will eventually. I haven't seen him much while we've been in Logan, and I didn't know if he was willing to put money into them when he had so many irons in the fire."

"Dale wants the second phase to go off like a firecracker, so yes. He'll be willing. You should tell him." Kevin shook his head and put down the cabin, crossing to the main design for the downtown buildings. "This is incredible. *Incredible.* You're a genius, Evan. I could sit and look at these for hours. I *want* to sit and look at these for hours. I have a million questions for you about why you did what you did to these."

Any other time, Evan would be happy to hear them. As matters stood… Evan crossed to Kevin and wrapped his arms around him from behind. "You can ask me later. Right now I have other plans for you."

It was highly satisfying, the way Kevin softened in

his arms. "Yeah? Like what?"

Evan nuzzled Kevin's ear, sliding his hands down to Kevin's waistband. "We're going to take a shower."

TERRY BLINKED AND turned around, the sensual spell Evan had been casting broken. "We're going to *what?*"

Evan gave him an exasperated look through his glasses. "Shower. I'd like to have sex with you now, which I assume you know is why I brought you out here, but we need to shower first."

Terry shook his head in disbelief. "How you ever get laid at all is a complete mystery to me."

"I don't usually have to have this much conversation. I prefer escorts. But of course, there aren't any such services up here. It's been quite stressful."

This whole scene was giving Terry whiplash. One minute Evan was too weird for words, the next he was dragging Terry into his orbit, and then he was back to weird again. "You use escorts. Exclusively? You never just go out and try to meet someone?"

"No, I don't go out and try to meet people." Evan shuddered. "Why would I ever want to do such a thing? Crowded bars, all that noise and smell, and then I have to make small talk when what I want is to find a man to have sex with? No. I'd rather pay a professional."

"Even though it's illegal?"

"It's ridiculous that it's illegal. If it were regulated,

escorts could unionize and ensure they had legal protections against poorly behaved clients."

He had a point, but the idea of never going out and meeting someone, really getting to know them and fall in love with them, left Terry cold. "Don't you ever want companionship? More than just sex?"

Evan gave him an impatient look. "Do we honestly have to discuss this right now? We could have been halfway through a shower already and that much closer to a blow job for one of us."

This was the craziest hookup Terry had ever had. Normally at this point in the date Terry was sabotaging things without meaning to, but he was so confused he was spending all his energy attempting to keep up. "I'm not exactly in the mood anymore. This is a little weird."

"If you let me get you naked, I promise, I can get you in the mood."

If Evan had made the statement with even a smidgen of a boast, Terry would have been out of there in a heartbeat, but Evan made this declaration with the same no-nonsense tone he said everything else as if it were a simple fact he couldn't help. Terry couldn't decide if he should glare at him, walk out, or laugh.

Before he could make up his mind, Evan put a hand on Terry's hip, drawing him closer. Not pulling their bodies together, but putting Terry into his orbit so when Evan spoke again, that intense gaze bore into Terry, making his heart beat faster.

"You have such a handsome face, but your eyes,

Kevin. They captivate me."

What was Terry supposed to say to that? "Thank you."

Evan was still staring at him. "I'm enthralled by you. I wasn't going to pick up anyone tonight, but you were so special, I couldn't resist."

Again, that should have been the cheesiest line ever, but from Evan, it sounded sincere.

Evan kept going. "I like the way you're put together. You have a good design. Excellent shoulders. Nice hips." His other hand rose to card fingers through Terry's beard before stroking his cheek, rubbing his thumb across Terry's lip. "The beard is wild. It makes me wonder if you're as untamed and rough as this hair once someone strips you down."

Terry had to swallow several times before he could speak, and he couldn't seem to raise his gaze higher than Evan's lips. "I…didn't mean for the beard to get this long. It…just happened."

"Even better. Your subliminal animal is rising. The question is, when I draw it all the way out of you, will you want to fight me, or follow me?"

This scene was getting out of Terry's league so fast. Or rather, it was skirting into territory he'd been to but didn't revisit lightly, and definitely not with a soon-to-be coworker. He needed to call a timeout, tell Evan he wasn't Kevin, that he was, in fact, the architect he was about to work with. To explain he wasn't against having sex with him, but maybe they shouldn't, since they were going to work together, and certainly they shouldn't do something weird and kinky that involved the word *animal*.

Except Evan's touch rendered Terry unable to move or speak. He couldn't look away, could barely breathe. When Evan's fingertips slid along the sides of his throat, he let out a sigh, a strange, guttural sound he hadn't known he could make.

Chuckling, Evan leaned in and kissed Terry, a brush of lips that lingered, encouraging their mouths open until their tongues tangled with one another. Evan teased at the line of Terry's beard. "You're not going to fight me at all. You're going to follow me every step of the way, aren't you?" He shifted his focus to Terry's shirt. "Let's start now."

It wasn't until Evan undid the buttons of the polo and clutched the hem in his fists that Terry realized Evan meant to undress him, right here in the basement. "Wait—"

Evan silenced him with two fingers, then lifted his hand and continued to undo Terry's belt. "Don't worry. I'll undress too. But I want to unwrap you first. I've been dying to see what you look like in your prime all night."

Don't worry. As it he could do anything else! "I don't think—"

"I don't believe this is the time for you to think at all, do you? You're about to have the best shower of your life, followed by an erotic massage, and then a blow job. And that's just the opening act. What in the world is there to think about?" Evan smiled and stroked Terry's neck, gentling him as if he were a spooked horse. "Now be good and raise your hands over your head."

Terry shut his eyes and shivered—and complied.

He opened his eyes again as he heard Evan toss their shirts aside before stepping back to cast an admiring gaze along Terry's body.

"Mmm, yes. I wasn't wrong. You have the perfect form. Look at those muscles. So defined, from all that manual labor." Evan hummed some more and ran his hands across Terry's chest, curling his fingers in his hair. "This is a lovely contrast, the hard muscles and the soft hair. Too many escorts shave their body hair. I'll enjoy this variety."

Evan's thumbs brushed Terry's nipples. Terry gasped, trembling.

Soft lips teased his ear as the sweet torture of his nipples continued. "Shower with me, sweetheart, and I'll tie your hands over your head and do wicked things to your body."

Terry's knees nearly buckled. "I…"

Evan's right hand stroked Terry's side, massaging his ribs. "You're so delicious, Kevin. Where have you been this entire time I've been in Logan?

Terry was wondering this a little bit too. Except this wasn't their last day together. Jesus, he had to tell him. "Evan, there's something I have to—"

His words died on his lips, turning into a soft cry as Evan stuck his tongue in Terry's ear. "I don't want to hear it. The only sounds I want to hear out of your mouth are you gasping and shouting as you come for me."

Holy fucking shit, this train wasn't just going off the tracks, it was diving right into the gorge. "Evan, I——"

Evan made out with Terry's ear again, and his nipple at the same time, and Terry got lost, trembling and sinking against Evan, leaning on him for support.

Time stretched, became fuzzy. As Evan's lips moved across Terry's ear, whispering words Terry felt but didn't hear, Terry also somehow lost the remainder of his clothes. All but his socks, and when Evan whispered that he should take them off, Terry did so in a haze. Then he stood still, naked, chilly, and dizzy, as he watched Evan strip down too, bare of everything but his glasses and a devil's smile.

"There. Now, see? It wasn't so bad." Evan held out his hand, and Terry took it, letting him lead him back up the stairs. Evan kept talking. "The shower is on the second floor. You're going to love it."

Terry felt so weird, walking naked through the cabin, but somehow holding Evan's hand, he could do it. He was cold, though, and he kept shivering.

Evan seemed amused by this. "You don't walk around naked that often?"

It was hard to talk after being told not to. Terry

shook his head.

"You should. It's so freeing." Evan stopped on the stairs and glanced back at Terry with approval. "You look good nude. So raw and masculine. You're going to look even more glorious wet. I'm going to have my hands all over you. Especially your ass."

Terry's legs felt like jelly as he followed Evan up the stairs. He had visions of Evan pressing him against the tile, sliding a hand over his cheeks, running a finger down his crack while the hot water sluiced over them and steam drifted around them. Terry let out a ragged breath. God, this was so insane. He still needed Evan to understand who he was.

When they reached the top of the stairs and Terry tried to open his mouth to explain, Evan closed his mouth over his with a dirty kiss instead. He pushed Terry's naked body against the wall, one hand kneading his ass, the other tugging at his nipple.

"You're so responsive," Evan murmured between licks into Terry's mouth. "I can't wait to wash you and fuck you. I'm going to take you so many ways. You want that, don't you, Kevin?"

Now. You've got to tell him now, before you lose your last threads of sanity. "I'm trying to tell you, I'm not—"

He gasped as Evan's fingers slipped into his crack, one finger teasing his opening as the others pressed against his perineum. "You want me to fuck you tonight. You want me to ride you hard, make you boneless."

Terry shut his eyes and clutched at Evan's shoulders. The last shreds of his panic were falling away, dying under the power of lust. "Yes, but—"

"You want me to tie your hands. You've been thinking about it since I mentioned it. How about I blindfold you too? You'll lie there and do nothing but feel my mouth on you everywhere. Look at how you tremble just thinking about it." He licked Terry's neck. "Let me leave bite marks on you. I won't go higher than your collar. But I want to mark you. I want you to remember how I fucked you."

Whimpering, Terry tipped his head to the side to give him access as Evan began sucking on his collarbone, the sharp suction of Evan's mouth ensuring Terry would look in the mirror later and see the evidence of this evening.

"Mmm. A nice start." Evan kneaded Terry's ass. "But I want the next one to taste like clean skin, not sweat. Into the shower now."

Terry gave in.

The shower was incredible, as Evan had promised and as Terry had designed: a fourteen-by-fourteen-inch rain-shower overhead, eight body-spray fittings on the surrounding walls, and a handheld unit for women who wanted to rinse their legs after shaving and for accessibility. The rain-shower and body-sprays could be turned off one by one with the control panel outside, and the handheld unit had several different attachments. A seat folded discreetly into the wall, though someone had brought in a freestanding stool too, and grip bars had been incorporated into the overall design. Terry had repeated the Christmas light theme in the bathroom as well, though he'd tried to keep it understated. Where the main rooms had soft strings of white lights, the master bathroom had white and blue lights, giving it a softly frosted theme. It had made sense to Terry, with the water. The accents were all white and chrome, so the room looked like blue-tinted ice.

It was one thing to design it, and another to live inside it, to be led naked and trembling into the steaming shower, to have his body hauled beneath the rainshower as Evan made love to his mouth and positioned his backside against one of the sprays. When Terry gasped in surprise, Evan laughed against his lips and ran his hands down Terry's sides, massaging the globes of his ass as the water shot into his crack.

"Nice, isn't it? I'm telling you. I want to do *wicked* things to the architect in thanks for what he's done with the shower and bath features of this cabin. But wait until you experience the handheld features."

Terry decidedly had *not* had erotic ideas in mind when he designed the shower, or the tub, or anything about the cabin. Unsurprisingly, before he could attempt to explain this, Evan claimed his mouth again, and Terry gave over to the sensation of hot water raining down around him, steam rising everywhere, Evan filling every space inside him, touching every part of his skin. When Evan nudged his cheeks apart, part of him thought, *Jesus, this is fast*, but mostly he rode the wave.

The last time he'd felt like this was when he'd met Dale, the night Terry's then-boyfriend decided they should try a threesome. It had been hot, enough to go for a few repeat rounds, but things had become awkward when Dale had wanted to date Terry. Alan had gotten jealous, though Terry had politely explained he didn't think he could handle more than one relationship at a time, and in the end the whole thing had blown up. The sex had been hot, though, and somehow Terry had always ended up underneath the both of them, spread open and gasping, their touches making him feel skinny and light, as if he didn't exist in his body any longer, that he was nothing but the sex itself.

This felt like that, Evan dragging him under some kind of sexual haze, except it was even deeper, and definitely kinkier. Terry had been with kinky partners— plenty of them—but there was something different about the way Evan made love to him. The calmness and quietness of the way he manipulated Terry, with slight dispassion but with control too. Terry found it intoxicating.

Resting Terry's arms over his shoulders as if they were pieces of limp spaghetti, Evan mashed Terry's ass flat against the water jet as he fucked into Terry's mouth with his tongue.

"Such a good, obedient boy." Evan nuzzled Terry's nose as he came up for air, biting his bottom lip, sucking on it. "Tell me, Kevin." Evan took a firm grip on Terry's ass, pulled him slightly open to let more water in. "Is your back door in business? Anything you need to clean out?"

Terry wasn't even surprised at the things this guy asked anymore, and he was giving up and going with the Kevin thing now. "It's fine. I'm good." He stared at Evan's mouth, wondering when they were going to get back to nipple play, and maybe those promised blow jobs. Though he supposed these questions and all this water-jet business meant he was getting rimmed, which wasn't bad either.

"Excellent. We can take care of everything right here, then."

Something hard and rounded and gently gushing water pushed at Terry's hole.

Terry yelped and tried to get away. "*Oh my God, what*—?" He made a high-pitched noise as the tip slipped briefly inside, and he shuddered as water entered him. He knocked Evan's hand and the thing away with a shaking hand, clenching his asshole tight. "*What in the hell are you doing?*"

Grinning, Evan picked up the handheld unit, which Terry realized to his horror held not the innocent spray attachment he expected or any of the other accessories he'd ordered, but instead a long, curved black wand with a rounded tip. A fucking enema wand.

"Isn't it the best?" Evan pushed a button and water gently shot out of the tip before falling to the floor of the shower. "I'm telling you, this architect is amazing."

Terry had *not* included that attachment—it had to be Dale, who Terry wanted to murder right now. "Do *not* put that in me again."

Evan winked and came closer, running the enema wand across Terry's neck. He didn't have his glasses on, and he was incredibly handsome without them—no more geeky Clark Kent, just straight-up Christopher Reeves. Wicked Christopher Reeves with an enema wand attachment. "Let me clean you out, and I'll fuck you with my tongue and make you cry. In front of a mirror so you can see how you look."

"*No*. Absolutely not."

Laughing darkly, Evan licked Terry's neck, sucking it. He massaged Terry's nipple with the wand now, shooting water against it as he rubbed circles around the areola. "Mmm, you have so many beautiful layers, Kevin. You're embarrassed, aren't you? Do you have, perhaps, a humiliation kink? I love it. You're so delicious."

Goddamn, this guy was way too perceptive. "Of course I'm embarrassed. I don't want someone I just met to give me an enema in his shower." And he still had the damn water in his ass. It wasn't much, but it was enough, and it felt weird.

"It's not exactly an enema, though. More of a rinse. Shoot it in, let it out, rinse off, good to go."

Terry thought he was going to pass out. "*In the shower.* You want me to do this *in the shower?* With you *here with me?"*

Yes. Boy, did that turn his crank.

Except no, it didn't. Jesus, what was wrong with him tonight?

Evan grinned. "Oh my God, I really want to do this now. You're so embarrassed. I love the way you look, all wet and panicked, big gruff lumberjack."

Jesusfuckingchrist. Terry shook his head hard enough to spray water with his hair and beard. "No. *No way.* I'm not doing that. Not with you watching."

He regretted those final words as soon as they were out of his mouth, even before Evan smiled slyly at him.

"But you'll do it without me watching?"

Terry shook his head again, but it was weaker this time, because he was transfixed by the feral look in Evan's eye.

Yes, go ahead, make me do it.

Evan zeroed in for the kill. "Do it for me. I'll give you a moment, and then I'll be back and give you such a reward, sweetheart. I'll eat your ass, suck your balls, your cock—you'll come like you've never come before. With your hands tied behind your back, facing a mirror, watching yourself. And all you have to do is stick this wand into your ass for fifteen seconds."

Terry meant to say no. He meant to tell Evan this was insane, he didn't do stuff like this, it was a weird fucking kink and he wasn't having any part of it. The problem was that was all a bunch of shit, he *had* done stuff like this, he *did* love stuff like this, and staring at

Evan, he fell under his spell all over again.

Don't panic. Just let go and enjoy this for one night.

"Five seconds." As soon as the words were out of Terry's mouth, he swallowed a whimper.

Eyes dancing, Evan ran the wand down the center of Terry's chest. "Twelve."

Terry's heart was pounding. *Why are you negotiating this? Why are you agreeing to this?* Except he knew the answer. Because he wanted this man to keep looking at him like this, touching him. Because the part of him that loved games had been packed away too long, and Evan had drawn it out to play. Because it didn't matter what got put in his ass or what he had to do. He was already under this man, ready to do whatever he wanted.

"Seven."

Evan stroked Terry's cheek with the wand. "Ten."

Terry let out a shuddering breath. "F-fine."

"There. Now don't look so scared. I'll keep you safe. Just let me see how embarrassed you are, all right? Because that really makes me hot." He pushed the wand against Terry's mouth. "Open up. I'll count for you this time, since the water will be in your mouth. But don't look away from me, and don't swallow. Try to be embarrassed. I want to see all of it, since you won't allow me to see the real show."

Terry *was* embarrassed. He opened his mouth, allowed Evan to push the wand past his lips, then closed them around the wand and let Evan fill his mouth with water. Evan counted slowly, and Terry stared at him the whole time, feeling awkward and strange, until finally Evan said, "Now, spit," and he did, the built-up water running slowly down his chin.

"Oh, that was wonderful. You looked so awkward, and you're dreading what you're about to do to your ass, aren't you? You're such a *gift*, Kevin."

Terry couldn't believe this was happening. It was so surreal, he wondered if maybe it *wasn't* happening. He couldn't be about to do what he thought he was about to do.

Evan clucked his tongue. "Don't look so scared. You have done this before, yes? You understand it's just a bit of bacterial-level cleansing, not some kind of shock scene?" Evan stroked his cheek. The one on his face, though the enema wand was massaging the other kind. "Kevin. There are two things I'm excellent at. Design and sex. Trust me on this."

Terry should have argued, should have insisted this wasn't sex. Should have taken this moment to reveal he wasn't fucking Kevin, he was fucking Terry. Should have clarified that he didn't use enemas as foreplay. He thought about all of those things. Then he looked up at Evan's face, and he got lost all over again.

"Here's your wand, Kevin." Evan passed it to him.

Terry accepted it with a shaking hand. "Thanks," he whispered, and got ready to do whatever Evan told him to do.

Chapter Three

TERRY PERFORMED HIS shower assignment in some kind of dream.

Evan issued instructions through the glass door. Terry could only see the shape of him through the frosted barrier, but he could hear him, albeit muted. His voice was…hypnotic. Evan made him count out loud. Terry ended up with fifteen seconds after all, and he did it three times, simply because Evan asked.

When Evan opened the shower door, Terry still held the wand in his hand, the metal rod dripping as his fingers quaked against his thigh. He stood beneath the rain-shower, where he'd been ordered to remain, and he shivered, not because the water had begun to run cool, though by rights it would soon. No, he shivered from shame at what he had done, at what Evan had made him do. And as he had been told, he looked up at Evan, letting him see how mortified he felt.

God, it felt so good.

Evan stroked his face, pushing him back fully under the water so it ran over his eyes and mouth. His stare was so intense it made Terry weak. "You look so miserable. Was it truly that terrible?"

Terry had never been so embarrassed in his life. Or so happy. "Yes."

"But if I asked you to do it again, right now, you would?"

In a heartbeat. That stare dragged Terry down, pulling him into something dark and wonderful that made his tongue feel thick, his limbs heavy, his brain dull and fat. "Yes."

With a wicked chuckle, Evan tangled his tongue with Terry's in a brief, carnal kiss beneath the water. "You're my new favorite person, Kevin."

Evan kissed him again, deeper, his hand reaching back to part Terry's cheeks so his other hand could tease his index finger against Terry's newly cleaned hole, and Terry relaxed to let him in, his only thought that he was so glad in that moment to be Kevin.

When they finished in the shower, Evan dried Terry, instructing him to raise his arms over his head and hold still so he could be patted down. Evan moved Terry to the counter by the double sinks and had him bend over, spreading his legs wide and watching in the mirror as Evan flossed the towel vigorously between his cheeks. When this, finally, made Terry blush, Evan patted his rump and smiled at Terry in the mirror.

"If I had a weekend with you, I could ruin you. You'd lose yourself completely to pleasure."

Terry was pretty sure he was already lost. "What—what are you going to do?"

Evan winked at him.

Then, despite what he'd just said, he *did* ruin Terry.

Right there at the sink, with Terry bent and exposed like that, watching himself in the mirror, Evan rimmed him. Pressed his mouth to Terry's hole, ran his tongue around the sensitive ring of muscle. It felt so good Terry shuddered.

Evan laughed softly. "You're so nervous. The wand made you loose, I can tell, but you're clenching." He met Terry's gaze in the mirror and winked as he kissed his ass cheek. "You don't like it when I speak so bluntly, when I point things like that out. But you like it at the same time." Evan stroked his thigh. "Do you want me to eat you out some more? Fuck you with my tongue, like I promised?"

Terry felt like his entire body blushed. "Yes. Please."

"Oh, but I like it when you say please."

Cheeks spread wide, cool air on his hole, wet, soft, moving inside…*so deep*… "*Oh my God*." Terry clutched at the counter and curled his toes into the tile, shutting his eyes, gooseflesh breaking out across his body as he heard the sounds Evan was making at his ass. Jesus Christ, he could *feel him* inside, and it was *so good*, he wanted to fall to his knees and weep. Evan kept going, overloading Terry's senses until he could do nothing but shudder and whine. His knees were jelly, his belly a nest of need.

His cock was rock hard and weeping, bobbing as Evan kept probing, stiffening his tongue into a spear and thrusting it deep, then licking at the ring of muscle. When Evan finally stopped, replacing his tongue with two fingers, Terry didn't hesitate, only opened as much as he could for them and fucked himself onto the digits, struggling not to pant.

Evan licked a line up the side of Terry's ass cheek, nipping the top as he gently fucked Terry with his fingers. Evan sucked at Terry's ass, hard enough to leave a mark. Then he ducked between Terry's spread legs and cupped his balls.

Terry hissed, clenching on Evan's fingers still inside him.

Evan sighed. "I want to blow you, but I'm not ready for you to come yet." He rubbed his face along the shaft.

Terry shuddered. "I…I can try not to."

"Do you think you could come twice?"

Normally Terry would say no. Tonight, with Evan? "Maybe."

"I don't think you're going to make it if we try to make you wait." Evan licked the length of Terry's shaft. "I'm going to fuck you anyway, even if you can't. I'll wait until you're desensitized, but I'm going to fuck you."

Terry nodded, sliding under again as Evan started to suck his cock. Then he realized Evan couldn't see him nodding. "Okay," he whispered.

"You're so good, Kevin." Evan massaged Terry's balls as he ran his tongue around the cockhead. "Tip your head down and watch."

It was difficult to move, but the order helped. Terry lowered his head and focused on Evan just in time to watch him suck down Terry's cock, going straight to the root. Terry gasped, overcome by the sensation and the visual. Evan was scrunched and twisted, naked and damp, one arm reaching back around so he could fuck into Terry's ass—and Terry felt that, two fingers inside him, teasing at those muscles—but Evan also anchored Terry to the floor so he could bob back and forth on the cock he was so patiently enjoying. Terry hissed, fighting the urge to fuck into his mouth. Except those fingers in him kept fucking deeper, Evan kept going, and eventually Terry couldn't help himself. He thrust between Evan's stretched lips, groaning against the tightness, feeling the stars building inside his head, until he was nothing but need, riding all of it until he exploded.

He came for what felt like ten minutes, shuddering as he pumped into Evan's greedy mouth. When he was spent, he felt limp, his legs barely able to hold him, his arms like jelly.

Evan pulled out of him, climbed out to stand beside him, and helped him to rise.

Terry obeyed in a daze, letting Evan move him, washing his cock with a soft cloth, leading him into the bedroom where he was placed on the bed and arranged on a pile of pillows, hands above his head, ass raised and knees drawn up. When Evan knelt in front of him, enjoying the view, Terry blushed, but he didn't hide his reaction or try to close his legs.

Evan stroked the juncture of Terry's thighs. "You're such a treasure. I had a feeling about you in the bar, but I had no idea what a diamond lurked beneath your surface."

Terry felt like he'd been injected with a bottle of sedatives. Every inhibition was gone from him now. "I don't usually let myself go like this."

"So it's only for me you behave this way. Even more delightful." Evan skimmed his hand up Terry's chest. "Do I still get to leave marks all over you, Kevin?"

Desire, heedless of the fact that Terry's body was still spent, pooled in his belly. "Yes."

Evan did. As Terry lay there, quiet and obedient, Evan methodically, maddeningly sucked at what felt like every inch of Terry's flesh, leaving bruises in his wake. On Terry's shins. The insides of his thighs. His hip. The sides of his body, his abdomen. His pectorals, his biceps. He flipped Terry over and left several all over his back and a few more across his ass. By the end, Terry wasn't hard, though his cock was trying. Terry was moaning, his desire to play the game overriding his body's insistence it had already had too much stimulation.

Evan lingered at the back of Terry's neck, teasing his way down the sides. Terry was kneeling on the bed now, Evan behind him. "Let me give you one mark where people can see it. Only one."

"No," Terry said, but it was a weak protest, because Evan was drawing his nipples into aching peaks.

"*One.*" Evan nuzzled at Terry's pulse. "Right here. So you know they see it. And you get embarrassed and think of me."

"There's no way I won't think of you."

Now Evan's nose was at his ear, his teeth grazing Terry's lobe. "Kevin, you delicious thing. But I want you to think of me and make that lovely, embarrassed face."

"Trust me, I will." Terry was making it now.

Evan nuzzled again, licking the pulse. "Let me," he whispered. "Then I'll tie your hands to your feet and let you watch as I rim you again before I fuck you. Please. Something you can cover, but that you *have* to work to cover."

Terry shut his eyes.

Evan tugged at his nipples, pinching the tips. "Say yes, Kevin."

Terry let out a ragged breath. "Yes."

Evan made a huge production of leaving his mark, making Terry turn his head to the side and exposing his neck as if Evan were a vampire and Terry were his victim. It was what it felt like, in a way, and while Evan sucked at him, Terry gasped, high-pitched noises escaping him. When it was done, he was so ashamed at what he'd allowed to happen he pressed a hand to his face.

Evan kissed his forehead, coming around to admire Terry's embarrassment. "Perfect. Just as I'd imagined." He patted Terry on the shoulder. "Sit there and think about your beautiful new mark. I'll be back with the ties, but I want to see a lovely, humiliated face when I return."

It wasn't difficult for Terry to follow those instructions. There was a mirror on the closet door opposite the bed, and he could see the mark, as well as the host of others. My God, what had he been thinking? What would *anyone* think if they saw these? How would he explain them?

What if they knew all the things he'd done with Evan?

Evan came back holding a handful of nylon restraints, but when he saw Terry's face, he dropped them. "*Oh.* Oh, that is *perfect*. What are you thinking about right now?"

That piercing gaze. Terry couldn't resist it. "I was thinking about how horrible it would be if other people found out the things I'd done with you."

Evan's grin made Terry shiver. He crouched to pick up the restraints, and Terry almost shied away as he came over, but Evan shook his head, softening as he stroked Terry's arms, gentling him. "Hush. You're fine. You're discovering your humiliation kink, is all. You don't need to worry. I won't hurt you."

Not discovering. Terry wasn't sharing that much information, though. "You're so brash. I don't know what you'll do next."

Now Evan looked wounded. "I wouldn't hurt you. I wouldn't push you beyond what you can handle."

"But you don't know me." *You don't even know my real name.*

"I know you better than you think I do. For example, I know that right now you really want me to tell you to lie back on the bed, put your hands above your head, and draw your feet up to your hands, holding them there so I can restrain them together. Then you want me to tease your nipples until your cock is ready for me again. You want to suck my cock, with your eyes open and looking at me, waiting for me to give you an order. You want me to fuck you, with your hands and feet bound, your body exposed. You want me to send you into a frenzy, keeping you at the edge of coming but not let you get there. You want me to humiliate you one last time, demanding you come with your face flushed and your mind full of confusion, torn between shame and arousal."

Terry was breathing heavily by the end of the speech. Yes, he did want all that. Every word. *Only for tonight. It's all right, so long as it's just for tonight.* He'd shut his eyes, but now he opened them, staring up at Evan in desperation.

Evan kept petting him. "That's all I'm going to do. Is that what you want?"

Face flushed, Terry nodded.

"Then ask for it." When Terry shut his eyes, Evan caught his chin. "With eye contact."

Terry met Evan's gaze, the heat of his embarrassment seeping through him. "Please tie me up and fuck me." When Evan only raised an eyebrow, Terry added, his voice small and defeated, "And humiliate me."

Evan kissed him, slow and lingering. "As you wish."

Terry had been tied up before, plenty, but it was nothing like this. It had never been with someone so confident, so easy, so…Evan.

He focused instead on loving his predicament, sinking into the sensations. He was like a turkey, trussed with his ass open, his limbs bound together in a single point at his head. Somehow Evan had the whole mess of ropes attached to the headboard, but he'd also made sure Terry was comfortable and safe. Then he sat back and admired the view.

"You're so open and vulnerable." Evan stroked Terry's hole, pressing a finger at the entrance until the muscle clenched. He winked at Terry. "Just imagine if someone walked in right now and saw you like this. Wouldn't they be shocked? Your friends on the work site. What would they say if they saw your legs spread wide, your body full of love bites?" He bent and licked beneath Terry's balls, making him quiver. "What if they saw me doing this? Imagine it, Kevin."

Terry shuddered. God, this man was *way, way too perceptive.* "No."

"I want you to imagine it while I fuck you with my tongue. Make a lot of noise, Kevin. They'll come watch you if you do, and I'll fuck you harder the more sounds you make."

Terry clutched at the edges of the strap. Then Evan's tongue was inside him, doing such wicked things, and he couldn't think of anything else but obeying whatever Evan said. He made noise. He grunted, gasped, pushed into Evan's face until he was panting, his cock ready once more.

Evan slipped a finger inside Terry, pulling him open wider. "Call them. Call them over, and I'll let them look inside you before I tongue-fuck you."

Terry protested. He refused. He struggled against his restraints…and then he did it. Weakly, his voice breaking, rough from the cold and now almost raw from everything else, he called out to his imaginary crew, told them to come and see what Evan was doing to him. He was so mortified.

He was utterly in heaven.

He let Evan see it, bask in it. Then he tipped his head back and rode the sensation of Evan going at his ass in earnest, adding fingers to his tongue.

By the time Evan got to the long-promised nipple torture, Terry was lost in a sea. He did whatever Evan asked, shamelessly begging, showing off his body to invented crowds as Evan took his nipples in his teeth, drew them into his mouth. He ran that wicked, devil's tongue down the center of Terry's chest, then up again, and then he climbed up to straddle Terry's face.

Terry sucked him, desperate and whining, so lost, flying on a pink haze as Evan whispered to him, making Terry look at him, forcing him to maintain eye contact as he invented an audience for them. Site workers. Random people from town. Anyone, everyone, come to watch Terry get trussed and fucked.

"They're all looking at you, Kevin. Give them all a good show."

Terry did. Eyes watering, he swallowed Evan, choking when he went too deep, learning his rhythm and when to suck air so he didn't gag. By the time Evan finished fucking Terry's face and slid back down to work lube into his ass, Terry was gasping, almost sobbing.

"Oh my God. I can't believe I'm doing this."

"You're doing so wonderful, darling. Here, watch me get you ready."

Terry couldn't help but watch. It was hot. Raunchy, lewd, more extreme than anything he'd done, being tied like this while someone slathered him with lube, but goddamn, it turned him the hell on. And Evan was right. This whole night had ramped him up like nothing else had.

It had been far, far too long. He was gagging for this. Metaphorically and literally.

He didn't want to think about it, though, so he broke the rule and looked up instead, which was when he noticed the lights. He'd forgotten that he'd designed them in here too—more fairy lights, these soft multi-colored, teased into the tulle surrounding the top of the four-poster bed. Evan had them turned on, which meant the room was cast in a soft, holiday-like glow.

"Look at me."

Terry lowered his gaze just in time to see Evan line up and push into him.

He cried out—not in pain, he was loose enough to accept him all the way—but he couldn't help it, he tensed, rocking up as Evan pushed forward, bracing his arms on either side of Terry and fucking into him. God damn, but it was a good angle. Terry gasped and let his mouth fall open, rolling his hips as much as he could.

"There you go." Evan kept fucking, a slow, deep, steady pace. "God, but you're so wrecked." He bent and nipped at Terry's lips. "I want to see you again."

The thin thread of Terry's brain that wasn't fucked out trilled a terrified laugh—little did Evan know how *much* they were going to see each other, but it wasn't as if Terry could say that now. He couldn't say anything. He could barely breathe, could only lie back and get fucked until he was a begging, pathetic mess.

Evan did finish him from behind—he unstrapped Terry and led him to an ottoman, and Terry went like a zombie, obeying his every command. When Evan gave him a few smart slaps across his ass, Terry only stuck his ass higher. There wasn't anything else to do any-more, only to give Evan everything he wanted.

They kept moving around the room, fucking everywhere, ending against the sliding door, facing the moonlit lake. Evan came inside Terry, in a condom, but Terry came against the glass, Evan pressed against his backside. His legs were so worthless after that Evan nearly had to carry him up the stairs, which didn't work because he weighed too much.

"I'll have to start lifting weights," Evan teased him.

"Sorry," Terry slurred back.

Evan bussed his forehead and tucked him into bed, climbing in beside him.

Terry was dimly aware of being stroked, kissed, petted, being given water and offered something to eat, which he didn't take. Then he slept, cradled in someone's arms. He didn't dream, he only floated somewhere warm and safe.

In the early hours of the morning, he woke.

The panic was mild, but Terry had enough experience with this sort of thing to know if he stayed, it would only get worse. He felt odd enough after regular one-night stands, but this was the craziest he'd ever had. By the time Evan woke, Terry would go well beyond caged animal. He'd feel awkward and unsettled, and then he'd have to extricate himself from this intense, blunt man to boot.

Except he saw the flaw in his logic too late, the lure of this promise of *just one night*. Running away would only be temporary, wouldn't it? Evan would meet him again, soon enough. He'd slept with the man he was about to partner with.

You should stay and straighten things out. Be an adult about this.

The very thought made him want to run screaming into the sun.

Terry sat up carefully, not wanting to wake Evan, and he slipped from the bed and down the hall without making a sound. Thanks to the skills of the building crew, the cabin didn't creak, and he was able to make it back down to the basement and his clothes without being detected.

He stared at the mockups for Christmas Town's second phase as he climbed into his clothes with shaking hands. Acknowledged again that they were incredible, that Evan did amazing work.

Yes, running was foolish. Yes, eventually he was going to have to face Evan and own up to what they had done together and admit who he really was, that there was no Kevin at all, only Terry.

However, none of that had to happen today.

Setting the basement door to lock behind him, Terry stole into the night and hurried back into town, towards the bar and his waiting vehicle.

EVAN WOKE TO find Kevin gone.

He'd left his phone in his pants in the basement, so he didn't know what time it was until he stumbled into the kitchen and found a clock—honestly, he'd expected to find Kevin too. It was only ten in the morning. As late as they'd stayed up, as hard as they'd fucked, he was shocked Kevin wasn't still asleep. Evan wondered at first if Kevin hadn't gone to take another shower, or maybe a bath—both enticing possibilities—but he was out of luck. When he saw Kevin's clothes were gone, he became concerned, but he told himself Kevin had to be outside.

Kevin wasn't anywhere, however. There was no trace of him.

Evan called Charlotte. "You need to help me find Kevin."

Her voice was thick and groggy. "Honey, I'm not quite awake, and you've got to give me more details. Who exactly is Kevin?"

"Don't you remember? The man in the bar. You taught me how to pick up straight people." He waved at the air in front him. "Actually, I decided your advice was terrible, so I used my own strategy. It worked wonderfully. I found Kevin and took him home."

"Oh, right." He heard rustling on the other end of the line. "Sorry, did that go well?"

"He was amazing. However, I lost him. He left without giving me a number or saying goodbye, and all I have is his first name. I need you to hunt him down for me."

"Hon, I hate to be the one to tell you this, but if he didn't give you digits, he didn't want to give them to you."

Evan thought of the soft way Kevin had looked at

him and dismissed this idea out of hand. "He's just being shy. All I want is to talk to him again. Can you find out where he lives, or get a message for me? Give him *my* number?"

Charlotte sighed. "I'll try. Tell me what you know about him. The nonsexual details, please."

Evan was upset to discover how little he knew about Kevin. All he could offer Charlotte, definitively, was that he worked with the Christmas Town project in some way, in construction on one of the sites. Charlotte was unimpressed with this lead, but nevertheless managed to produce a list of three Kevins and links to their profiles on the Davidson Incorporated page.

None of them were his Kevin. Not even close.

"Look again," he told her, but she wouldn't have it.

"I've looked, babe. Those are the available Kevins. Take them or leave them."

"I'm leaving them. They're not my Kevin."

Because he was so upset, Charlotte hunted down all the Kevins in Logan and the surrounding area, but she came up with nothing—only another list of men who did not turn out to be Evan's Kevin. Evan scoured the Davidson Incorporated website, looking at every image of every employee, thinking maybe somehow the name was wrong, that Kevin was some kind of nickname, but he had no luck there either. It was as if Kevin didn't exist.

He began to despair, which was bad, because when Evan despaired, he couldn't work.

Charlotte tried to cajole him out of his funk, but Evan wasn't having it. He felt lost, betrayed, and confused. How could this have happened? Had he pushed Kevin too hard? He was sure he hadn't. He *knew* Kevin had enjoyed himself. It had been so perfect. *Everything* about their night together had been exquisite, and now…now it was simply over, forever? No. He refused to accept that.

Except he had to, because he had no route left to him to Kevin's heart. Or his anything.

When his work stoppage went on too long, his boss came to make a plea for Evan to get over his broken heart.

"Charlotte explained the Kevin situation to me. I want you to know, we've all been doing our best to find him. In the meantime, though, I need you to keep working on the project." Dale sat in Evan's kitchen, trying to get Evan to eat some of the food he'd brought with him. It was a gourmet-style soup and sandwich a friend of his had made. The hairstylist Charlotte had mentioned, who also made Evan's food.

Evan didn't care who had made it, unless it had been Kevin, come to apologize for ignoring him. He sighed and pushed the plate away. "I can't understand why no one can find him. This town isn't that big."

"I have my best people on it, several of them local. Lifelong locals. Arthur Anderson knows everyone in the tri-county area, and he says he doesn't know anyone who fits that description, but then we have been drawing in people for job opportunities, so perhaps he's from farther away. If he's working on the Christmas Town project, though, he has to turn up eventually." Dale gave him a severe look. "There won't *be* a project, however, if my designer can't finish his job."

Evan waved impatiently. "Yes, I know. I've been doing my best to work, I truly have. Mostly I've been fussing with the models, because it's what I do when I'm nervous. Would you like to see?"

"I'd love to see any progress you've made, yes."

Evan led Dale downstairs, trying as he always did not to think about how it had felt to show Kevin the models, of how Kevin had reacted, of how Kevin had *understood* his designs the way no one else ever had. He sighed. "Lately I've been obsessed with the lighting. It means so much, even during the day, and you can make lights do a lot of thematic work for you in the summer when you don't have snow. Plus with LED, it doesn't have to cost as much."

"I always appreciate it when you can save me money."

It was so hard to look at the models and not think about Kevin. In fact, it was because they'd talked about lighting so much that Evan was obsessed with it now. "If you flip the switch on the side by the model of the bank, it should turn on."

Dale flipped the switch, but nothing happened. He frowned, then peered at the underside of the table.

"Did it get unplugged?"

"Maybe. I might have bumped the table and jostled it." By *might have bumped* he meant that he had been kicking it when he was full of helpless rage over not being able to find Kevin. "I'll check."

Evan got on his hands and knees and lifted the skirt underneath the table—and that was when he found the notebook.

It was a small, black Moleskine Squared, well-worn with the elastic band meant to keep it closed nearly frayed in half. Evan blinked at it, amazed. He hadn't seen one in this condition before. It looked, frankly, as if it had been run over by a truck. Oh—there were tire marks. Apparently it *had* been run over by a truck. But this wasn't his. He had Moleskine notebooks, of course, but none of his were in this bad of shape. This had to belong to someone else.

Kevin. This might belong to Kevin.

With trembling hands, Evan sat on the floor and cracked the book open carefully, as if he had unearthed an important artifact, and if he disturbed it improperly, it might disintegrate in his hands. His heart skipped a beat at the insides of the notebook filled with the telltale scrawl of a builder—this *had* to be Kevin's book, it had to be. He flipped as hurriedly as he dared to the front, praying he would find a phone number, or at least a full name.

He found both—but it wasn't the name he was looking for.

If found please return to Terry Reid.

Evan's heart sank. This *had* to be connected to Kevin. He could *feel* the connection, as surely as he could feel the right way to design a room. So why was some other asshole's name in the front of this book?

A shadow fell over him, reminding Evan Dale was still with him. "Oh, hey, what's Terry's notebook doing here? Did you meet him already?"

Evan glanced up sharply at Dale. "Who's Terry?"

Dale nodded at the notebook in Evan's hands. "Terry Reid? The head architect of Christmas Town? The guy you're going to be working intimately with, as soon as I can get you to finish the work I need you to do here so I can send you back to Minneapolis?"

It was as if Evan could hear the hallelujah chorus inside his own head. How had he forgotten something this important? *The architect knew Kevin.*

And Evan would get to know this architect when he got to the next phase.

"I'll finish up my work this afternoon," Evan promised. "You just keep looking for Kevin."

Dale raised an eyebrow in surprise, but he only smiled and held out his hand. "Sounds like a deal to me."

Chapter Four

THE EVENING BEFORE Terry had his first meeting with Evan back in Minneapolis, he had too much to drink at Levi's house and shared far too much information about what had happened in Logan.

He'd accepted Levi's invitation in hopes being with the Daniels family would distract him from his impending doom. It had worked while he and Levi manned the grill together and served hot dogs and burgers to Laurel and the kids, while he'd listened to Levi lament at how quickly his children had grown and wonder at how Jackson could be going into kindergarten in three weeks. Terry had been fine while Levi had read to the kids as well, when he'd helped Laurel with the dishes, even though she'd tried three times to get him to sit down. If it could have continued like that, if when Levi had come back down the stairs he'd let Terry keep listening to Laurel tell him about the crazy case she was working on at her firm, he'd have gone home, watched late-night cable to counteract his insomnia, and gone into work simply sleep-deprived. But as soon as the kids were down, Levi had grabbed a six-pack of Terry's favorite microbrew, dragged Terry to the den, and poured Steel Toe Rainmakers into him until he explained, as Levi put it, why he'd been so damned edgy ever since he came back from Logan.

"You were fine when I left you at that bar, I swear. Then you came back to the Cities, showed up to the office all jumpy and weird, and every time someone comes into our cubicle area you act like they might be an axe murderer."

Terry stroked his cheek, where he did have a beard, but now it was a much more refined and trimmed strap and mustache. He'd tamed his split ends and gotten rid of the bleached tips.

He rubbed the lip of the bottle he was holding and stared intently at the label, trying to find a denial that worked. "There wasn't an axe murderer."

"But something *did* happen, didn't it? Why're you so jumpy?"

Terry took another drink. Any day now the design team would join the architect team, and he'd have to face Evan. That was why he was so jumpy. He'd been doing his best to forget it, but now he had Levi dragging it out of him, lubricated by alcohol.

Levi wasn't letting up either. "Did one of those townies pull something?"

Evan's intense gaze filled his mind's eye. "No. It wasn't a townie." Immediately realizing his mistake, he added, "*Fuck.*"

"Uh-huh." Levi settled into his chair, propping a foot onto his knee. "Now it comes out. Start talking."

This was bad. This was so bad. "I don't actually want to talk about it."

"Tough. You're a hot mess and getting messier. I care about you as your friend, but even if you wanted to be an ass and keep me in the dark, you've got to lead not one but two teams next week, including wrangling that loony dude Myles." When Terry flinched, Levi zeroed in. "Okay. I just hit something there, I can tell, but I don't know what. You might as well tell me, man, because you know how this is going down. I'm keeping after you until you spill everything."

Terry knew from experience Levi was telling the truth. Also, as much as he didn't want to have this conversation, he also *did* want to have it, in a way. Levi was right, he was a hot mess and getting hotter. Or messier. Or both.

He drained the rest of his beer.

Now Levi looked worried. Really worried. "Tell me this—am I bailing you out, or am I punching someone?"

Terry felt like shit. Fuck the embarrassing details. Maybe it was time to talk to *someone*, and Levi was as good as he was going to get. "Can you give me a ride home? Because I think if I get a little bit drunker, I can tell you. Though you might not want to hear this."

"Dude, at this point I don't care what you tell me,

so long as you tell me. The ride is yours." He popped the cap off another beer and passed it over. "You can have the rest of the beer and whatever other alcohol I have, if you can still sit upright and finish the story."

Terry nodded. Then he drank, took some deep breaths, and started to talk.

"As soon as you left, Evan Myles came over and hit on me."

Levi blinked. "Shut up. Are you serious?"

"Yes."

"That had to be something. Unless he's more suave in person? Everything I've heard about him is that he's socially clueless."

"Oh, he's a disaster. He read the name on my shirt and assumed I was a local construction worker named Kevin."

"So, what, you let him have it and it got ugly?"

"No. I went along with the gag, and then he started insulting Terry Reid, except he didn't even know that was me. Somehow this inspired me to go with him to his cabin. I had dreams of a big reveal, I think. I wanted to hear all his idiot designer ideas so I could shoot them down."

"I take it that didn't happen?"

More drinking. "No. It turns out he really likes my work, it's just the fishermen cabins he feels I pulled my punches on, and once I saw his redesign, I have to admit he was right. Plus I got to see his ideas. His models anyway. They're incredible. I see now why Dale hired him. He's insane, this guy, but he's crazy in the right directions, if you know how to aim him."

"This all sounds good so far. Where does the story go south?"

Terry rubbed at the side of his neck, at the place where he'd had to buy foundation and wear shirts with creative collars to hide Evan's hickey. For almost a week. "When he got me into bed and it got..." he blushed, searching for the word that would convey his message and preserve his dignity, then gave up, "...kinky."

He was ready for Levi to make a joke, but if anything, his friend became more serious. "Did you consent?"

Terry was sweating, gripping the arm of the chair. He couldn't quit staring at the carpet. "Yes. He didn't hurt me. And it wasn't that kind of kink either. It was..." he shut his eyes, feeling his face heat to near-furnace level, "...humiliation stuff."

"Hmm." Levi was quiet, letting that hang in the air before he continued. "I take it this was something new for you?"

The laugh that came out of Terry sounded deranged. He drank to drown it. "I really don't want to talk about this."

"And yet I'm thinking you have been bursting for *not* talking about it. So, *not* something new for you. Was it good, though?"

Terry swallowed. "Yes. At the time it was fine."

"Only fine?"

More drinking. "Very well, it was incredible. *At the time*. But once it was over, I freaked out."

"Is he aware you freaked out?"

"No. He was asleep. I got dressed and ran out." Terry shoved a hand into his hair. "This…this is a thing I do. I'm not proud of it. You already know I'm bad at relationships, but whenever they get kinky, especially if they get kinky fast, I panic faster. Normally it's not an issue, and it wouldn't be one here. Right now this is simply another case of me running away. It's even cleaner than usual. I didn't leave my number or ever tell him my real name. He still thinks I'm Kevin." Terry stared miserably into the carpet. "Except tomorrow he's going to find out he was fucking Terry Reid all along. While we're supposed to be working on the project. And there's nothing I can do about it."

Levi's eyebrows raised into his hairline, and he leaned forward to rest his elbows on his knees. "Huh. Well, damn. That's going to be a hell of a mess no matter how you slice it." He tilted his head to the side thoughtfully. "Unless he considered it a one-night stand too and just sort of winks at you. Then it's you getting drunk here a few more times and moving on. Though this fuck-and-run habit of yours is a little concerning."

Terry was well aware he had a problem, which was why he chose to ignore that part of the conversation. "I don't think it's going to be as simple as you say. Evan kept telling me he wanted to see me again."

"Yeah, but people say that during sex all the time. You probably wanted more in the heat of the moment too, then look what happened."

That was true. Terry bit his lip and frowned, wondering if it was possible he had blown this whole thing out of proportion. Then he thought of how intense Evan had been, not only during sex but before, and he shook his head. "No. I think he's going to at least want to talk about it."

"Damn." Levi leaned back, rubbing his chin as he shook his head. "So all your freaking out at work, what was that? You're saying you *don't* want to talk, or you're nervous because you know it's going to happen? Both?"

"That's just it. *I don't even know.*" The alcohol was seriously loosening Terry's tongue. "He wasn't what I thought he was going to be, Levi. *I* wasn't what I thought I was going to be. Things just…happened. The whole world fell away. After the adrenaline wore off, though, I panicked, so I left. Which was stupid, because I knew the whole time I was going to have to face him again." God, the more he talked, the more he felt like a shit-heel. "I'm a mess. I'm a terrible person."

Levi removed the beer from Terry's hand and replaced it with a bottle of water. "You're not terrible. You're predictable. I knew this had something to do with romance. You always run from men and women you're interested in. But I'm serious, this is something you need to address. When George is in town for the holidays, you should talk to him."

Now Terry was annoyed. "I do *not* want to date your brother, Levi."

"I'm not talking about dating George. I'm talking about *talking to him*. Seeing him. As a therapist."

"Oh, for fuck's sake." Terry frowned at the water in his hand. "Where did this come from? I thought we only had beer in here."

"You were so busy staring a hole in the carpet you missed Laurel bringing it in earlier. I texted her for some emergency supplies."

Laurel was such a good woman. Terry wiped at his eyes. "You have such a wonderful marriage. I can't even hold down a relationship for more than six months." He aimed the water bottle at Levi. "I'm not seeing a therapist, though."

"Fine, fine. We'll save that for another night. Drink that water, buddy. Okay, let's review. Myles is about to join our team and figure out you're the one he got kinky with. Obviously I will back you up on whatever you want or don't want from him. You want help telling him to stay the fuck away?"

Terry thought about how Evan had looked at him, how he'd stroked his skin, how he'd whispered to him in the dark. He shut his eyes and drank furiously from the bottle of water.

"All right, so do you want help navigating the transition from being Kevin the hot construction worker to

Terry the genius architect he gets to work with and bone on the side?" When Terry only whimpered and clutched the plastic bottle until it crunched, Levi threw up his hands. "Dude, I love you, but I'm glad I don't have to date you."

Terry let out a heavy breath. "It's that he's so intense. He swept me off my feet so quickly, and I know as soon as he's back in my life it will happen again. Plus this time it will involve my work as well."

"So play for middle ground. Only see him for work at first, and if you have trouble holding to that, use me as your buffer. You know I'm good for it. It's been a long time since my days as defensive end, but I still know how to protect my quarterback's blind side."

"I'm a lousy quarterback. I shouldn't be a quarterback of anything."

"Protecting my friend then, how about that?"

Terry hemmed and hawed awhile longer, trying to say he shouldn't bother Levi, then Levi getting more and more insistent Terry allow him to be bothered, until finally Terry broke down and said yes, he'd let Levi help. They finalized a battle plan as Levi drove Terry back to his condo. Mostly Levi did.

"I'll bring him in to your office tomorrow first, so it's only the three of us. That way when he realizes who you are, you don't have an audience, but you have me with you. I'm gonna let you lead, but if you look like you need a save, I'm coming in."

"Okay," Terry agreed, with a confidence he didn't

feel.

Levi didn't let him off that easy. "Hit me with the plan again, big guy."

"I'm going to tell him I'm open to exploring something with him, but not until the project is finished, because I don't mix work and pleasure. Which isn't a lie."

"Damn straight. And if he tries to push you?"

"I keep saying no, and if he won't back down or I get too nervous, I signal to you."

"The signal is?"

Terry tried to remember. "I don't know."

"I'm asking you. We didn't set anything. How about you say, 'Levi, please take care of this.'"

"I don't think I could say that."

"Then look at me like you're drowning, and I'll sort it out. Odds are good I won't be able to stay out of it that long anyway."

It was the best plan Terry could hope to get, all things considered, but he still didn't sleep that night, not until twenty minutes before his alarm went off. He dragged himself through the shower, poured black coffee, and ordered an egg sandwich at the breakfast cart, which he took to his desk and didn't eat. In fact he didn't do anything but pace around his desk until Levi showed up, looking ridiculously rested for as late as they'd stayed up.

"I've got two kids under the age of six. I've been sleep deprived so long now my body thinks five hours of sleep is some kind of spa treatment." Levi put his hands on Terry's shoulders and ushered him into his chair, pushing his uneaten sandwich and a new cup of coffee in front of him. "Eat. I asked them to bring in the final notes for the meeting, and we're going to go over them, not spool endlessly over a problem we solved at two in the morning."

Terry ate, managing to choke down over half the sandwich. He drank enough coffee he thought he might be able to stay awake through midafternoon, though he conceded most of his power today was coming from cold terror with a side-dash of anticipation. He was going to see Evan again after almost three weeks. They were going to work on the Christmas Town project together. They might do more together.

He hoped Evan wasn't too angry with him for not coming clean about who he was that night, that Evan believed him when he explained how many times he'd tried. He hoped he was able to set his own boundaries without Levi having to interfere.

He hoped he didn't throw up this egg sandwich.

When the receptionist buzzed to let them know Myles and his team had arrived, Terry had to put his head between his knees.

Levi patted him on the back. "Keep taking deep breaths. I'll knock before I bring him in, and I'll drag it out a few seconds so you have a chance to pull yourself together. Just remember. You can do this."

I can do this. I can do this. Terry repeated this to himself over and over as he waited for Levi's return, giving up sitting, instead pacing in front of the window, but when the knock finally came, he panicked after all.

Oh God. I can't do this.

Then the door opened, and Levi led Evan inside.

"Mr. Myles," Levi began, coming into the room first and telegraphing heavy *calm the fuck down, it's going to be fine* signals at Terry, "I'd like to introduce our team leader and the lead architect on the Christmas Town project, Terry—"

"Terry Reid, yes, I know." Evan pushed around Levi and made his way toward Terry—there he was, tall, intense, gorgeous, awkward, everything Terry remembered and somehow more, even his glasses seemed thicker—and stuck out his hand. "Hi. Evan Myles. I admire your work of course, and I look forward to working with you, and so on, but more importantly, I have a favor I need to ask of you."

Terry blinked at him, still holding his breath, waiting for Evan to figure it out, perplexed, in fact, that he hadn't. Or maybe this was his strange way of calling Terry out. "Um…yes?"

Evan closed the distance between them, bearing down on Terry with his intense hazel gaze. "Tell me everything you know about Kevin."

Terry stared at him. His mouth went dry. "What?"

"Kevin. He's a construction worker in Logan, at the site." Evan eyed Terry critically. "A little taller than you, and more built. Lighter hair, big beard. Knows quite a bit about building. Bisexual, if that helps narrow it down."

What in the...*what*? "I'm sorry...is this a joke?"

Evan seemed annoyed. "Look, I know you know who I'm talking about. He said he knew you, and I have proof." He reached into his satchel and pulled out—

Terry gasped. "My notebook! I've been looking all over for that. Where—?"

"*Kevin* had it." Evan put it back in his satchel, triumphant. "I'll return it once you tell me his name and phone number."

Terry couldn't stop staring at Evan. This had to be a joke, right? Any second now Evan would laugh and tell Terry this was what he got for hiding this whole time, or...anything, really. Except Evan did none of these things. He simply kept waiting.

For Kevin's name and phone number, apparently.

"You're serious," Terry said at last, completely mystified. "You don't...you're *serious*."

"Oh, you won't believe how serious I am." Evan folded his arms over his chest. "You're giving me that name *and* number. I'm going to do whatever I have to in order to get them both."

Terry just kept staring, his jaw falling open.

Levi, unable to stand it any longer, burst out laughing.

EVAN WASN'T SURE what was going on, but he was starting to get annoyed.

So was Reid, who finally stopped staring at him like an idiot, turned to the man who'd brought Evan in, and glowered. "This isn't funny. Stop laughing, Levi."

Levi wiped his eye with one hand. "The hell it ain't. Myles, you've got him good."

Got him good? What did that even mean? Evan had no idea, so he ignored the comment and glared at them both. "Kevin's full name and phone number. Do you have some reason you can't share that information with me?"

Reid pinched the bridge of his nose while Levi covered his mouth in a fit of giggles before prodding his superior with his foot from the chair he'd collapsed into. "Yeah, Terry. What's the reason you can't share that information?"

"What the hell happened to my *backup*?" Reid ground out.

"Oh, we are next level, lover boy. We're talking pay-per-view. I am here for the *show* now."

Lover boy? These two were an item? Whatever, Evan couldn't care less, except that their office romance was keeping him from Kevin. "I assure you, I don't want his name or number for nefarious purposes. I only want to reconnect with him. We met a few weeks ago, but he left before I could get his contact information."

Reid continued to stare at him while Levi giggled

behind his hand.

Evan decided the only way to get through to these people was to be quite blunt. "We had sex, if you must know."

Reid's face and neck became flush with pink as he turned with an inscrutable expression. "*Levi, I want you to handle this.*"

Levi stopped laughing. "Wait—*wait*. You mean this is serious? He really doesn't know who you are?"

What kind of comment was that? Of course Evan knew who Reid was. Honestly, the two men seemed like a mess. This is why Evan worked alone. "Is it so difficult to share contact information?"

They were ignoring Evan completely now, Levi regarding Reid with concern. "So, what, are you going to say something?"

Reid was becoming more and more panicked. "No, I'm not, and you aren't either."

"Then what exactly are you proposing we do about this?"

"*I don't know, that's why I told you to handle it.*"

Levi pulled Reid aside and began to speak in whispers Evan couldn't hear, which gave him a moment to study the pair of them. Levi was tall and put together and handsome, very pleasing to look at. He wore three-piece suits and his shoes gleamed. Reid wore a lightweight sweater and khakis, and his shoes had frayed seams. His hair was short and brown and messy, the thin line of beard on his cheeks slightly uneven.

His eyes, though. Pale, smoky blue, like steel, and so soft. They seemed…familiar. Why?

Before Evan could dwell on this thought too long, Levi and Reid left their huddle. Reid's shoulders were tight with anger, and Levi kept patting him on the back.

"Terry, calm down. I got this. Go lie down in my office or something. Just don't jump out the window."

"I'm going to call your wife and tell her what an asshole she married." Reid stalked out of the room.

"You do that, and I won't fix this," Levi called after him, not sounding remotely concerned.

Evan didn't know what Levi was supposed to fix, or what kind of scheme these two were pulling if Levi was married, but what he did know was if Reid walked out of the room, so did his chance to find Kevin. When he tried to follow him, Levi rose from his chair with smooth, languid grace and stopped him with a hand on his arm.

"Easy, tiger. Let him go. There's no talking to him when he's all worked up like that."

What choice did Evan have? He watched Reid leave. "He seems very moody."

"He can be temperamental, yes, but he's a good guy." Levi put his arm around Evan's shoulders. "Look, Terry needs some time to himself. What do you say you and I have a long lunch, right now, just the two of us, and get to know one another?"

Evan pushed Levi's arm off him and took two

steps away so the contact didn't happen again. Right now? Levi wanted to go to lunch *now*? Evan glanced around, regretting rushing to this appointment without Charlotte. "Aren't we supposed to be going to a meeting?"

"Forget the meeting. I set your team up with our team in the conference room, and they can push paper at each other until everyone feels better about themselves. If you want, we can talk a little bit about your designs while we're at lunch, but the truth is, nothing's going to happen until Terry's in the room. Between you and me, so long as your design is good, he'll go for it. If your design is shit, forget it."

"My designs are always perfect."

"See? Meeting adjourned. Now. I wanted to try this great new seafood place over on Hennepin. Shall we take an Uber, or would you like me to drive us there?"

Evan didn't want to go, but somehow they ended up in Levi's car anyway, a silver BMW SUV that impressed Kevin until he saw the interior was strewn with toys. With a chagrined expression, Levi shoved a stuffed animal and box of crackers aside to make room for Evan. "Sorry, kids. What are you going to do?"

Evan decided it was best he not share his thoughts on children. He wondered if he could salvage this lunch date by getting some of the answers he'd come for in the first place. "Do *you* know how I can reach Kevin?"

An odd expression passed over Levi's face. "Well,

for starters, I can tell you you're going to have to slow your roll a little."

Ah-ha. "So you know him too?"

Levi navigated out of the ramp and toward the exit as they spoke, pausing to swipe his card at the gate. "I'm not at liberty to say much, but I can tell you Kevin scares easily. You gotta lay the pipe *carefully,* man."

"I can't very well do that if I don't know where he is." Evan sighed. "Also, I don't know how to charm people. I'm direct. It's the only way I know how to be."

"I get that about you. I really do." Levi turned onto the road that would take them over to the interstate. He seemed to consider something for several seconds, then said, "As far as how to get to Kevin, I'm going to be straight with you. The best way to do that is to go through Terry."

Evan pursed his lips. "I don't care for Reid. He has some skills as an architect, but he seems terribly unsteady."

For some reason Levi found this funny, though he covered his mouth to hide his laughter and sobered quickly. "Yes, well. You're going to have to work with him, and as I said, he's your key to Kevin. Why don't you let me tell you a bit more about how to deal with Terry over lunch?"

Evan had zero interest in learning more about Reid, but he was trapped in this car now, and in any event, it was clear this was the bridge he must cross for gaining access to Kevin. It didn't make any sense to him, and he was seriously put out that the only progress whatsoever he'd made was confirmation that Kevin's best friend seemed to be Terry Reid.

Fine. Terry Reid would become his best friend too.

Chapter Five

T ERRY HAD NO idea what had ever possessed him to sleep with Evan Myles, but he knew for damn sure it wasn't ever happening again.

He worked himself into an acute state of panic while Evan and Levi were at lunch. He kept waiting for Levi to come back and give him an update, and when waiting made him too crazy, he went to the team meeting because it was either that or bang his head against the wall of his office. The meeting was largely ridiculous, mostly a collection of uneasy underlings too hesitant to make decisions without Evan and Terry present. They made some headway with Terry there, but Evan's team wouldn't go forward with anything until he arrived, so Terry ended up taking all the files to his office, where once again he conceded that though the man might be an ass, his talent couldn't be denied.

Terry glanced up from the design sheets as Levi returned, blessedly without Evan. "These are seriously good. Moreover, I suspect they're only roughs. I still want to punch him in the face, but his work is unparalleled. I'm going to revise things based on what I've seen here alone." He closed the folio and glared at the cover. "I can't fucking believe he didn't even *recognize* me."

"Not only that, but he doesn't much like you, not as Terry." Levi flopped into a leather armchair and rested his elbow on the arm, propping up his head. "I sold you like the prize pig at the county fair, but he wasn't buying. He thinks you're unstable."

"I don't want to be bought. And where does he get off calling me unstable, anyway? His precious Kevin ran off on him and hasn't called."

"His precious Kevin is you. Don't hate him too much."

Terry held up a hand. "It doesn't matter. I'm lucky he doesn't remember. He's never going to find Kevin. I'll do the project with him, and then we'll be finished with one another. End of story."

"You seriously underestimate the man's determination to reconnect with his Cinderella."

"That analogy doesn't work. How can he try my Moleskine on people? It's *my* Moleskine. It has my damn name on it."

"I know, that's what's so crazy. I think you could go up to him and come clean that you're Kevin at this point and he wouldn't believe you. I think the guy has some kind of disability or something that might be keeping him from recognizing you. Did you see those glasses? He tripped twice at lunch and said he has trouble with his equilibrium. Maybe he has vision or other processing issues too."

Terry remembered the way Evan listed and stumbled that night, realized Levi's hypothesis fit, and felt guilty for being angry. "Well what am I supposed to do? Come clean?"

"Yes, that would be the adult approach. Why didn't you let me tell him who you were? I felt ridiculous pretending otherwise. Also, did you know he somehow got the idea you and I were having an affair?"

Terry stared at him. "*How?*"

"I called you lover boy, apparently. Ironically, teasing you about Evan. That went over his head and he decided you and I were lovers, and when I mentioned my wife, he assumed we were illicit lovers. I've corrected his assumption, though he's still confused about the lover boy comment. I think he didn't ask for clarification because it didn't fit his mission of all things Kevin." Levi steepled his fingers. "Amusing as all this is, Evan's a good man, and he doesn't deserve this. Tell him the truth."

The very idea made Terry tense up. "It's not that simple."

Every shred of amusement left Levi's body. "Terry Reid. You're either going to explain things to your coworker, or you're getting on the phone with George and he's counseling your ass. You decide."

Terry knew Levi was right, that he needed to explain things to Evan, but he really did get cold sweats every time he thought about it. This whole thing was so out of hand. He honestly was ready to get it over with, but even if he wanted to tell Evan, the man had gone home for the day after their lunch, so he couldn't have any further conversations about the design work or Kevin.

He was off the hook, for now.

Despite his escape, Terry didn't sleep much again that night, mostly tossing and turning as he replayed Evan failing to recognize him and then disliking him to boot. He thought too about how they'd have to start working together the next day, unless, as Dale had warned him, Evan pulled one of his moody fits and didn't come into work. Terry couldn't decide if he hoped for that or not. Part of him wanted to put off the encounter. Part of him wanted to get this whole business over and done with.

All of him, whether he liked it or not, was hurt at not being identified, even though it made life easier for him. He didn't look *that* different.

Yes, the beard had been big. He supposed his voice had been raw from shouting on the site.

Fine, he'd allow it had also been dark that night too. Since then he'd sat at a desk for three weeks, eating takeout instead of eating Frankie's packed lunches and homemade breakfasts and working on a site all day. However, he wasn't *shorter.*

How in the world am I supposed to tell him I'm Kevin?

Perhaps Evan would figure it out once they had prolonged contact. Perhaps he wouldn't have to say anything at all and it would come out in due course. As Terry lay awake, he imagined working beside Evan, his partner asking him why he was so familiar. In his mind's eye, it was so easy to confess then. Waiting for the natural course of events seemed the best way to go, the more he thought of it.

Even so, he paced his office the next morning, wondering if Evan would even show up. Anxious about what would happen if he did.

Evan did arrive, promptly at the meeting time. Once again, he didn't recognize Terry as the man he'd slept with. Evan was polite, but he looked at Terry as if he hadn't held him against a shower wall and coaxed him into being obscene with shower attachments. The only attention he paid Terry at all was that he seemed to keep glancing at his eyes.

"I hear you went over the project notes with my team yesterday." Evan nodded at the portfolio on Terry's desk.

"Yes." Clearing his throat and trying not to think about Evan and showers, Terry picked up the documents, flipped through them. "I was impressed. They're drafts, yes?"

Evan's expression was guarded. "I don't normally finish my sketches until final approval is given."

Yes, but you make all those models. Terry couldn't point that out without giving himself away, though. Which technically he should do, according to his plan. So why was he hesitating? Levi was going to murder him when he found out he was stalling again. His headache was coming back. "Well, unless Dale has some kind of objection, I'm all for your designs. I have to adjust a few things on the plans to make them work, but that's not a problem. I've already calculated the alterations."

Evan frowned. "You need to make adjustments? Show me where." He unclenched his jaw and added, "Please."

Terry opened the design drafts and his working drawings and laid them side by side on his drafting table, flipping on the light above. "Okay—so, for some of the downtown buildings there won't be any trouble with your designs. But there's so much variance in the construction there, and between you and me the Logan building code is shit. If we're going to have this many tourists running in and out of these buildings, we need more reinforcements on these posts anyway, which is why I had those refits done that way. See?"

Evan leaned in as Terry pointed with his mechanical pencil. "I see. I hadn't thought of that. My apologies."

"Not your job to think of it—don't worry about it." He tapped the end of his pencil on the paper as a new idea occurred to him. He glanced at Evan, still feeling the edges of awkward, but starting to lose himself to the work. "Would you mind if I tried something out while you're standing here?"

Evan looked slightly taken aback. "I—that's fine."

Terry wasn't sure what to make of that reaction, but he was more worried about losing the thread of his idea, so he focused on his drawing. "The city says they're giving us carte blanche to do whatever we want, but I'm trying to be respectful of the town at the same time. It's going to be a big change for them to get as many tourists as we're sending them. They'll be glad for the boost in their economy, but I heard from the people I stayed with how it's divided the town."

"Who did you stay with?"

Terry's pencil paused as he tried to remember if Kevin had told Evan anything like that. He didn't think so. "Marcus Gardner and Frankie Blackburn. The lawyer and stylist. Though I think Marcus is running for city council now as well."

"I think I met them, possibly. I don't know. I tend to forget people."

Terry, gaze away from Evan, rolled his eyes and kept sketching, reaching for an eraser as he got to a section he needed to adjust. "I like the way you use the lights on not only the edges but the windows, and the drape on the corners is good. I dislike the way my support posts ruin the line, so I see why you removed them. So I'm wondering, if we did this…" He pursed his lips. "Except I worry it's too much renovation."

"Stop thinking like an architect. Here. Give me that." Evan nudged him aside and took the pencil and eraser, removing Terry's addition and changing it yet again. "Why does it have to be literal? What's wrong with a false front? You don't have to actually extend the storefront, only this section to make it appear that you did. We could do that much with fiberboard and paint it."

That was true, but…"Won't it look cheap?"

Evan gave him an incredulous look. "Do you honestly think I'd let it look cheap?"

Fair point. Terry studied Evan's adjustment, impressed the more he examined it. "It looks like a real Nordic storefront now. I'm almost glad we had the support beam issue."

"I was thinking the same thing. Would you mind if we made the same design on all the storefronts, even the ones that don't need this disguise?"

"Absolutely. Like you said, this won't cost much of anything, and I think both Dale and the residents will really go for it." Terry dusted his hands and nodded in satisfaction at the drawing. "Shall we tackle the interiors? I don't think they'll be quite this smooth, but I'm feeling confident now. Let's push on."

He was feeling great, so much so he could almost get over the ache of Evan not recognizing him. Maybe they could simply start over from scratch. Perhaps that would be the best plan after all.

Evan frowned at Terry. "I've never had an architect be so agreeable."

Terry averted his gaze to hide his blush, fussing with the drawings. "Why wouldn't I be? Your work is good, and I'd like to implement it as much as I can."

"Your work is also quite excellent."

Terry's ears burned.

The day flew by. They got through several interiors and put some finer touches on three exteriors, sending the drafts to their teams to finalize and submit to Dale for final approval. It was still awkward, but getting less so, and Terry decided he could get through it, that it wouldn't be the best time he ever had, but the work would be good, and in the end he would be okay.

Then, as they were wrapping up, Evan caught him by the wrist as he tried to leave and said, "I'd like to take you to dinner."

Terry nearly tripped over his feet, and he *did* run into the back of the door. He rubbed his head as he turned around, staring at Evan in disbelief. "You…what?"

Evan didn't let go of Terry's wrist. "I want to take you to dinner. To thank you for today."

Terry's heart skipped a beat. It was so difficult not to get sucked under that gaze. "I…all right."

The hand on his wrist relaxed. "Good. Because I need to ask you about Kevin too."

The words were like a slap against Terry's face. He shook his head, pulling away from Evan's grip. "No. I need to go home." He put his hand on the doorknob.

Evan pushed it shut again and kept his palm against it to stop Terry from escaping. Terry glanced at him on impulse and sure enough, there was that intense stare, bearing down on him once more. "I miss him."

Intellectually, on some distant plane in Terry's mind, a part of him understood it was ridiculous for him to feel jealous of Kevin, since they were one and the same person. He knew, too, that here again was another perfect moment to reveal himself—in fact, logic pointed out if he said he was Kevin, that jealousy would evaporate in an instant.

Yet it *did* hurt. Why couldn't Evan recognize him? Beard, no beard—they'd done more than have sex that night. They'd talked too. Evan was missing more than the sex. He was missing the man he talked to, who was also the man he was talking to right now.

So tell him they're one and the same person.

The thought made Terry want to throw up. It also made him feel guilty, and then, because he couldn't bear to hold all those feelings, simply angry. He told all his intellectual arguments about why Evan responded the way he did to go fuck themselves. Terry was overwhelmed and confused by the fact that even though he wanted Evan to care about him, he couldn't stay this sense of panic building inside him. He was furious that Evan couldn't see through any of it and help him out.

He wanted to bury this nonsense now, once and for all and eradicate it from his heart.

Fishing out the smile he reserved for people who asked him to explain how being bisexual wasn't the same as cheating, Terry aimed it at Evan full blast. "Well, he doesn't miss you."

Telling himself Evan deserved to look that pole-axed, he shoved the man aside, wrenched the door open a second time, and escaped before the idiot could say anything else to piss him off.

WELL, HE DOESN'T miss you.

Reid's parting shot haunted Evan the rest of the day, all through the evening, and into his dreams, where instead of Evan making love to Kevin only to have him evaporate like mist in his arms, he made love to Kevin only to have him stand over him afterward and laugh beside Terry Reid before the two of them linked arms and went away. The idea that Kevin wasn't simply shy, that he wasn't actively avoiding Evan—that he had forgotten him and *moved on*…well, it was too much to bear. Evan woke from the second nightmare in a cold sweat, thought about taking a shower, and then gave up, because while they always made him think of Kevin, now showers made him think of Kevin *mocking him.*

Or worse, *not even thinking about him.*

He made some tea, got out his stylus, and drew on his tablet, then tossed them both onto his drafting table. He was too depressed to work.

He lay on the couch, listless, staring out the window at his balcony, the only mark of the passage of time the shifting of the sun and his phone ringing, though eventually he got up with a heavy sigh and turned it off. He had to get up to urinate a few times, which he resented, and he shifted to lie on the bed after a while as the couch wasn't comfortable. Toward what he assumed was afternoon he heard banging on the door and a female voice—Charlotte, no doubt—but after a period of time she also left.

His stomach gurgled, but he ignored it as well. He'd drink some water in a minute.

The problem was, if he moved much more, if he let himself think at all, he was afraid he was going to cry.

He was right, that was exactly what he did when he went to get the water. One minute he was staring at the glass, watching it fill, and the next he was trying to decide why his hand was wet, and why the glass was blurry—then he'd dropped the glass before he ended up on the floor, holding his knees, rocking back and forth, marveling at how hard it was to breathe.

He wasn't sure how much time passed between that and when Dale appeared in front of him.

Evan stared at his employer for several seconds in surprise, then remembered. "That's right. You have a key."

"I do. Part of your contract after the last time you went into a black hole." Dale settled onto the tile, cross-legged, and regarded Evan with a patient expression. "Normally I like to give you more time before I come find you, but Charlotte seemed particularly concerned when she called me."

Evan wiped his eyes, but the tears kept falling. "I

seem to be upset. I'm not fully sure why." A pinch in his chest reminded him, and he thought about sending Dale away because he didn't want to explain, but he was too tired. "I have deeper feelings for Kevin than I knew. Which is problematic, because apparently he has none for me whatsoever."

Dale's eyebrows rose. "Did you locate him?"

Evan fixed his gaze on the black grout between the white tiles. "No, but I'd remembered when I found Terry Reid's notebook that the architect was supposed to know Kevin. When I met him, I discovered that was true. Except Reid says Kevin doesn't miss me at all." The tears began falling faster, and the tight feeling in Evan's chest increased. "He was quite rude about it, in fact."

Dale frowned. "Wow, really? That doesn't seem like Terry."

"I don't like Reid. I did my best to be polite to him. I thought we were doing well, but then he…" The tightness in Evan's chest was unbearable. He *never* felt this way. Not anymore. He clenched his hands into fists. "I'll find a way to work with him, don't worry, but I can't work right now."

"I'm not concerned about that at the moment. I'm worried a lot more about you. Is there anything I can get you?"

Evan rubbed at his throat. "I *was* trying to get a drink, but then I started crying and startled myself."

"One drink of water, coming up."

Dale brought Evan the water there on the floor and sat beside him while he drank it. Evan felt calmer as he sipped. Dale was soothing and handsome. Evan wouldn't have minded having sex with him, but Dale didn't have sex with employees, and the first approach Dale had made toward Evan was for a job. Dale was an excellent employer, the best Evan had ever had, so he didn't mind. Much.

Evan glanced at Dale over the top of his glass. "I thought you'd moved to Logan. Why are you in Minneapolis?"

"I'm in the Cities while you and Terry work on the draft for the next phase of the project. I'm still splitting my time between here and there until Christmas Town is more fully established, anyway."

Oh. "Sorry I'm slowing you down."

"I told you, I'm not concerned about that."

Evan drank more water and leaned against the cupboard beside him, trailing his index finger along a groove. "I meant to tell you. Charlotte said another firm tried to hire me away."

"Did they now." Dale grinned. "You sent them your list of requirements?"

Evan nodded, a slow smile breaking out on his face. "She let me listen in on speaker when they called to ask her if it was a joke. When she told them that was the special clause addendum of my contract with Davidson Incorporated, the CEO sounded like he was choking."

"Ooh, look at you, getting calls direct from the CEOs now."

"We don't respond unless it's from them. The replies aren't any fun otherwise."

"I'm going to have to give Charlotte grief for holding out on me. Usually she shares those offers with me and we have a good time laughing over their angry responses to your refusals."

Evan sighed. "She's been a little busy, looking for Kevin."

Tears welled up again. Would he actually die from this? It felt possible.

Dale squeezed his knee. "You're going to be all right, Evan. I want you to leave this to me, now."

"He doesn't want me." It hurt so much just saying the words.

"We don't know that yet. Let's see if we can find him first. Though I'm surprised at how quickly you got attached to him. Normally you don't attach to the men you're with at all."

"I know. I think it's because it wasn't my normal arrangement. I'm only using escorts, no matter what, once this is over. I'm going to need to rewrite my contract and ask for one for remote locations so this doesn't happen again."

"Well *that* will certainly make those phone calls from CEOs more fun, when we send them your addendum clauses. But before we go that far, why don't I have a conversation with Terry. Because something doesn't feel right here."

"I don't want it to hurt anymore."

"I understand. I don't want you to hurt anymore either. So let me see if I can fix this, okay?" Dale nudged his arm. "You're going to eat something for me too. No arguments."

Evan didn't want to eat anything ever again. Then he remembered what a good cook Dale was. He opened one eye. "Are *you* making it?"

Dale winked at him. "You bet."

Evan sighed. "Very well."

IT HAD BEEN a long time since getting called into his employer's office had made Terry nervous, and a summons from Dale had inspired that feeling exactly never. However, the terse, "Reid, in my office please," had cut across the room and zinged straight to the base of Terry's spine. He couldn't begin to guess why, but he didn't waste time hurrying to the double doors and letting himself inside.

"Yes, Dale? Is something wrong?"

When Dale flattened his lips into a thin line and asked him to take a seat, Terry knew something was.

"I need to ask you something," Dale said, leaning on the edge of his desk and looming over Terry ever so slightly, "but before I do that, I want to explain a few things to you. You might have noticed we're at another standstill on design work today, with Evan absent."

Terry had noticed, yes. "Is he all right?" He startled at the icy flash in Dale's gaze. "Sorry—have I done something to upset you? Would you mind telling me what it is? You're making me nervous."

"In a minute. First, I need to finish explaining. As I said, Evan isn't here. Work stoppage for him is common, and it happens for a variety of reasons. It happens less now that we've come to understand one another and he pretty much has everything he wants and needs, however ridiculous it might seem to everyone else, but when he first started working for me, we once lost a week of work because he couldn't find a bag of Twizzlers in his apartment. Now we have grocery shopping and cleaning worked into his salary. Because when Evan is able to work, he's dazzling. You have to know how to tune him, though, like a musician playing a fine instrument. I hired him away from a Fortune 500 company, and multimillion-dollar corporations try weekly to steal him back, but they don't know how to speak his language, so they don't get anywhere. They all *say* they'll give him whatever he wants, but despite what some people think, Evan isn't an idiot. He knows I will do whatever I need to in order to take care of him, the same way I will all my employees. His old companies didn't treat him the way I do, and he's well aware of this."

Dale rubbed the back of his head. "In hindsight, it's my fault for not giving you a proper Evan primer before having the two of you work together. Normally he has no issue working with people, and I never would have guessed the two of you would have issues—I thought your designs were meshing beautifully—but then, we are in extraordinary circumstances. The bottom line is this, Terry. Apparently you are connected to someone Evan, hell, *all* of us have been trying to find for almost a month now, and I understand you said something rather sharp to him about that person. He was so devastated, I have to believe the two of you butted heads and you snapped at him, which I must ask you never, ever to do again, under any circumstances. I was up until three in the morning trying to find something he would eat because he hadn't for over twenty-four hours, and he only ate because I told him it was that or the hospital. He was weeping, which completely shocked me—I didn't know he even *did* that. I'm not sure how Evan attached to this Kevin person so quickly, or why. I'm not asking you to force someone who doesn't want to see Evan to do so. However, if you could at least let *me* talk to him, I hope you can trust— Terry, are you all right? *Terry?*"

Somewhere in the middle of Dale's speech, as he talked about how absent-minded and yet brilliant Evan was when properly managed, Terry's chest had started to hurt. When Dale reminded Terry how he'd snapped at him, Terry's ears had begun to ring. When Dale got to *hospital* and *weeping*, Terry got dizzy, and by the time he was talking about how attached Evan was to Kevin, Terry thought he might be having a heart attack.

Dale crouched in front of Terry, pressing the backs of his hands to Terry's face. "You're as white as a sheet. What's going on?"

Terry couldn't take it. He could have held out if Dale had shouted at him, accused him of things. Begging, though. *Just like Evan, who you snapped at, and look what you did, you animal.* Terry shut his eyes, drew a shaky breath, and let it out.

"I'm Kevin."

Dale stilled. "Sorry—what?"

The white-hot terror made Terry want to evade, try to lie, but what was the point? He couldn't lie to Dale, and he obviously couldn't snap at Evan again. "I'm Kevin. Or rather, there is no Kevin. I'm the person Evan thinks is Kevin."

The whole story came pouring out of him, not only how they met, but what they'd done. It was Dale, and they had a rather intimate history, so Terry didn't hold back anything. He told Dale how well he'd worked together with Evan, but how Evan hadn't recognized him, how much that had upset Terry and how without meaning to he'd lashed out.

"I'm so sorry. I'm a terrible person. He was only doing what Levi told him to, trying to get close to me to get close to Kevin. I didn't realize how much that hurt until we'd spent the afternoon together, how he could talk with me the same way he had that night and still not understand who I was. Then I felt ridiculous because I didn't *want* him to know who I was. I panicked. I wanted him to leave me alone, so I lashed out and left. I'm so sorry."

Dale had ended up perched on the edge of the desk again, but his stance was a lot gentler now. He waited until he was sure Terry was finished, then shook his head in stunned disbelief. "Wow. That's...*wow*. So we've been looking for *you* this whole time. I never would have guessed." He raised an eyebrow at Terry. "I knew about the other part, though."

Terry blinked at him. "What other—?" He blushed. Hotly. *The humiliation kink.*

"What I do need to know, *Kevin*, is what we're doing now."

Terry threw up his hands. "That's just the problem. I have no idea. I've been living in terror of him recognizing me, and then he showed up and *didn't* recognize me, and now..." He couldn't finish that sentence, distracted by the memory of how it had felt to work beside Evan, of Dale's stories of how much care he took of him, of the knowledge of how sexy his intense looks were. Terry cleared his throat. "I don't want any of this to interfere with the project."

"Perhaps you missed the part where I said Evan is obsessed with Kevin to the point of making himself sick and is unable to work?"

"Yes, well—what's he going to do when he finds out his precious Kevin is *me*? Will he ever even hold a stylus again?"

"You matter in this too, you know." Dale folded

his arms over his chest. "I've never seen him this way, and I've never seen you come unglued like this either."

Yes, well, there was a lot about Terry that Dale didn't know.

"I never knew the rival for my affections would be my own mistaken identity."

"Tell me this much. If you didn't have the project, if this was me figuring out you were Kevin and asking you as my friend to give my other friend a chance, would you do it?"

Terry shivered and hugged his stomach, averting his gaze. Damn that panic. Why wouldn't it go away? "I can't answer that because we *do* have the project."

"That's a cop-out reply."

It absolutely was. Terry sighed. "Fine. I would *consider* it. But he's so intense. I don't know that I could go on a date without a list of peace accords set in place first."

"You don't understand—talking about peace accords? Now you're starting to speak in a language Evan's actually comfortable with." He scratched his chin. "Hmm."

Terry frowned at him, uneasy. "What are you planning?"

"Not planning anything. Just had a thought on how I could make things easier, is all." Dale pushed off the desk and clapped Terry on the shoulder. "I'm going to talk to Evan, see when he might be ready to come back to work."

"What are you going to do about the...Kevin issue?" Terry's heart felt like it was going to fly out of his chest. "Are...are you going to tell him?"

Dale raised an eyebrow. "I think you should tell him, yes, but I'm not going to betray your confidence. I'll leave it up to you."

That Dale would keep his secret was both a relief and a burden. But then he remembered Levi's ultimatum. "I don't want to tell him yet. I will, I promise, just...not yet."

"Can you tell me, out of curiosity, what it would take to make you feel comfortable arriving to the point where you *could* tell him?"

Terry threw up his hands. "I don't know. I'm still having a difficult time processing the fact that he doesn't know who I am by looking at my face."

"He doesn't remember faces, or names. And I know a lot of people struggle with those issues, but I mean that he *really* can't recall them, especially faces. It's not that his vision is bad. It's different."

So it was like Levi had guessed then. Which meant Terry being offended by Evan's failure to recognize him was like being angry a blind person ran into you on a sidewalk when you had your face in your smartphone. And yet. "I *still* am not ready. But I'll try to get there, I promise. As soon as possible."

"That's fine. In the meantime, get done what you can on the designs, but bear in mind, it might be another week or better before we move forward."

"A *week*?"

"Yeah, like I said, I've never seen him like this." Dale smiled, though to Terry's mind the gesture looked a little strained. "Don't worry about it. Getting Evan back on track is my job, and I've gotten pretty good at it."

Except the reason Evan was off the track in the first place was because of Terry, and the thought distracted him the rest of the day.

Chapter Six

D ALE CAME OVER every day and cooked for Evan, and he made him eat, which Evan resented but also understood. After a few days Evan let Dale bring Charlotte along, who didn't make any sarcastic comments, only hugged him tight and said if he ever did that again she'd kill him, except then she got gooey and sappy afterward, which wasn't like her at all. Dale told Evan he'd made her cry.

The idea of Charlotte crying was frankly terrifying, and he'd said as much. Dale informed him, with a straight face, it was absolutely that.

As he made food for Evan, Dale also shared stories about Terry.

"I wanted to give you some background on the guy, since you'll be working so closely with him." Dale chopped his vegetables casually as he spoke, tossing them into his soup and stirring them as appropriate. "Don't tell him I told you this, but I met him at a hookup."

Evan hated Terry *more* now. "That's completely unfair. You've had sex with *him* and not *me*?"

Dale waggled his eyebrows over the top of his spoon as he tasted his broth. "Oh, yes I have. Terry's pretty sweet. *Deliciously* responsive. Never met anybody like him until Gabriel."

Evan stared at him blankly, then remembered. "Oh. Your librarian."

"My partner, yes. Terry was dating someone at the time, someone who wanted a threesome. *Un*like Gabriel, however, Terry's partner got upset when I fell for him and wanted to date him. Even though Terry politely declined a relationship with me, his boyfriend never got over it, and they broke up."

"The boyfriend sounds like an idiot."

"Afterward, Terry and I became friends, and when I found out what a brilliant architect he was, I hired him."

Evan rolled a potato spitefully into the package of celery. "He *is* good. I can't deny that."

"I've actually worked with you and Terry for about the same amount of time, but Terry is often away on sites, and you're usually not in the office, and when you are, you work on different floors of the building. So it's not surprising you haven't met before. The thing about Terry, though, is that while I don't have a special addendum to his contract...at the end of the day, he's more like you than he isn't."

Evan found this highly offensive. "How *exactly* is he

like me?"

"For one, you have Charlotte, and he has Levi. I don't know how much Terry is *aware* he's being managed, but Levi absolutely knows. Terry tends to forget to eat the same way you do. I had to have him stay with friends of mine while he was on site in Logan or God only knew what would have happened to him. Even as it was, he lost a lot of weight. He's gained some back because Levi's wife sends lunch for the two of them. I make sure Levi is paid accordingly. The biggest way Terry is like you, though, is that he loves his work. I don't just mean that he enjoys it. He gets lost in it the same way you do."

"Hmm." Evan wasn't certain this qualified as *exactly* like him, but he couldn't help remembering the way Reid had looked when he was focused.

"The other thing I wanted to tell you, though, is that Terry shares your difficulty with people. You wouldn't know it to talk to him, but he's the opposite of you in how he expresses it. Where you're blunt and sometimes offend people without meaning to, he can end up trying to please everyone. It's actually a lot more dangerous for him, since people use him, deliberately or simply because people like it when someone tries to make them happy. He bends over backward not to have anyone be angry with him, and he famously never raises his voice, even when he should. It's why a great deal of Levi's job is managing Terry—he's a brilliant architect in his own right, and I'm always glad to have him on a project, but he also serves as a gatekeeper. If someone gets too close to Terry and manipulates him, he sends them away."

"Levi took me to lunch the first day we met."

"Yes. He was checking you out. Levi loves you. He wants to take you to lunch again once you're feeling better."

Evan considered this information as Dale finished the soup. Now a great deal about Terry seemed logical. It was also difficult to continue hating him. "I must have made him very uncomfortable, then, for him to be angry with me."

Dale shrugged. "I don't know about that. I've been thinking a lot about it myself, and the way I see it, I think he felt so inherently comfortable with you he forgot to try to please you."

Evan replayed their argument at the door and shook his head. "That's definitely not what happened."

"No? Then there must be something else going on, something we don't understand. It's not like Terry simply to be upset or angry because you asked to see someone he knows. Even if you did ask a little insistently."

Evan was silent for several seconds, then said what he had been, for days, too afraid to say aloud. "Maybe Kevin truly does hate me."

Dale tapped his spoon on the side of the pot. "I'm going to tell you something, Evan. You're not going to freak out, and you're not going to ask me questions until I'm done talking. Are you ready?"

Confused and slightly wary, Evan nodded.

"I've met Kevin."

Evan's eyes went wide, and he drew a deep breath. All his questions came rushing to his mouth at once, and Dale cut them off with a look and a well-aimed spoon.

Evan sighed.

"I've met him," Dale continued, stirring the soup idly, as if he hadn't been sitting on the most important details all evening while blabbering on about Reid instead, "and I believe I understand the whole situation a lot better now. Unfortunately, I can't give you much more information than what I've just given you without breaking a confidence. *However*," he said quickly when Evan started to interrupt again, "I don't want you to think he hates you. That's simply not true."

The idea that Dale knew Kevin, had *information* on him, was a lot to process. Evan did his best to digest it, but at the same time, he searched for a line of questioning Dale might answer. "Is there anything about him you *can* tell me?"

"Yes. You should get to know Terry better. A *lot* better."

Evan lifted his head and glared at Dale. "That's exactly what Levi said."

"I did tell you Levi knows Terry best. He also knows Kevin as well."

How was it everyone knew Kevin but Evan? "Why

do I have to get to know Terry to get to Kevin? Why are they a package deal?"

"This is one of those mysteries whose answer will reveal itself with application."

Evan curled his lip in disgust, staring out across his apartment.

"I can tell you one thing more, though."

Evan glanced sideways at Dale. "Hmm?"

Dale winked at him. "Like I said, I don't think he hates you. At all." He grabbed a ladle and began scooping soup into bowls. "I can still add the escort clause if you want, though. I'll have to be creative about it so my lawyer doesn't have a conniption."

I don't think he hates you. "No...not just yet."

Evan thought a great deal about what Dale had told him once he left, and for the first time he didn't feel listless and hopeless. Slightly confused, but he felt as if he finally had the puzzle pieces in front of him, potentially. It was like Dale said. The mystery would be solved with application. It was odd to think Reid was the application, but Evan trusted Dale, so he'd attempt it.

This meant he needed to go back to work. If he were honest, he needed to go back to work for Dale and the sake of the project. It was going to be tense, getting everything ready. He'd text Charlotte and ask her for the notes, and he'd do what he could to get into the office next week. Right now the thought made him ill, but he'd find a way to do it.

He slept that night, though not well. He dreamed he was chasing Kevin, who kept turning into Terry, and Dale and Levi urged him on while Charlotte handed him project notes. He woke in the middle of the night and started drafting some ideas on his computer, and he played with a model for most of the morning. Charlotte came by in the afternoon with a box full of files for him to go over in addition to the things she'd uploaded to the server. She was, to his relief, back to her more normal self.

"Put some damn clothes on," she told him when he answered the door in a pair of boxer shorts. She swept past him with three bags in one hand and the crate in the other, which she handed to him on her way by. "You knew I was coming. You could have gotten dressed."

"I did. I put on shorts." He set the crate on the counter and flicked through it with mild interest. "Some of this is good, but some of these drafts are garbage."

"Then get to work fixing them so we can go forward. All we've done at work is eat donuts and make betting pools on when you'd show up. Unless the architect stops by. He's thrown away the betting book twice. We made the third one digital."

Reid? "Why did he throw it away?"

"Something about being disrespectful to you." She rolled her eyes and passed him the smallest bag. "Here. Half a dozen of your favorite Glam Dolls if you give me a hint as to when you're coming back so I can even my odds."

Evan perked up. "A Varga Girl? Pinup Girl?"

"And a Scream Queen, a Night Moves, a Calendar Girl, and a Pucker Up." She pulled the bag out of his reach as he tried to take it from her. "No donuts until you give me a hint."

"Probably next week. I'm shooting for Monday, but I can't promise."

"Good enough." She handed him the bag and sat on a barstool, watching as he put two donuts on a plate. "I got you coffee too. Some for both of us. In a thermos in my bag. Grab some mugs and I'll pour."

The coffee was good, and the donuts were excellent—he had the Pucker Up and the Night Moves—and when he was done, he rode the sugar high to the couch, where he sat resenting his boxer shorts and going over the notes he'd made from the online files.

Wiping sugar from his lips, Evan gestured to the printout in front of him. "I like all of this, but we need to ask questions about these seven items. I have a bulleted list of things I want to go over."

Charlotte tilted her head at him. "You do know you're going to need to talk to Terry about this, not me."

Everything kept coming back to Reid. Evan sipped his coffee. "Yes. I'm aware."

"He's not bad. He's fussy, and he's ruthless for making people redo their work, the same as you. Actually the two of you are the same in a lot of ways."

"Can we talk about the damn work instead of Reid?"

Charlotte held up her hands. "Sure. Jesus, didn't know it was a touchy subject."

She didn't bring up Reid again as they finished going over the work, and she didn't linger long after, only pulling one of the meals Dale had prepared for him out of the freezer, putting it in the oven, and setting a timer on his phone.

"You're going to text me later that you ate," she said as she left, and he waved her away, not looking up.

Honestly, they were all so annoying. Though they brought great treats and good food, so he didn't mind much. He poured more coffee from the thermos—it was *exceptional* coffee—and ate two more donuts. He also stripped out of his boxers, finally, and went back to work naked, as nature intended.

He worked for hours, losing himself in the notes and drafts, pausing only to text questions to Charlotte and to pull his dinner out of the oven. He ate distractedly, pouring over a redesign on his tablet. Reid had been busy, retooling all the exteriors based on the conversation they'd had. There was also, for reasons he couldn't begin to fathom, a file with notes for redesigning the fishermen cabins.

Evan sat on the couch, spread the revised plans over the coffee table, and frowned at them. They were, essentially, remodeling notes based on his conversation with Kevin. They needed a little tweaking here and there, but the drawings were all but construction-ready now. When had this remodel become part of the second phase?

Did this mean Kevin was somewhere, part of the team? Did it mean he had told Terry this much about their night together?

What *else* had Kevin told Terry?

Evan sipped at the last of his coffee, thinking perhaps Charlotte might lose her bet after all. Maybe he'd go in to work tomorrow. Just for the afternoon.

He'd moved the fishermen cabin plans to his drawing table and was deeply involved in a design edit when he heard a knock on the door. The knock came three times before it fully permeated, and he glared at the portal, resenting whoever was intruding. Charlotte again, most likely, or Dale. He sighed, not even bothering to turn down his music or grab so much as a pillow to cover himself. They'd wanted him to work, and he was working. Couldn't they leave him alone?

"I don't need food, I have more work than I can possibly do, and I'm tired of both of you. What do you want?" He shouted this through the door, then opened it, glare armed and ready.

Except it wasn't Charlotte or Dale on the other side.

It was Terry Reid, holding a bouquet of flowers, a bakery box, and a tool bag full of sculpting supplies.

TERRY OPENED HIS mouth to apologize for intruding on Evan's evening, then could only manage a squeak as Evan stood in the doorway completely nude. Nude except for his insanely thick glasses, which wasn't a look Terry would have thought could be sexy, until right now.

"Reid? What are you doing here?" Evan frowned at the flowers. "Why did you bring me…?" His eyes lit up at the label on the bakery box. "Cupcakes?"

Terry couldn't make his mouth work. Some distant brain cell offered up the reminder that Evan had told him he liked to work in the nude, which was…fine, but mostly all Terry could think was the cabin hadn't been this brightly lit, and that Evan was well-hung even when completely flaccid.

Evan took the box from Terry, and thankfully held it at an angle that partially cock-blocked Terry, literally. "Come in." He glanced down at himself, as if just now realizing he was inappropriately lacking clothing, and sighed. "I suppose now I have to put on clothes *again*."

Please, put on your clothes. Terry occupied himself staring at random objects on the walls, the countertop, and did a serious contemplation of the ceiling as Evan meandered naked around his apartment, Terry prayed searching for an article of clothing. He couldn't help the occasional peek at Evan's ass, which was also well-lit and round. It also fit, he remembered, perfectly in his hands.

He cleared his throat and shifted the flowers and

box of supplies. "I'm sorry to interrupt your evening, if you're working."

"Oh, I'm always working." Evan had stopped searching for clothes and was nosing through the box of cupcakes. "Where did you get these? They look amazing."

"A Cupcake Social. They're over on 28th Avenue." *Clothes. Don't forget the clothes.*

"Oh, I've heard of them! I've wanted to try their stuff, but I haven't yet."

Yes, Dale had told Terry that Evan had a weakness for baked goods. "I got a variety. Some are traditional, like the Red Velvet and Snickerdoodle and Dreamsicle, and of course Black & White and Blondie. But I threw in some of their more avant-garde ones too: Balsamic Strawberry, Chili Chocolate, Chocolate Covered Bacon, Irish Carbomb, and Lemon Lavender."

Evan had completely forgotten about clothes now, and sat down on the couch to stare at the cupcakes neatly arranged in the box. "These look so good. I only wish I had coffee to go with them."

"Do you have a coffee maker? I could put some on."

Evan gestured vaguely at the kitchen. "There's a pour-over somewhere and some filters, and I think Dale left beans. He likes to make his own when he's here. I order it from the deli downstairs."

Terry hunted through some cupboards and found the metal pour-over single-serve system, some filters, a grinder, and a bag of beans. "How strong do you like your coffee?"

"Strong." He had his finger in the icing of the Irish Carbomb. "These are incredible."

Terry considered asking if he wanted a plate, then decided that would be a silly question. "Do you have a vase of some kind?"

"I don't think so."

"I'll use this pitcher then."

"Why did you bring me flowers, anyway?"

Terry focused on arranging the flowers in the glass pitcher to hide his blush. "To apologize for being rude to you."

"Oh. Not necessary, really. I need to apologize too, I suppose."

"No, you don't need to apologize at all. I think mine alone is fine."

"More than. Nobody's ever given me flowers before. The cupcakes are nice too. Dale and Charlotte bring me baked goods all the time, but I didn't expect it from you, and you aren't trying to get work out of me, so it feels special." He paused and glanced at Terry. "*Are* you trying to get work out of me?"

Terry waved his hands and shook his head. "No, no. Like I said, I'm only here to apologize. I promise. But—" He set the kettle on to boil and picked up the box of supplies, bringing it over to Evan. Terry ignored the nakedness as best he could. "I did want to give you these. Also as an apology, but I thought you might find them useful both for work and your hobby of making models of things." He set the box on the coffee table and sat in the chair opposite Evan as he pulled items out one by one. "Some odds and ends, really. A different craft foam to try, and a knife with a curved edge. Plus these paints go right on the foam, and they come with felt tip markers you can fill, or you can use them as traditional paints, with brushes. This fiberglass is scrap from a site I was on a few months ago, but the weight is nice and perfect for models. Plus there's some random stuff. You don't have to keep any of it."

Evan, eating a cupcake, peered into the box of supplies, and Terry was saved from having to watch by the whistle of the teakettle. While Terry poured the water, Evan asked, "How did you know I made models, though?"

Terry nearly dropped the kettle. "Ah. I…heard about it. From people."

"If you saw the ones I have in my office, I hope you don't think they're representative of my work. The ones I have here at home are far better. I have the whole town of Logan. You should have heard Dale complain about transporting it. It's worth it, though. The models have helped me visualize some of the changes, and I can see what they're going to look like before we make them."

He'd updated the models? "Can I see them?"

"Of course. I'll show you everything, including the notes on what I've edited so far from what Charlotte sent. It's so handy you're here, actually." He licked his fingers and reached for a second cupcake. "Once I'm done eating and have had some coffee."

"No problem."

Evan shot Terry a forlorn look around the icing of the Balsamic Strawberry. "Do I *have* to get dressed? If we're going to work, I'll do so much better if I can stay free."

Terry rubbed a hand over his beard and looked anywhere but at Evan. "I—I don't think it's a good idea, no."

"Not a good idea for me to get dressed? Excellent, thank you."

Good Lord. "For you to stay *naked.*"

"Why not? We're both guys."

"Yes, but I'm bisexual. And you're attractive." Annoying, but attractive.

Evan's eyes went wide, and he shifted sideways on the couch. Abruptly he listed and had to steady himself. "You're bisexual *too.*"

Now they'd breached the Kevin topic. Terry focused on pouring more water over the grounds. "Many people are."

"I normally don't meet so many in a row, and you know each other. You and Kevin." Evan chewed his bite of cupcake, smiling. "You find me attractive?"

"Objectively, yes, you're handsome. Baffling, exasperating, maddening, but handsome." He finished the cup of coffee, removed the pour-over, and carried the mug to Evan. "All things considered, though, I would feel more comfortable if you weren't completely nude."

Evan accepted the coffee with a sigh. "Fine, but my performance will suffer. I don't know how you stand it, working fully clothed."

"I've managed to muddle along somehow."

"Have you *tried* working naked?"

Terry went back to studying the ceiling. "Can we please discuss something else?"

Though Terry braced for another round of cajoling and was half prepared to end up being seduced out of his clothes, to his relief Evan put his coffee down, swiped a pair of boxers from behind a pillow, and rose to step into them before sitting back down. He didn't seem pleased about his situation, but he didn't make any further attempts to bring the matter up. He simply finished his food, dusted off his fingers, and reached for a pile of papers on the coffee table, passing them over to Terry.

"These are from your notes from the original downtown designs. The sketches we talked about for the false fronts. I've added in a few design elements I thought might be worth considering. There are three versions. Raw, what the town would look like undecorated. Summer, a Christmas Town without snow and especially in a warm season. Then of course there's Christmas, December or an extended holiday season. Those designs are best with snow. I asked Dale if he'd be willing to purchase a snowmaker to coat the roofs and trees strategically, but he said that's a third phase move. So I'm still working on making the designs look good even if it fails to snow. I'm still hoping they might buy one for this season, though. I think we might be able to talk him into it."

Terry thumbed through the designs, impressed by Evan's work. "Isn't it highly unlikely it would fail to snow that far north?"

"For Christmas? Yes. But it's not unheard of. The thing is, if they open in November or October, which they're hoping to do, there's an even higher likelihood. Plus I want to be able to freshen up dirty snow." He tapped the top of the Christmas design page. "The real trick is developing the theme I haven't touched yet: Winter Off-Season. Dale wants to entice people up for Winter Wonderland in January and February. He wants people to come for quieter getaways and for hunting. He knows it will be slower, but he doesn't want the town's economy to pancake then. The marketing team wants to package it possibly as a corporate retreat, but it's difficult because a blizzard could unexpectedly cancel or extend the getaway."

Terry nodded as he skimmed his fingers over the pages, imagining the buildings he'd seen in Logan decorated in the various incarnations. "What do you need from me, as the architect, to make sure you can implement these schemes? I mean, it's clear you want this kind of flower-box thing under every window, and loops in the scrolling under the false fronts where you can attach some of this garland stuff. Do you want the signs to stick out far enough from the building so you can hang things from them? You have these light strands in every scheme but the raw one—do you want them to be built in? Because I can do that. We can set it up so they change colors too. I can get you a master panel for the whole city square—hell, I can include the square itself—and you can program it to light up specific places, all of them, special colors, you name it. It's going to cost to install, and the system will be pricey, but the manpower it will save the town is intense. That Logan Repair team, Arthur Anderson and Paul Parks, should be able to keep it maintained."

Terry was getting into this now, lost in the possibilities, but when he realized Evan hadn't said anything, Terry turned toward him, worried he'd upset him. From the way Evan stared at him, it was difficult to tell.

"What?" Terry asked at last. "If you don't like it, obviously we won't—"

"*Are you serious?*" Evan leaned into Terry, staring him down harder now. "You aren't even going to comment on how I refitted your design again? You're just going to fuss over my window boxes and rig me some custom lighting out of my wet dream?"

Terry tried to look away, but Evan was a tractor beam. "You didn't change much. You left the supports in place, the ones I showed you. You even kept in mind the idea of protecting the town's sense of pride and so on. Everything else is negotiable, really."

Evan leaned over Terry so much he fell backward onto the couch. Evan's eyes were wild, and his voice sharp and loud. "What about the pride in your *work*, architect? Your original design? You outrank me, and look what I've done with your precious lines."

It was almost impossible to think, with Evan glaring down at him with so much intensity. Terry swallowed. "I...I don't think like that. About rank. I think about the project. I think about the client. What they want. And my team, what ideas they have." His gaze, unbidden, fell to Evan's lips. "Your...your ideas are good. So...so good. I would never get in the way of that."

Evan leaned farther forward, his body blocking the light. Terry closed his eyes, focusing on his breathing, which had become difficult. He had a brief fear that Evan was going to kiss him. More terrifying was that he almost wanted the kiss to happen.

What if he does? What will you do? Will you make out with him as Terry, as well as Kevin?

Yes, Terry's traitorous body whispered, and he held his breath.

But when the couch shifted, it was because Evan had stood up, not leaned in the rest of the way. The light streamed in Terry's face again, and he opened his eyes, confused and blinking, in time to see Evan walking away from him.

"Come over here and see the models I made," Evan said, sounding a little gruff.

"All right," Terry replied, shaking off his dizziness as he sat up, telling himself he wasn't disappointed.

Chapter Seven

WHEN TERRY FINALLY left that night, Evan lay awake in bed for a long, long time.

He'd shown the architect the models, they'd gone over the notes again and accomplished quite a bit of work, which was wonderful, on one level. But Evan had been distracted the entire time, to the point that when Terry asked him if he was feeling all right, Evan had lied and said he was tired and had sent Terry home. The truth was, he was wired with more thoughts than he knew how to process right now, all of them centered around the enigmatic, troubling individual whose cologne still lingered in his nostrils.

There were so many things about Terry Reid that nagged at Evan, but two stood out as most disturbing. The first was that Evan had never, ever known an architect to be so agreeable, and he could see what Dale meant about Terry going out of his way to please people. As allegedly celebrated and talented as Terry was, he should have had more pride, more sense of protecting his craft. Evan felt as if *he* were the only one protecting it most of the time. So often Evan had been ready to be shouted at over the way he'd ruined Terry's lines, but no, Terry had simply accepted the changes and asked how he could make more. That alone was unreal.

But it was the second upsetting thing about Terry that had Evan reeling. Lying in the shadows with his eyes closed when Evan loomed over him, Terry had looked oddly like Kevin. With his voice pitched low and quiet like that, he sounded the same too.

They had the same eyes. In the office, Evan had been fixated on the color of Terry's eyes, but with Terry's face in shadow, it was as if Kevin had appeared before him, minus the beard.

Evan told himself he'd simply been thinking about the man too much, that even he had to admit his obsession had gone too far, and so the next day, despite far too little sleep and a high sense of agitation, he called and asked Dale for a ride into the office.

"Oh, you're coming in so soon? I didn't place my bet on you until next week. But then, I made that bet before Terry came to see you last night."

Why Dale would have known that would change Evan's mind was suspicious, but he was too irritated to ask about that now. "Can we stop for breakfast on the way in? And coffee? I'm tired of the deli."

"Sure. Is it okay if I ask why you're calling me and not Charlotte for a ride?"

"She's going to be angry I made her lose the bet, and I'm already cranky enough."

"Makes sense. I'm going to be an hour, though, because I'm finishing up a meeting. Can you handle deli coffee until then?"

With a sigh, Evan conceded to a small prebreakfast coffee and bagel at the deli, which he ate in the back of the restaurant behind the screen of a *StarTribune*. He read each section quickly, then let his gaze hover unfocused on the black and white of the ink on newsprint until Dale slid into the other side of the booth.

Evan lowered the paper and studied him critically. "Why did Terry look like Kevin when he was lying on my couch with his eyes closed?"

Dale raised an eyebrow, then picked up another section of the paper. "On your couch, was he? Interesting."

This wasn't an answer. "Why does Reid look like Kevin?"

Dale continued to read the paper. "Why do *you* think he does?"

That was just the problem. "He doesn't. Kevin has a long beard. He's thinner. He's..." The rest of the details blurred in Evan's mind. "He's Kevin."

Dale glanced up with a smile. "You really never have been good with faces, have you? I remember the time Charlotte cut and dyed her hair and it took you half the day before you figured it out, and only when she'd been trying to get your attention for fifteen minutes. You came in to ask me who the new girl was and why she was so annoying. You can see the same person with simple cosmetic changes and think you're seeing someone brand new."

Evan didn't care for this reminder. "People are too complicated to remember, especially when they change things on me without prior notice." He folded his paper and took the one from Dale, folding it as well. "I'm hungry. Let's go get breakfast."

For some reason Dale regarded him expectantly for several seconds, then let his shoulders droop as if in defeat. "I was thinking we hadn't been to The Bad Waitress in a while. Sound good?"

It sounded very good. "Let's go."

They managed to score a booth, where Evan ordered the Delmonico Eggs Benedict and two pancakes on the side along with some coffee, and Dale got the Flying Saucer Omelet. Evan pushed his glasses higher on his face and took in the ambiance of the restaurant. It was always busy, but he liked their decor and sense of design, so he didn't mind.

"Terry emailed me your notes from the changes you two made last night." Dale sipped his coffee, looking pleased. "I really like the way you two work together."

"He's so much more agreeable than I expected." Evan ran his finger around the rim of his mug. "He brought me presents too. Flowers and food and tools. Did you show him my models?"

"No, I can't say that I did."

How had he known so much about them, then? Because Terry had brought just the *right* tools. He did have a few models at the main office, but his best ones were in his condo.

Evan couldn't seem to lift his gaze from his mug, caught in the coffee's inky depths. "I haven't asked him about Kevin." The rest of his thoughts hung in the air a moment before he could articulate it. "Last night when we worked together, until the end, I didn't think about Kevin at all."

"What happened at the end?"

Yes, what *had* happened? Evan still couldn't figure it out. "We were arguing because he kept saying he was going to give me everything I wanted in the design and a few things I hadn't asked for, and it was wonderful, obviously, except it made me nervous because architects don't behave that way. I pushed him onto the couch, saying something like *come on, fight back*, but all he did was close his eyes, and…and that's when I thought he looked a little bit like Kevin."

Now Dale had that expectant expression again. "Is it that they only look the same? Are there other similarities?"

Evan was agitated, unsure how to answer. "I have strong feelings for Kevin."

"I'm aware. You don't normally do relationships, but you wanted one with him after one evening together."

"I connected with Kevin. There was something tangible there, like when I have the threads of a project between my fingers." He opened his napkin and pulled out his fork, twirling it absently. "I had so much more I wanted to talk to him about in the morning. It still bothers me that he's gone, that you, Levi, and Terry know where he is, but I don't."

Dale bit his lip, then took a deep breath. "Do you want me to tell you?"

How strange that so little as a few hours ago Evan would have said yes, but now that Dale was seriously offering, all Evan could think about was the way Terry had looked with his eyes closed. The way he'd smiled nervously at the door, holding his offerings awkwardly. The way he'd kept glancing at Evan's naked body even as he tried not to.

He had the oddest feeling about all this. He couldn't name it. In fact, the more he thought about it, he realized he was deliberately trying not to name it.

Evan set the fork down on the table carefully. "There's something big you're not telling me. Something obvious I'm missing because it's one of the things I always miss."

"Yes."

"So what do you have to say if I admit I'm a little attracted to Terry as well as Kevin? Are you going to tell me you don't allow office romances?"

Evan expected Dale to tease him about cheating on Kevin, but Dale didn't. He only stared at Evan with something sort of like surprise but also slightly reminiscent of constipation, and then he stared at his place mat until their food arrived. He didn't eat, only continued to stare.

Since he was hungry, Evan ate, figuring Dale would talk again when he was ready.

Once Evan had taken about three bites, Dale said, "I think you should go on a date with Terry."

The very idea made Evan drop his fork. "I'm not sure about that. I said I was a *little* attracted. Also, I'm loyal to Kevin. What if he finds out?"

"I think it'd be good for him. Either it will spur him into action, or it'll help you let go."

Evan wasn't sure about that. "What if Kevin doesn't step up, I can't let go, and the date with Terry doesn't work out?"

"Then I buy you a lot of desserts and breakfasts, and you go back to your escorts."

Evan hadn't had an escort over since he'd returned from Logan. Was that healthy? "I haven't ever been on a date, though."

Dale smiled a wicked grin as he popped a bit of egg into his mouth. "I could send you and Terry on a team-building evening. What do you want to do, dinner and a show? You can decide if you take him to your place after to show him your *models* or not."

The potential reality of a date with Terry had Evan stammering, let alone taking him back to his condo. "No. I should keep my focus on Kevin."

"I think it's healthy to keep your options open. And *no*, before you make any wise-ass comments, this has nothing to do with me being poly. I don't doubt your reaction to Kevin, but it *is* unusual for you. What if you have that reaction to Terry also, and Terry is willing to give you his phone number?"

"Yes, but I'd have had that reaction to him by now. I've been in contact with him far more than I had Kevin."

"You'd been drinking the night you were with Kevin, right? You don't think that might have colored things a bit?"

Evan picked up his fork and twirled it again. "Are you implying I made advances on Kevin he didn't want?"

"I'm implying maybe the alcohol gave your memories an embellishment worth reconsidering. Not discounting, but considering. Especially given the way you're reacting to Terry."

"I'm not reacting to Terry. I'm confusing him with Kevin in my head." Evan regarded Dale carefully. "There really is something big I'm failing to understand, isn't there? Something that causes you to make weird faces at me like the one you're making right now whenever I bring it up."

Running a hand through his hair, Dale slouched into the booth. "It's complicated. I'm tempted to tell you. I could tell you. I *should* tell you."

Once again, Evan had a powerful urge to shut his

eyes and ears to make sure he didn't hear the truth. "I don't want to hear it. Not yet."

Dale nodded. "All right. Solve the puzzle on your own then. In the meantime, finish your breakfast."

Evan did finish, but he was distracted by the thought of what big thing he wasn't seeing. He both didn't want to think about it and couldn't stop wondering what it was. He was also obsessed with the idea of a date with Terry—what would that be like? He'd never had a date before. The night with Kevin wasn't exactly a date, was it? It was a different kind of date, if so. What would a more typical date be like? What would one be like with Terry?

When he and Dale left for the office, Evan wasn't closer to figuring out any puzzles and couldn't imagine what the potential date with Terry would be like, or what Kevin might think of it, and so he arrived a pile of frazzled nerves. Because he was so preoccupied with his thoughts, he kept his gaze down as he headed toward the doors, trying to walk in a straight line and failing despite the guide line on the sidewalk.

He was so preoccupied, in fact, that he didn't see Charlotte until she was in front of him, arms folded as she tapped her foot and regarded him with arched eyebrows.

"Um, *excuse* me, what happened to Monday?"

Oh. The bet. Evan wasn't in the mood to listen to her, so he ignored her and continued to walk to his office. Evan was all ready to duck behind his door and lock it when a familiar voice called his name.

"Oh—Evan, hey."

Terry. Evan turned toward him, but unfortunately he was still walking, which meant he fell sideways into the wall.

Terry winced and hurried over to steady him. "Careful. That's right, I forgot about your balance thing. Are you okay?"

Evan nodded, rubbing his shoulder, studying Terry. He looked good. Smelled better. "Did you need something?"

"Yes—actually, I was about to fax you, but everyone got excited because someone saw you with Dale in the parking lot, so I came to find you instead. Are you sure you're up to being at work?"

Being at home would have driven him crazy, so yes. "I'm fine. How can I help you?"

"Right." Terry pulled a thick file from under his arm and nodded at Evan's office. "It'd be easier to show you. Would it be okay to bring this inside and spread it on your light table?"

Looking at Terry's notes calmed Evan for the first time since that moment on the couch when he'd conflated Terry and Kevin, and he quickly lost himself in making minor edits, asking questions, and in general descending into the joy that was designing things with Terry Reid. Because as usual, the architect went out of his way to make the structure work to Evan's vision, even though it should be the other way around. It blew

Evan's mind, this idea that someone would be willing to crawl inside his head and not only tease out all his ideas but help him make them a reality.

"I think this is really coming along." Terry leaned in close to Evan, their hips brushing as he indicated the plans for the master light panel with his pencil. "I can't wait to show everyone in Logan. We've made enough changes now that I wonder if we shouldn't show them once we get final approval from Dale."

Evan smoothed his hand over the plans spread across the table. "I think we're ready for the final approval stage, don't you? Especially if we need to get the Logan board to give it an okay before we proceed to finer details."

"Probably so." Terry sighed a little sadly and gathered the papers. "I admit, though, I hate the idea of finishing. I've enjoyed working on this with you more than any project I've ever collaborated with."

Evan couldn't meet Terry's gaze. "Well...we still have the fishermen cabins."

He did glance at Terry then, and the smile on the architect's face made his heart do funny things again. "That's true, we do."

They were halfway down the hall to Dale's office when it occurred to Evan he'd never told Terry about his balance problem, and he wondered how he knew about it. He would have asked, but by that point too many people were bothering them, mostly complaining to Evan because he ruined their bet. All but one woman who had bet against the odds he'd come back today and had cleaned up. She stopped and tried to Evan to give him a big hug and kiss, an effort which was immediately rejected.

Terry sent them all away, angry.

"I'm sorry." Terry spoke with more gentleness to Evan, but he was still clearly upset. "I hate that they were betting on when you'd come back to the office. It's incredibly rude and I told them so, but no one seems to care."

Evan was more interested in Terry's reaction than anything else. "I don't mind, but they're annoying when they drag me into it. Also, the hugs are intrusive." Protective Terry was quite attractive, though.

Maybe Dale was right, a date would be a good idea. He'd work up his courage and ask him out in a few weeks.

When they went into Dale's office, their employer was on the phone. Terry started to back out, but Dale waved them inside, indicating they should wait. He was leaned back in his chair, feet on his desk. Mostly he was listening, saying, "Oh yeah? And then what did they do? That's hilarious," and things like that at intervals. He smiled a lot too, more than Evan had ever seen. Finally, though, Dale sat up and winked at Evan and Terry. "Hey—baby, I hate to cut you off, but I need to get back to work. I want a full report later, though." A pause, and his expression softened further. "Yes. I'll come up as soon as I can. But you know, you can come down here too…" He laughed, touching his cheek, and Evan startled because for a moment Dale looked young, almost like a little boy. "Okay. Okay—love you, honey. Take care. Give my love to Arthur and the others."

Dale put his phone down and turned to them, trying to put on a business face, but he still seemed dopey. "Sorry. Talking to Gabriel. It looks like you guys have some final plans for me?" He rubbed his hands together and stood, coming around his desk and flipping on the light to his table. "Let's see them."

Terry spread them out, and Evan hovered to the side, waiting while Dale studied the plans, interjecting when he began asking questions. Mostly, though, Dale was excited about their changes, though he agreed with Terry they'd done enough alteration it was important to show the Logan officials. How he wanted that to happen, though, blew Evan away.

"I think the two of you should run these plans up to Logan and make the presentation yourself."

Evan blinked at Dale, and Dale stared back at him meaningfully.

Ah. This was his version of the date. *Sneaky, Dale.* Except Evan wasn't sure what he thought about this at all.

Terry seemed to have no problem voicing his thoughts. "You want us to do *what?*" He took a step back and put both hands in his hair, looking panicked. "What, go all the way up to Logan, *now?* Just the two of us?"

"Why not? You're the architect and the designer. No one knows the project better. This way if they want changes made, you can do them on the fly. If you want me to approve something, call—though I'm hoping to be back up there as soon as possible myself. I need to clear up a few things on the construction end, and then once they approve this, we need to get started. Honestly, what I'd love would be for the two of you to stay up there during the build. You know there's going to be issues. You said you wanted to adjust the fishermen cabins—start on the project up there, and call up whatever team members you need as you need them. Take the big cabin for yourselves, and turn it into your personal workspace. I'll arrange for Frankie to make you meals again."

Terry had gone completely pale. "Did you…just turn this from a weekend mission into a *months-long assignment*?"

Evan didn't like the way Terry was so upset, especially since it seemed centered around Terry being with him. "We can do the cabins later if Terry doesn't want to right now."

Now Terry looked embarrassed. "That's not what—I don't mean…" He cast a glare at Dale. "You're a weasel."

Dale grinned. "I don't know what you're talking about."

Evan didn't either, but he felt uncomfortable. "I

think it would be fine to send the plans up with you, if Terry doesn't want to show them. Or you and I could go, Dale." He tried not to let it show how disappointed he was, but he was still feeling tired from the night before. Perhaps he should go home after all.

A hand on his arm drew him out of his thoughts, and he glanced up too quickly, making himself dizzy. Terry was the one touching him, but Terry wasn't looking at Evan, only at Dale. "Can I talk to Evan for a minute?"

"Of course." Dale gave them a salute and headed for the door. "Take all the time you need."

He left, and then it was Terry and Evan alone.

Terry was still holding Evan's arm.

Terry noticed this and let go. He paced back and forth a bit, then began to babble. "I don't want you to think I didn't want to go to Logan with you because of you." He shoved his hand in his hair, rubbed at his beard. "I'd be happy to go with you. I just...Dale surprised me, is all."

Evan wasn't sure what to say, so he didn't say anything. He held on to the edge of the table and watched Terry pace. He was handsome even when he was upset. Different than Kevin, but Evan liked it. He wanted to go to Logan with Terry. Wanted to stay in that cabin with him.

Wanted to possibly have sex with him. Even if that did betray Kevin. He tried not to feel bad about that.

He didn't feel very bad about that, to be honest.

What if Kevin was there too? This was getting so complicated.

He was thinking he should call an escort and clear his system, see if someone would be willing to be on call to come up to Logan, when Terry turned to face him again, giving him a look that melted all thoughts of other men out of Evan's head. *Those eyes.*

"Do you think we should spend that much time together, the two of us?" Terry asked.

"I really do work naked."

Terry's gaze raked Evan. "That would be highly distracting."

Desire yanked at Evan's belly, drawing all his focus. "You'd like to see me naked?"

"I have seen you naked. I already know it's distracting."

"I haven't seen you naked."

A strange look passed over Terry's face. Something like guilt. "There are things I should tell you, but I'm not ready."

What in the world did that have to do with getting naked? "Do they mean we can't work together in the cabin?"

"They mean I need to not be distracted by how good you look without your clothes."

Oh. The fluttery feeling came back to Evan's chest, stronger than ever before. So he affected Terry. Funny how Evan found himself full circle to where he'd been when he woke up this morning, but knowing Terry felt the same way somehow changed the whole game.

"I'll do my best not to distract you, then," Evan said.

The thing was, Evan was lying.

TERRY WASN'T ENTIRELY sure how he'd ended up packing to move up "indefinitely" to Logan, let alone *moving in* with Evan, but he did know everyone in his life was conspiring against him.

Levi collected Terry from the meeting with Dale and Evan, and once he heard the lowdown, wasted no time helping Terry get organized to head north again. "Sounds like a great idea. You love Logan, and you love working with Myles."

"Not under these circumstances, I don't. Dale's gone insane, and apparently you have too. Just because Evan and I have been working well together doesn't mean we should move into the cabin and risk him finding out his project partner and Kevin are one and the same."

"So your plan is to never tell him?" Levi settled into the chair across from Terry's desk. "That sounds incredibly adult."

Oh God, Levi was going to bring this up again. Terry had been spared after his last screwup with Evan because Levi had been called out of town, but he should have known better than to imagine he could get off scot-free. "I didn't say I wouldn't tell him. I'm thinking of the project, is all."

Levi gave him an arch look. "You have well and truly broken our agreement, but don't think I've forgotten. If George were in the country right now, I'd have him on the phone. The hot second I can put you in the same room with him, I will. Be ready."

When Levi was on Terry's side, he was a force. When he antagonized him, he was a terror. "Then maybe I shouldn't go to Logan. Help me get out of it."

Levi shook his head. "Boss man seems really set on this. If it would make you feel better, I'll call Frankie and see if you can stay with him again instead."

It would make Terry feel better, yes, but he suspected Evan wouldn't understand. Terry sighed and ran a hand through his hair. "What do we do if Evan finds out I'm Kevin and goes into another work-stoppage mode?"

"Honestly? Then we work around it. We have enough in place we don't need his input. This is Dale wanting to be extra, going above and beyond the call to make sure the city council and the committee people are as happy as possible. He loves the idea of you two solving problems on the fly, helping his favorite small town." Levi clapped Terry on the shoulder. "Once you're up there, you'll be fine. You bloom in Logan, as long as someone's feeding you and doing your laundry, and all that can be arranged. The only reason you're panicking is because things are getting cozy with Evan. Also because you haven't told him the truth. *So tell him the truth.*"

The very idea made Terry ill, and the truth of why began to whisper at the edges of his mind.

What if he finds out I'm Kevin…and that I'm nowhere near as wonderful as the Kevin in his mind?

The bottom line was that Terry wasn't confessing, and with Levi refusing to bail him out, this meant the only thing left to do was pack. Terry would tell Evan in Logan at some point, when he was ready, when the timing felt right. Or it would come out naturally in Logan. Something would work out, or it wouldn't, but in the meantime he'd do his job and do his best to avoid naked Evan sightings.

The rest of the week at work he was consumed with preparations, leaving his team with instructions and putting together his away kit. It occurred to him if he was staying with Evan, there were some things he didn't need to double up on, so he decided he should check in. This involved getting the man's phone number from Dale, but it also required having Dale call first so Evan would actually pick up the phone, since he didn't recognize Terry's number. It also meant Evan called Terry before he had a chance to do so.

"Terry. Dale says you needed something?"

Why did Terry feel so flustered? "Yes—I wanted to check what tools you were bringing and what was already in the cabin, assuming you left some things there. It seemed a waste to bring double."

"Oh, good idea. I usually let Charlotte take care of

that, but if you tell me what you want, I'll pass it on to her and make sure it gets there."

"Never mind. I wouldn't want to put either of you out. I'll just—"

"You're not putting me out, and this is what Charlotte does. She's used to it. What do you want?"

They went back and forth, discussing what they required for an extended stay. For the first five minutes Terry assumed Evan was writing it down, but when it turned out he wasn't, they started over, this time with Terry as secretary. Half an hour later they had a respectable list of things they'd need to launch Christmas Town in Logan. Except Terry still felt uneasy.

"Are you sure it's all right if the two of us live together in the cabin? I could see if I could stay with Frankie and Marcus again, and come over to work—"

"Why? That's ridiculous. We need to work together. Why shouldn't we live together?"

"I don't want to crowd you or get in your way. I know your work process is delicate—"

"My work process is great with you. You won't be in my way. I'm looking forward to this, in fact."

Warmth blossomed in Terry's chest. "You are?"

"Of course I am. Aren't you?" Now Evan sounded uncertain for the first time.

Terry tripped over himself to put Evan back at ease. "I am. I love being in Logan, and I enjoy working with you a great deal. But I guess I worry a lot too. I don't always relate well to other people."

"You wanted to stay with that...somebody. Frank?"

"Frankie and Marcus. They're friends of Dale's who live in Logan." Terry smiled at the memory. "Yes, well, I didn't want to stay with them the first time I went up there, either. I wanted my own place, but Dale wouldn't let me have one. He insisted I stay with Frankie and Marcus, and he was right, in the end. I still don't feel comfortable with a lot of people around, but those particular people are lovely."

"Funny, Dale tried the same thing with me. He wanted me to stay with someone too. I told him no, because I wanted to be alone." Before Terry could get nervous again, Evan added, "Not this time, though. This time, I want to be with you."

Terry swayed on his feet. Was that flirting? Was Evan flirting?

Had Evan given up on Kevin...to focus on Terry?

Which was obviously the same thing, except Evan didn't know.

Oh God.

Terry pressed a hand to his cheek, which had become abruptly warm. Levi and Dale's admonitions haunted him now. *Tell him. Tell him who you are. Open your mouth and say you're Kevin. Do it.*

Oh, sweet Jesus, I can't.

Terry swallowed, his knees feeling unsteady. "Th-thank you."

"Dale will send all the big things up in a van, but

he'll give us a company SUV when we leave next week. Except I can't drive, so that means you'll have to be behind the wheel the whole way. I promise to keep you entertained, though. Let me know what music you like, and I'll get a playlist ready. You can send me some links in email from Spotify. Sound good?"

Terry was overwhelmed already, and they weren't even in the car yet. "Sure."

"I can't wait for next week, Terry. It's going to be great."

Yes. It was going to be something, that much was for sure.

Chapter Eight

E VAN WAS SO excited to go back to Logan he could barely stand it. This was pretty much a literal truth: he couldn't focus, and he couldn't land on anything to do with his nervous energy. He was driving Charlotte crazy.

"Here." She handed him his cell phone with his contacts open. "Call one of your escorts. I was thinking you should try Chris. You always seem to calm down after an evening with him."

She was probably right, but he couldn't bring himself to place the call any more now than he could since he'd come back from Logan. It was difficult to think about having sex with one person when you were thinking of someone else.

Or two someone elses.

The pent-up energy dogged him though, and the day before they were scheduled to leave, Evan broke down and called Terry. He didn't really have a pretense in mind, so he raced for something to say as Terry answered.

"How are you doing? Are you packed, ready to go?"

"Mmm, yes." Terry sounded a little sleepy. He yawned too, then apologized. "Sorry, I didn't sleep well last night."

"Why not? Is something wrong?"

"Ah—no. I was just…worrying about things."

"What things?" Maybe Evan could help.

"Nothing. Really, don't worry about it."

It didn't sound like nothing, but Terry seemed stressed talking about it. Evan wished Terry were at his house so he could see him. Talk to him.

Hey.

"Would you like to come over?"

"What? You mean now? To your place?"

"Yes. I don't have anything to do. I wish we could leave today. Let's do something together."

"Did you want to work on something? I can bring my notes—"

"*No.* I don't want to work. I just want to be with you, Terry."

"Oh." There was rustling, and Evan thought Terry might have dropped the phone. "Sorry."

Why was Terry so weird? He made Evan feel weird. "Do you not want that?"

"No—I mean yes—" Terry laughed nervously. "You caught me off-guard. I'd be happy to come over. You surprised me, is all."

"Why is it surprising that I'd want to hang out with you?"

"It isn't, I… It's just that you keep offering to do things with me, and I don't expect that. Especially since I feel like all do is make mistakes with you."

"I don't know what you're talking about. You need to work on your self-esteem." Evan shifted his grip on the phone. "Come over, Terry. Bring your things for Logan, and we'll leave from here in the morning."

Evan liked the way Terry stammered and got embarrassed, his tongue-tied reply making it clear he'd heard the idea of staying overnight and thought of sex. "I don't think—Evan, I don't—"

"I'll give you my bed, and I'll sleep on the couch. Just come, please."

Soon Terry had packed up his car and come over, parking in the visitors' section of Evan's parking garage. Evan met him at the door, trying not to look as if he'd been bouncing on his feet as he danced around his condo for the past forty minutes. Which, indeed, he had.

"Come in." He collected Terry's things from him, and when his guest fussed too long lining up his shoes by the door, Evan took his hand and tugged him into the room. "I've been waiting forever. Forget the shoes."

Terry laughed. "You're like a little kid. I feel like I've come over for a playdate."

"Oh? I never had those. Is this really what they're

like?"

Evan turned his head as he asked that, and because he was walking, he got dizzy and started to lose his balance. Gasping, Terry caught him and righted him, but when it was clear Evan was still woozy, he led him to a couch.

"Be more careful." Terry sat beside him and stroked his arm, looking concerned. "Every time I'm with you, you do this."

That made no sense. Evan poked Terry's shoulder. "I think I've done it with you once."

For some reason this made Terry blush, and he let go of Evan's arm. He also frowned. "What do you mean, you never had a playdate? Was that a joke?"

Evan shook his head—carefully. "I didn't. The kids at school always said I was odd. Eventually my parents homeschooled me because I was bored, so I didn't have to deal with the kids acting strange, but I had always hoped one day someone would move to school and be my friend like in the books."

Terry seemed confused. "In what books?"

"In books I read. There was always a new kid at school who befriended the lonely kid. Or sometimes it was the other way around. Anyway, no one ever did that for me. I wrote several of my own books and made my own friends, though."

Now Terry's mouth fell open. "You...wrote books?"

"Well, they were comics." Evan tapped his cheek.

"They must be in the condo somewhere. I wouldn't have thrown them out, and all my things are here now. It's why I have such a big space."

Evan hadn't expected Terry to look this eager. "Would...would you let me see them?"

"Sure, but you can't laugh. The art style is really terrible. I was twelve. Well, sixteen by the last volume."

"There are *volumes*?"

"Obviously. I didn't have any friends, so I had to invent them."

Terry just looked so *weird* today. "I really want to see your comics, Evan."

It only took fifteen minutes to find them, and then Terry was spread out on Evan's bed, reading.

"These are *great*." He was on his stomach, feet in the air as he paged through the binders with the yellowed pages carefully saved within protectors. "I don't know what you're talking about. This is a great art style. I like the story too."

"It's not a bad style, I guess." Evan was reading too, starting a volume as soon as Terry was done with it. "The weird thing is I don't think I could draw people this well now. It's been so long since I've done anything but render landscapes and buildings."

"I've never been able to make people look right. I can't make them consistent. Every time I was required to draw people in my art classes, I got terrible grades. Someone in my graduate program tried to teach me once, but I'm unteachable. She broke up with me shortly after too. She says it wasn't related, but I always felt it was somehow the last straw."

Broke up. Why that rankled Evan, he didn't know. Obviously Terry had dated people. Evan had slept with people. Maybe it bothered him because Evan *hadn't* dated anyone, and he couldn't stop wishing he knew how to date Terry. Damn these total strangers who had managed to have relationships with this man so casually.

Terry glanced at the time. "Oh my gosh. We've been doing this for three hours?"

"It's okay. I haven't minded." Evan's stomach rumbled, and he rubbed it. "Maybe we should order something, though?"

They debated their delivery options, placed an order, and went back to reading. When Terry went to the plastic bin to get the next volume, he frowned. "I don't think this is the same story."

When Evan saw what Terry held, he blushed. "Oh. That's the one where I wrote myself a boyfriend."

The look Terry gave Evan did very dangerous things to his insides. "Can I read this one as well?"

"I wrote this one during college." Evan was having a difficult time looking up from Terry's mouth. "It gets quite dirty."

Terry's mouth tipped into a wicked smile. "Mmm. Dirty drawings?"

Evan blushed. "Well, yeah, but I don't know how good they are."

"Let's find out."

It was awkward to read this series with Terry, but exciting too. The plot was rushed—Evan remembered this now, how he'd been so frustrated because he couldn't connect with anyone. That was the story of his life, but he'd been hoping going to college would change the game, and it hadn't. Nothing had changed until he met Dale and Charlotte. But in the pages of this comic, Dominic had fallen instantly in love with the mousy, reclusive, self-insert hero, then made love to him on pretty much every page.

"Sorry," Evan said as they moved on to volume two, which had given up all pretense and turned into a straight-up porn comic. "I forgot how sex-obsessed this was."

"Did you hear me complaining?" Terry turned a page and studied the panels. "You're really not bad with human figures. I'm so jealous. Also, this is hot."

Evan was feeling hot as well. His arm was touching Terry's, and their legs were pressed together too. "I'm serious, I couldn't draw like this now."

Terry bit his lip as he smiled. "Now you have me curious. I want to see." When Evan started to balk, Terry nudged him gently with his elbow. "Come on. I'll make you feel better—I'll draw too. I promise, no matter how bad you feel about your work, mine will make you look godlike by comparison."

Evan *really* didn't want to do it, but Terry kept urging him, so he did it mostly to show Terry what a bad idea it was. Except Terry hadn't been kidding. He absolutely couldn't draw people.

Evan shook his head. "I've seen you sketch out the whole of downtown Logan from memory, but when I watch you draw people, it's like you're an entirely different artist."

"My seventh-grade art teacher did a whole quarter on drawing personal portraits and portraits in general. He told me I was an utter failure as an artist. I nearly stopped drawing because of that year." He sketched in a background behind his terrible people, a town square reminiscent of Logan. "My godmother is a college art professor, though, and she made me come stay with her for three weeks that summer and audit a class she was teaching. It happened to be landscape design. What can I say? I fell in love."

Evan paused his drawing for a moment, stewing in his jealousy over someone giving him that kind of attention when he was that age. But then he supposed he had more than his share of it now, so everything had just been delayed. "I taught myself until college, but even there I did my own thing more often than not. I went early, starting when I was only seventeen. This is probably part of why I couldn't get a date or a group of friends, the more I think of it."

"Well, you seem to have friends now."

"Not really. Just Charlotte and Dale, and I don't know that they're friends exactly. I feel like they mostly take care of me." He sighed as he shaded in the neck of one of his two characters. "They have to do it because I'm so high-maintenance. I've always said I don't need anyone, that I'm fine on my own. Except I think I'd rather have friends. The problem is I have no idea how to get them."

"You have me, so that's a start, and I have news for you. Don't rely on me for anything. I can give you a run for your money on being a mess." He tapped Evan's paper with the end of his pencil. "When we're in Logan, I'll introduce you to Frankie and Marcus. Then you can have two more friends."

Evan couldn't stop the stupid grin on his face no matter how he tried. "Okay."

The doorbell rang then with their delivery, and they stopped to eat. Neither of them was awkward about anything any longer. Afterward, they watched a movie together, sitting side by side on the couch, almost touching. Terry didn't seem to mind when Evan wanted to talk about the movie during the movie—in fact, he talked back so much they kept having to pause it to finish their conversation so they didn't miss the plot. By the time it was over, it was so late they needed to go to bed.

Which was when Terry surprised him.

"Look, you don't need to sleep on the couch." He blushed as he said it, holding his toothbrush and not making eye contact with Evan. "We're both adults here. We can sleep in the same bed, and nothing is going to happen."

While it was true Evan wouldn't make any moves on Terry, he knew he wouldn't get any sleep if he was next to the man he kept fantasizing about. Of course, he wasn't going to get any sleep anyway. Also, the idea of getting to sleep next to Terry was far, far too tantalizing. "Sure," he said.

His voice only broke a little bit.

He lay there for quite some time, on his side facing the closet door. Terry was awake too—he could tell because Terry kept moving in the bed. Finally Evan gave up and started talking.

"Is this what it's like? To have a sleepover?"

He heard Terry roll onto his back. "I guess, yeah. Pretty close. Except there's more giggling at this part, and a parent in the other room who comes in when the giggling is too loud and tells you to go to sleep because it's three in the morning."

Evan rolled onto his back too. "We do need to go to sleep. It's a long drive to Logan, and I can't help you at all." He regarded Terry's profile in the darkness, which was blurry without his glasses. "I'm excited to live with you in the cabin. I feel like every day will be a slumber party."

Terry smiled. "I'm excited too. I guess that's why I can't sleep. But you're right. I need to try harder."

"Do you need white noise? I have a white noise machine I use sometimes. It's pretty helpful."

"Sure, I'll give it a try."

Evan turned the machine on, adding a few drops of

lavender essential oil. He made a mental note to take the machine along with them to Logan.

He also thought, as he drifted off to sleep, how much Terry looked like Kevin, in the dark.

IT TECHNICALLY ONLY took three hours to drive to Logan from Minneapolis, but Terry soon learned that was a measurement of time that didn't include Evan Myles.

Getting loaded into the company SUV was difficult enough. Terry hadn't brought that many things, having sent all his bulky items ahead, leaving him with little more than a large duffel. Evan was another matter. Terry had thought they could take Evan's things to the office and transfer them to the SUV, but when he saw how much Evan intended to take, he changed his plans and took his car over to pick up the other vehicle, leaving his keys with Levi, then came back to Evan's condo to load up. Evan tried to help, but Terry feared that balance issue and insisted on doing it all himself. When he finished, Evan treated him to an iced mocha from the deli, and at last they were on the road.

They weren't more than fifteen minutes out of town before Evan saw an interesting advertisement on a billboard for an upcoming town, and suddenly they were planning a side trip to stop at an incredibly random and slightly sketchy antique mall. This happened again near Rush City and Moose Lake, but once they left the interstate and began heading north on the narrow country roads taking them to Logan, things went decidedly off the chain.

"I love these tall trees so thick and close." Evan craned his head nearly upside down to peer at the line of pine trees standing sentry beside the highway. "There's nothing like this in California—there are the redwood forests, yes, but it's not like this. Nothing is like this."

"So that's where you're from, California?"

"Yes. From a small town three hours northeast of the Los Angeles metro area. Oh, there's somewhere selling honey. We have to stop."

They did stop—at the honey stand, at a farmers' market they happened to see a sign for, and at every store they saw along the way. The trip took over five hours, and eventually Terry stopped texting Frankie to tell him when they'd be arriving and sent his location and let himself be tracked.

"Where are you from?" Evan asked this as they were in the final stretch of the drive, down a road that wasn't on the usual route but one which Terry had run a quick scan through Google Maps and confirmed wouldn't lead them into anything interesting.

"I grew up in Rochester."

"Oh, you're from New York?"

Terry laughed. "No way. Never been there. Rochester, Minnesota."

Evan seemed genuinely surprised. "I had no idea

there was another one."

"Well you should know about it. It's where the Mayo Clinic is, and it's where I'm from. I went to college at a small liberal arts school in Iowa, did my master's at Iowa State, came to the Cities to find a job. Worked a few places before I ended up with Davidson Incorporated."

"So you never wanted to leave the Midwest?"

Terry shrugged. "It's not so much that I was against leaving. Mostly I never left. I'm not exactly adventurous. Going to Luther and ISU were safe choices, as was coming to Minneapolis. All my jobs were ones I got through friends. Risks aren't my thing." He glanced at Evan. "Have you done much traveling?"

"I guess. I went on trips with my parents, and I studied design in Paris and London before coming back to work in L.A. But I never went on trips on purpose. They just seemed to happen."

Terry hadn't known Evan had studied in Europe. He suddenly felt incredibly plebeian. "I think the townspeople in Logan would be incredibly impressed to discover they were being remodeled by someone who had studied abroad."

"Maybe." He craned his neck around again, pointing at a small shack at the end of the road. "I keep seeing those. What are they for? They look like outhouses, but some of them don't have doors. What's going on?"

"I think they're shelters for kids to wait for the bus.

It gets cold here in the winter."

Evan grinned. "This is so great. Dale flew me up here last time. I'm going to make him drive me from now on."

Terry was pretty sure he knew why Dale had sprung for the plane ticket.

When they finally pulled into town, Terry was famished. "I need lunch. Frankie was going to take us to the café, but we're so late we might have gone past his lunch break. We'll stop by his shop and see if he's still free."

Evan had already climbed out of the car and was looking around the town square. He frowned at a tree near the pavilion in the center. "I think I need to edit my design."

Terry grabbed his hand and tugged him toward Frankie's salon. "We can edit later. Come meet Frankie first."

Frankie did indeed have a client in his chair, but he paused his cut to stop and greet them. "Hi there, Terry. Good to see you." He tucked his shears into his apron pocket, wiped his hands on a towel, and extended one to Evan. "You must be Evan Myles. It's so good to meet you. Frankie Blackburn. I'm a stylist here in Logan, married to Marcus Gardner, who owns the law office next door. We'd love to have the two of you over for dinner tonight if you're free."

Terry rubbed his stomach. "I was hoping we could grab some lunch. We never managed it on the way."

The woman in the chair had been watching them intently, and she interjected now. "You should head over to the café. The split pea soup special is something else, but they run out by four every day. Try it with a hot ham and cheese. You won't regret it."

Evan perked up at this. "What about dessert? Do they have a good dessert?"

The woman looked affronted. "Of course they do. Fresh apple turnovers made with local apples. Those run out even faster, though."

Evan took sharp hold of Terry's wrist. "We need to go to lunch. Right now."

Terry tossed a helpless glance at Frankie as he was hauled out the door again. "Text me what time you want us for dinner?"

Frankie waved at him, smiling. "Will do."

Evan was singularly focused on the car. "Do you know where this café is?"

"Of course I know where it is. You're telling me you don't?"

"I haven't been many places in Logan. Dale took me on a driving tour once, but otherwise I mostly stayed in the cabin, except the one time Charlotte and I went to the bar."

The very idea of this boggled Terry's mind. "You mean you spent the entire time you were here for the first phase alone?"

Evan was at the car now, holding on to the door, so he looked at Terry when he replied. "No, sometimes

Charlotte came over, or Dale. Mostly Charlotte, though."

That was nearly the same thing. "Did you do nothing but work?"

"Sometimes I watched television. The cabin has satellite and surprisingly decent internet."

Terry couldn't believe this. "Well, this time you're going to see more of the town. It's important to the idea of the design."

Evan grimaced. "I know. Dale said the same thing. I don't do well with people, though."

"It's okay. I'll handle the people. You just stick close to me."

Evan smiled, the gesture sending a shiver of awareness down Terry's spine. "Okay."

The café wasn't busy when they arrived, and to Evan's relief they had not only the soup but the turnovers too, so they settled in with orders for both, plus the ham and cheese sandwiches and cups of coffee. They had a booth in the back, and while they ate, Evan told Terry how he wanted to redesign their lights on the square now that he'd seen the large tree near the pavilion. He'd started to sketch out his idea on a napkin when Terry noticed someone peering over the top of the booth behind Evan—all that was visible was the person's nose, eyes, glasses, and hair, but it was distracting and slightly concerning.

"Um…can we help you?" He couldn't determine the individual's gender or age from a haircut and pair of eyes, but they didn't seem to be a child.

Evan turned around too, startling as he saw his stalker so close. "Oh. Hello."

Their observer rose higher, revealing a full face, and Terry recognized the features of an adult woman with Down's syndrome. She screwed up her face in a commanding expression, rising on her knees so they could see her putting her hands on her hips. "What's this I hear you saying about remodeling the town square? You have to get permission for that."

Terry was about to explain, gently, that they did have permission, but Evan answered with his usual bluntness before he could. "We do have it. We work with Davidson Incorporated. I'm Evan Myles, the head designer, and this is Terry Reid, the head architect."

"Oh, that's all right then." The woman's face broke out into a beautiful smile, and she held out her hand to Evan, her tongue protruding slightly. "Linda Kay Parks. Head greeter at the Walmart in Eveleth, but I want to get a job working for Christmas Town." Her grin turned almost feral as she leaned in and winked. "Can you get me in, cutie?"

"*Linda Kay.*" A brown-haired man with red highlights hurried over from the register, face flushed. "I'm sorry if my sister said anything inappropriate. She can be *very rude.*"

Linda Kay stuck out her tongue at her brother, then turned back to Evan. Apparently she was going to ignore Terry. "This guy is my twin brother, Kyle. We're nothing alike, but his husband is a real cutie, just like you."

"Oh my God." Kyle's glare was the kind only siblings could muster.

Once again, Evan spoke to Kyle before Terry could try to smooth things over. "Linda Kay was fine." He turned back to her, serious. "I'm sorry, though. I don't think I have the kind of influence to get you a job. You should talk to Dale Davidson. Do you know him?"

"Know him? Dale and I are like *this*." Linda Kay held up both hands and attempted to cross her fingers, and when this failed, crossed both arms instead.

"Oh, well there you are then. What do you think you'd be suited for, besides a greeter?" Evan scratched his cheek thoughtfully. "I mean, I don't really know what's available, but I'm curious."

Kyle had stopped regarding his sister with exasperation and was watching Evan with interest.

Linda Kay flicked her hair. "I'm an excellent singer."

"Well, I'm sure we need entertainment, but I imagine the competition will be intense. You'll want to practice."

Now Kyle looked alarmed. "She's coming over to *your* place to practice, I'm warning you right now."

Linda Kay seemed to think this was a fine idea. She patted Evan's arm. "You can come pick me up and show me around the place."

"I can't drive. Plus, we'll be pretty busy with work.

But if you can get out to the lake near our cabin, singing over the lake would be good practice." He frowned. "Sorry, I just assumed you were a singer. You seem like one."

If anything, this made Linda Kay's chest puff up more. "I'll practice in my dad's fields. Every day."

"Come on, Linda Kay. We need to let them get back to their lunch." As Kyle herded her away, he smiled over his shoulder at Terry and Evan. "I'll see the two of you at dinner."

Evan looked puzzled, so Terry explained. "Kyle Parks and his husband Paul are good friends of Frankie and Marcus. I guess they'll be at dinner tonight. If they're going to be there, I wonder if Arthur and Gabriel will be too."

"Charlotte was right. There are a lot of gay men up here."

Terry hadn't thought about it before, but Evan was right. "There do seem to be an extra high number. I guess there's a segment of the population not happy about the fact that Dale, an openly gay man, is the developer up here. They fear he'll make this a gay paradise."

"I wouldn't call it that exactly, but Charlotte says the marketing department is already trying to bill this as the place to come and fall in love with your gay sweetheart." Evan ate his soup thoughtfully. "She says she's going to start a campaign. The Ladies of Logan, she's calling it. I'm not entirely sure what the campaign is for, though. I forgot to pay attention."

"Having met Charlotte, I can only imagine how that will go down. All the women will fall in love with her."

"I don't know. She's great at getting dates, but falling in love is another story." He grimaced and poked at a chunk of potato. "Guess that's why we're friends. Two of the same kind."

Guilt crept up on Terry at the look of dejection on Evan's face. "Hey, don't talk like that."

"It's the truth." He put down his spoon, brightening as the waitress approached them. "Oh, good, our turnovers."

Evan was smiling. So why did Terry feel like his smile wasn't meeting his eyes?

They finished eating, some of the light coming back to Evan as he declared the turnovers were as good if not better than any gourmet dessert he'd tried in the Cities, and then, at last, they were on the way to the cabin.

Terry told himself it was ridiculous to feel nervous, that nothing was going to happen and Evan *clearly* didn't recognize him and at this rate never would. The problem was, of course, that Terry knew the truth of what had passed between them, and as Evan gave him a whirlwind tour, it took everything in Terry to quell flashbacks from that night, which now felt like it had happened in another lifetime to another person.

Which in a way, he supposed it had.

"What's wrong?" Evan stopped at the top of the stairs and faced Terry, who hadn't followed him up. "Did you want to take more time on the first floor? You didn't seem as interested in the architectural details as I thought you'd be, so I figured you'd want to get settled before we went to this dinner."

Terry blinked in confusion. "Architectural details?"

Evan gestured around them. "Of the cabin? You know, the one you designed?"

Oh. Terry glanced around, realizing he was supposed to have been seeing the place for the first time. The guilt that had caught up to him at the café swamped him, and he had to sit down on the bottom step.

Evan hurried to his side. "Are you sick? Do you have food poisoning?"

Terry leaned into the wall, shutting his eyes. "I'm a bad person, Evan."

"You aren't, though. You're a really great person." His hand rested on Terry's thigh. "I…like you a lot."

He sounded so shy and hesitant, he broke Terry's heart. "There's…there's something I have to tell you." How many times was he going to say that before he actually told him? *A million. A billion.* No. He'd tell him now. He'd blurt it out and take the fall. He started to sweat simply thinking about it, but he made himself forge forward. "You might hate me once I finish, but I need to tell you. I have to. I just—I—"

He didn't get to babble any further, because cool

lips stopped his mouth.

When Terry gasped in surprise and turned, Evan took gentle hold of his face, deepening the kiss, but not by much. It was as polar opposite of the kisses they'd shared that night as kisses could get. When Evan finally pulled away, Terry felt dizzy, but he also couldn't help unconsciously leaning in after Evan for a few beats as he moved out of range. He hadn't wanted the moment to end.

Evan's fingers caressed Terry's cheeks before he lowered them. "I couldn't ever hate you."

It was too much, that they were playing this out all over again here, now. *I have to tell him.* "You might, if you knew what I was trying to say."

"I doubt it. And what you're attempting to tell me is upsetting *you* a lot. I don't want you to be upset." He leaned in and nuzzled Terry's nose tenderly. "I want to kiss you again. I've been wanting to do that for a while."

Terry could feel himself going under. "I don't want you to be angry that I didn't tell you."

"I promise I'll remember you tried to tell me."

Terry stopped feeling panicked and started to be annoyed. "That doesn't make any sense."

"Why not? Clearly I'll know what it is right away. Am I wrong?"

"Oh, you'll know."

"There. Problem solved. If it works out, you can tell me later, but don't do it now. Because it would get in the way of me kissing you, wouldn't it?"

Terry paused, considering his answer. Evan laughed, and Terry swatted him. "It's not a joke."

"Sorry. But it is pretty funny, this situation." He grinned and brushed his lips over Terry's. "I can't believe I got to kiss you, and you didn't run or tell me I was weird."

"You're not weird." Terry ran a hand down Evan's chest, leaning on his shoulder. "You're wonderful."

Evan ran fingers through Terry's hair, drawing him in close again. "See? Why in the world would I want to ruin a moment like this?"

Why in the world, indeed.

Chapter Nine

E VAN HAD KISSED Terry.

The thought kept playing inside Evan's head as he put his clothes into drawers and tucked his suitcase inside the closet, as he got dressed for dinner and went downstairs to get his models out of the boxes and set them up properly. He kept catching himself smiling at strange moments, smiles he couldn't wipe away.

It had been such a nice kiss. He'd never kissed anyone like that before, so sweet and soft.

He wasn't certain why he'd done it, except that he'd been thinking about it ever since the night before. Every time they stopped on the drive up he'd kept hoping there'd be a moment when he could try to kiss Terry, but it hadn't felt right. On the stairs had felt like the first time it might be okay, and even then he hadn't been sure. It had worked out, though, really well. The only trouble had been whatever it was Terry had wanted to tell him.

Evan didn't know what that could be. All he knew

was he had the same nagging feeling of unease he'd gotten when Dale had offered to tell him, and now *what Terry wanted to say* was tucked in the back of his mind as the same dark box as *Dale's truth about Kevin*. Instead, Evan focused on wondering when he might get another chance to kiss Terry. Did the fact that Terry had let Evan kiss him mean Terry had feelings for him?

What if Terry runs off like Kevin did?

Evan's blood ran cold.

Terry couldn't leave. They had to work together on the next Christmas Town phase. To be safe, though, Evan decided to proceed with caution.

It would be so much easier with Charlotte here.

"Everything okay?" Terry asked from the doorway.

The very sight of him made Evan's heart flutter. He also swayed dizzily at the abrupt turn of his head.

Terry hurried forward to steady him. "Don't do that. You'd think you'd know better."

"Normally, I do. But I forget when I'm surprised." Evan gestured around them. "What do you think? This is the room where the models are meant to be displayed. That corkboard wall is where I usually pin up my designs."

"I think it's perfect. This is going to be a huge help as we work." Terry tucked his hands in his pockets. "You know, this cabin truly suits you. Though it would have been better if I could have designed it with you. The same as the fishermen cabins."

"Well you have me now," Evan pointed out.

"That's true, I do." Terry rested his hand on Evan's arm. "I'm sorry for earlier, for losing hold of myself."

Was he sorry about the kiss too? Evan studied him, searching for the answer. "I don't mind."

Despite Evan's assurance, Terry seemed troubled. "I truly do have something important I should tell you, though."

There was that uneasy feeling again. "Why do we have to talk about it right now?"

"Because…" Terry's blush stained his cheeks. "Because if you're going to do things like kiss me, it's important you know the truth."

"Yes, but this truth makes you look like you want to throw up." It made Evan nervous too, and he didn't want to think about why. He'd rather kiss more instead.

Terry laughed sadly and ducked his head. "Well, I'm a little ashamed of myself."

All right, now Evan was *slightly* curious. "Why? I don't understand. Is this thing you need to tell me something you did?"

Terry frowned. "I… Well, mostly it's a misunderstanding."

"Your misunderstanding?"

"No, yours."

Oh no, the sense of doom was back. Evan wanted to end this conversation. "Well, then why are you so nervous? This isn't your fault. It's mine. So don't worry about it."

It didn't matter how much Evan reassured him.

Terry simply looked wretched. "I should've clarified things long ago. I just didn't know how, and now…"

Evan stared at Terry, attempting to decide if this was a mess because Evan was bad at relationships, Terry was, or they both were. He wished again Charlotte was here, or even Dale. Except Dale would try to tell him. Like Terry was doing now.

Which made him think that probably he should let someone tell him. So why *wasn't* he letting anyone tell him anything? Why did he have a feeling Evan and Dale's confessions were related? Why did that make him feel so panicked?

Why did it make him think about Terry's steel-blue eyes?

A headache began to form between Evan's eyes, and he pinched the bridge of his nose. "I think I want to lie down for a bit before we go to this dinner."

Did Terry look disappointed? Relieved? Evan didn't stick around to analyze his expression. He simply disappeared into the master bedroom, pulled back the sheets to his bed, and climbed into the familiar nest.

Terry's eyes followed him into the darkness.

Or were they Kevin's?

Evan's headache never went away, so he was in a foul mood as he emerged from his room to go with Terry to the dinner party.

It was an awkward drive over, but as soon as they turned down the street where Frankie and Marcus lived, Evan became too distracted to focus on anything else.

"This is some amazing architecture. I think Dale told me about this, but I never got to see it in person."

Terry also came out of his funk, grinning as he gestured at the houses. "Aren't they great? Frankie got me inside a few when I stayed with him this summer. Some of the renovations would break your heart, but a couple are gems. According to Frankie, though, everyone on the street is interested in retrofitting their houses to match the original style, and they want the outsides of their houses in particular to look showy so tourists come down this street. Marcus found them a grant. I think part of the reason the whole crew is coming to dinner is so they can sweet-talk us about doing a side project."

"It sounds like fun." Evan rolled down the window and leaned out to get a better look and ended up waving awkwardly at an enthusiastic resident, who quickly ran away to call to a neighbor. "Uh-oh. I think we've been spotted."

Indeed they had, and when they climbed out of the SUV, they were greeted not only by Frankie, Marcus, Arthur, Gabriel, Kyle, and Paul, but by half the neighborhood. Too many people called out to Evan from too many directions, and he got dizzy, which was when Terry clamped a hand on his arm and told Frankie they needed to get inside and sit down.

Frankie and Marcus's house had looked the nicest from the street, and it was quite something inside as well. Evan had ideas on how he'd redesign some elements, but overall he found the place, and the people, charming.

"Did you get settled in the cabin?" Frankie asked, passing out glasses of wine from a tray Marcus had carried in for him, though Arthur got beer and Kyle stuck to mineral water.

"We did, thank you." Terry accepted his glass and took a sip. "The basket of food on the counter was so thoughtful, and I assume the food in the fridge and freezer was from you too?"

"It was from all of us, actually." Kyle leaned into his husband's side. "From us and the LGBTQIA group that meets once a month. We made meals at the cabin last weekend while we had our meeting there. Oh, and thanks again for being so kind with Linda Kay. She really liked you, Evan."

"I'm gay," Evan told him.

Kyle grinned. "She was pretty sure of that herself, and sighed a lot over it too. Don't worry too much over that, though. My sister likes a little bit of drama here and there. She's also leading about three men on at her social center at the moment, so there's that."

Terry rubbed at his beard, frowning. "Have you guys still not been able to set up a center of your own?"

Arthur, a shorter, robust man whose red hair seemed natural, threw up his hands in frustration. "No, and not for trying, either. Obviously Dale, Paul, and I would build one in a heartbeat, but it's a matter of funding and politics. I'd donate the land, and we'd all chip in for the supplies, but somebody's got to pay the taxes on the place, and Marcus is always the spoilsport, pointing out the people afraid we're queering up the county as it is won't like us putting up a building for queer people to gather in. Plus we're thinking of having the shelter on our property."

Marcus was a lawyer, it turned out.

"Have you thought about having the center not be *only* LGBT?" Terry swirled his drink thoughtfully. "Maybe that would calm people down."

"It would, but it would also take away from the purpose of the establishment, which is to make a safe space for queer people in this area, something sorely needed." Evan was pretty sure the tall, curly-haired man with glasses who was speaking now was Gabriel, mostly because he was sitting so close to Arthur. "I still think the best course would be to have the center be in town. Anywhere else and you run the risk of vandalism and assault when the members visit. We'll run that risk now, but it'll be less in a populated area."

"We could make that part of our plan," Terry suggested. "I wish Dale would have said something."

"It's personal, so he was probably reluctant." Arthur pulled Gabriel in closer. "Town council would have to approve it, see, and he doesn't like to get in their business."

Terry waved a hand to shoo the objection away. "We'll put it in the proposal now. That's part of our job, to liaison with the council. We'll let Charlotte and Levi sell it when they come up with the rest of the team."

They chatted about the Christmas Town project for a while, or rather Terry and the others did, and sometimes they coaxed Evan into the conversation. It was a lot of new people for him to process at once, and frankly he wished Linda Kay had been present. He'd have gone into another room with her and let her speak animatedly to him one-on-one.

When Frankie said he needed to get dinner ready, Evan was surprised Kyle rose and claimed him, saying he was stealing him away to help put some finishing touches on the dinner table. Except when they went into the other room, they went right past the table and into the kitchen, where they sat at the smaller table and chatted while Frankie worked.

"You looked like you could use a few fewer people," Kyle said, when Evan regarded him in confusion. "Would you rather we chat with you, or would you prefer to be left alone?"

Evan was flustered. "I don't want to be left alone especially." He was disappointed to be taken from Terry, but he supposed it wasn't as if they were talking anyway.

Kyle winked at him. "I'll get Gabriel for you, and I'll help Frankie."

Evan wasn't sure how to object to this, so it wasn't long until the curly-haired man with glasses was sliding into the chair beside him, smiling politely. "Hello again. It's nice to meet you at last. Dale's talked so much about you."

Right, this was Dale's...husband, or something. Evan wasn't sure about that. He frowned, worried he'd offend Gabriel if he asked. He didn't want to ruin this new friendship the first thing he did.

Gabriel's smile was kind. "You look so nervous. You don't need to be."

"I don't want to say the wrong thing." Evan decided honest, at least to an extent, was the way to go. "I do that a lot. I usually upset people. I don't do people well."

"And here we threw six new ones at you at once. Sorry about that." Gabriel crossed his legs and leaned back in his chair. "As for upsetting me, it's difficult to do. I work with children all day and fussy patrons of all ages, plus I'm married to Arthur Anderson. You need a warhead to shock me at this point."

Evan couldn't take it any longer. "Are you married to Dale too?"

Gabriel's smile took on a bit of a glint, but he didn't seem upset. "I am. My legal marriage is to Arthur. Dale and I have our own type of union. It's not exactly a secret in Logan, because I think everyone knows we have some kind of relationship, but they've agreed not to talk about it. Which suits us. We don't need a public marriage, and our relationship doesn't have to be public. Among our friends, I have two husbands. No one else matters."

Honesty was working well. "I will probably forget and say the wrong thing in front of the wrong person."

Now Gabriel looked like Charlotte. He had her evil grin and everything. "That's fine. I just hope I'm around to see the reactions. I suspect it'll be entertaining."

It was easy talking to Gabriel, and Evan didn't know why Dale hadn't told Evan to go to his husband instead of Frankie's, but it didn't matter. By the time dinner was officially ready, Evan felt calmer, and he didn't mind, much, when it was loud and noisy at the table. He ended up seated near Gabriel and Terry but across from Kyle, though the latter spent much of the time teasing his husband. Paul seemed a little shy unless he was talking with Arthur or Marcus, at which point he became more animated, though not as much as the others. Paul would probably be okay too.

He supposed this meant he liked them all but Marcus, who he hadn't gotten to know yet.

"Did you have a good time?" Terry asked as he drove them home.

Evan nodded. "I did. They were very nice."

"Told you." Terry smiled. "They liked you a lot, Gabriel especially."

That made Evan feel good, because he'd liked Gabriel the best too. He hugged himself, trying to be discreet about it. "I've never had an evening like that, with a group of friends."

Terry's smile faded to a more sorrowful expression. "You always say things like that, that you've never had something that to me is so common. Here I was envying your studying abroad, and you're thrilled to have a sleepover and dinner with friends."

To have friends, period, who weren't workmates managing him. "They're all happening because I'm with you."

Terry was quiet after that. Evan enjoyed looking out the window, imagining what Logan would be like with their remodels and upgrades, making modifications to his plans and taking mental notes until they were on the road to the cabin. "I like it up here. It bothered me last time because I felt like it was too long and I missed my habits in the Cities, but I feel like this time might be different. Not just because of you, either. If I can keep from upsetting my new friends, and you, this could be very good."

"I wish you wouldn't talk bad about yourself like that."

"Like what?"

"Like you're some kind of social leper. You're not."

Evan turned to him—too fast, and he had to shut his eyes and wait for things to stop spinning. "I'm not trying to get your pity or make myself sound terrible. I'm stating facts. Until Dale and Charlotte, I didn't have any friends at all. My family has always thought I was strange too. I didn't mind too much, because I don't need people, really, but it is nice to have people to be with. I don't know that I always want to be around so many at once like tonight, but I would like to keep these friends. I just have to not drive them away. The trouble is, I usually don't know why people leave."

Terry's hands tensed on the wheel. "Kevin didn't leave because of you."

Oh, good, now they were both tense. "I don't want to talk about Kevin."

Terry laughed bitterly. "Serves me right. First all you wanted to do was talk about him, and now that I'm ready, you don't want to."

They pulled up to the cabin, where a timer had turned on the outside lights for them. Christmas lights, of course, but they were a string of white lights, so they were subtle. It was mid-September, but with the lights on, it felt like winter. Evan followed Terry into the house, thinking how festive the place would look in the snow. It was already significantly cooler than it had been in July. Soon he'd need a hat and gloves as well as a coat to be outside at this hour.

Terry peered through the window at lake and the sky full of stars. "You're right. It's beautiful up here. I forgot how much I enjoyed Logan until I was here again. Of course, we haven't become swamped with work yet. I can see why Dale is upstate more than he's not, though. It's not just about Gabriel, either. This place pulls on you."

Evan agreed. "I want to make it beautiful enough to pull on lots of people."

"But only so many at once, and at a rate and volume the town can handle. That's not our job, thankfully. We just have to design things and make building plans." Terry put his hands in his pockets, staring out at the lake. "I won't bring it up more than this, but I need to say one thing, and then I'll leave it alone. Kevin didn't leave because of you, like I said. You didn't do anything wrong. Kevin has...issues. He scares pretty easy."

How did Terry think he could bring that up and they wouldn't talk about it? "Then it *was* my fault, because I scared him."

"No. He could have told you that. He could have contacted you after to explain. He could have done a lot of things. Kevin is a bit of a coward, always wanting other people to take responsibility so he doesn't have to."

"I was trying to take it. I didn't mind."

Terry seemed so sad. "I know, but this is what I mean. None of this was on you. I don't want you to think that. That's all."

Evan felt a bit better, actually. "What about you? Do you scare easily?"

Terry looked embarrassed, but he smiled. "I try not to let people know, but yes."

"I won't scare you."

Terry laughed. "You scare me every day, Evan." When Evan recoiled in alarm, Terry held up a hand. "It's okay. I've grown used to it. I know you mean well, so it's fine."

Evan couldn't relax, though. "I don't want you to run off."

"I won't run off."

"Yes, you say that, but if I'm scaring you all the time—"

This time it was Terry who cut off Evan with a kiss, but he trembled.

Evan sighed, though his hand settled on Terry's hip. "See? You're scared right now."

"Of myself. Not you." Terry shifted closer, his beard scratching Evan's neck. "I do feel guilty not telling you everything."

"You can tell me later."

"Then I suppose we'll have to make each other promises, that you won't be upset when I tell you everything later, and I won't run off if you scare me."

It sounded like a perfect arrangement to Evan.

Chapter Ten

TERRY HAD EXPECTED another kiss, but he didn't get one.

He'd expected a lot more than a kiss, to be honest—he'd expected to get seduced, undressed in the entryway, led naked through the cabin, and taken to Evan's bed. A repeat of his night as Kevin, essentially. Instead, once they were back inside, Evan only squeezed his hand, pushed his glasses higher onto his nose, and told Terry he'd see him in the morning.

That was it.

Terry had barely slept, tossing and turning in his bed. His bed which was not, blessedly, the bed he'd shared with Evan the last time, and when he finally caved at five and got up, he took a shower in the bathroom near his room, which was *not* the sexed-up master bedroom spa complete with enema wand. Then he went in search of coffee.

The kitchen was truly well-stocked, and he munched on a croissant and wandered onto the deck while he waited for the coffee to brew. God, but it was a lovely morning and such a beautiful view. Why *hadn't* this become a tourist destination already? Probably the remote roads and the fact that it was so far away. Except a lot of places in the north were far away, and plenty of people had cabins there. Usually, though, they were clustered around packets of civilization. People liked to be rustic, but within reason. They wanted this view, but they wanted that sinful shower and some gourmet coffee and the knowledge they could go grab a nice meal later. They wanted to go fishing, but they wanted to shop too.

Dale had planned for all those things, and Terry had built shelters for the dreams. The café was due to start its remodel next week. The empty storefronts on Main Street would be refitted with the new designs. Paul and Arthur had already started work on the light panel Terry and Evan had designed before they arrived, since Dale had faxed them the design as soon as it was approved, and they had plans to wire the whole street when the time was right. Everything was coming together.

Terry felt so invested in this project, more than he'd felt since he could remember.

When he went back inside for his coffee, Evan was there, wearing a robe. Terry had a feeling Evan wasn't wearing anything underneath and only wore the robe for Terry's benefit. Evan waved a greeting at him as he entered. "Oh there you are. I assumed you were awake because of the coffee. Come on. I'm in the model room. I have some ideas I wanted to go over with you. But I think we might need to go to the real thing before we know for sure."

Terry poured two mugs of coffee. "How long have you been awake?"

"About two hours. Come on."

Terry followed him down the stairs to the model room, which was set up in an exact replica of the town once again, though now there were flags with notes stuck with pins in several places.

Evan gestured to several on the town square. "When we made our plans, we were going by my models, but driving past these places last night, at the points I've marked, I think we need to reconsider some of our designs. The corner here will obstruct the line of this building, even with the remodel, and this tree is bigger than I thought, plus it will obviously only grow larger. The hill here is a steeper slope than I'd remembered. Also, I want to walk the length of it with you, to imagine some changes and have you tell me how feasible they are."

Terry sipped his coffee to cover his excitement. Had Evan always looked this sexy when he worked, or was the kiss getting to him? "Sounds good. We could grab breakfast at the café while we're out and about, if you want."

"I don't want to sit. I have too much energy. I want to work on this."

Terry did too—with Evan. "I bet we can get them to make us sandwiches, and we can take them to go. You can check out the café's details while we wait."

"I did that yesterday, but I suppose I didn't do it with you. We can make some notes." He smoothed his hands over his robe. "I should get dressed."

"Here, don't forget your coffee." Terry held it out toward him.

Evan shook his head. "If I carry it while I walk, I'll spill it. I'm too agitated this morning."

"Then I'll carry it for you."

Terry did, following Evan to his bedroom. He lingered in the doorway, unsure if he should set the mug down, hand it to Evan, or what. He thought of the seduction that hadn't happened the night before, and he felt flustered, wondering what it all meant.

It must have shown on his face, because Evan came over to him, brushing a kiss on his cheek as he took the mug from his hands. "You need to leave while I get dressed. If you stay, you'll distract me from work, and I won't be able to keep my promise to myself."

Terry's cheek burned where Evan's lips had touched. "What's your promise?"

"That I'll go slow with you, so I don't scare you."

Terry practically floated down the hall, and he blushed like a schoolboy.

He still felt the glow as he drove them to the café, where a waitress named Patty was indeed happy to make them sandwiches to go, and she threw in a thermos of coffee on the house. "It's chilly out there this morning. We might get an early snow again this year."

This comment drew Evan's interest. "How early does it snow here, normally?"

"Oh, it depends. Usually it's October, though. Doesn't always stick around, but generally we have at least a flurry by then."

Evan glanced at Terry, but Terry was already making notes. "What's the average temperature, do you know? In October, or even September. Though I guess I could look it up."

Evan had his phone out. "Mid sixties in September, fifties in October. But it drops to the thirties in November."

Terry scratched his chin. "We could probably start reliable artificial snow in mid-to-late October. I think Dale's going to say most people won't be excited about Christmas Town until Halloween clears, and not with gusto until after Thanksgiving, but I know what you're thinking, and I bet it will work. I'll make the notes, and we'll look into it."

Evan had the distant glaze he had when he was deep in thought. "Dale's almost caved on the snow machine. I don't know how the machines work, though, so let's not get too ahead of ourselves. I'd want it on all the roofs for sure, and the trees. In summer I have an artificial material in mind, but the real thing would be excellent in the winter season. How do we find out?"

Patty looked intrigued and excited. "For anything involving a machine, you want Paul and Arthur over at Logan Repair. They know everything, and if they don't, they'll learn."

Evan turned to Terry. "The Paul and Arthur we met last night?"

"The very same. I'll take you by their shop. We can hit it on our walking tour as you check some of those places that concerned you." He put a twenty down for Patty, payment and an insanely generous tip. "Thank you so much for breakfast and the coffee. We'll be sure to be back for lunch."

She passed him a slip of paper with a phone number. "You text me when you're hungry, tell me what you want, and I'll send somebody to find you. Don't worry about the bill. I'll start you a tab. You boys have fun. We can't wait to see what you do to Logan."

The day went by in a beautiful blur. Evan was laser focused on his task, albeit distracted on the way by other details he'd forgotten. Terry kept his notebook out and wrote everything down, though occasionally they stood a moment and debated whether the alteration would work or how best to do the workaround. They tended to attract a lot of attention from passers-by, sometimes enough that townspeople would stop and offer their two cents, though usually people simply stood and listened or whispered, often smiling. A few of them frowned, and Terry assumed they were part of the resistance effort Dale had mentioned.

By the time they made it to Logan Repair, the rumor mill had announced their arrival for them. Paul and Arthur greeted them with warm smiles, and in Arthur's case, a wave as he set down his screwdriver. "Been wondering when you'd show up."

"We've been making a study of things on our way." Terry set his notebook on the bench and got out the thermos of coffee and bag of plastic cups, noting Patty had packed more than two. Was she psychic? He glanced up and noticed Evan was wandering around the shop, taking everything in, lingering to watch the repair Paul was working on. Terry decided it would be best to leave him be and do the talking with Arthur. "Evan had some questions about snow machines. Do you guys know anything about how they work?"

Arthur stroked his beard. "Hmm. Can't say that I do, but you've got me curious now. I'll do some digging. Actually, I'll have my nephew do it with me. This is right up his alley. When do you need to know by?"

"Oh, next few weeks or so. This is a final design element, really, more of a finishing touch."

"Dale does like that sort of thing, though, and I know he wants this first Christmas Town season to go off with a bang. He and Gabriel are having one of their Duluth getaways this weekend, so maybe I'll knuckle down and see if I can get you answers before they get back and construction begins on Monday."

Evan had stopped wandering and was focused exclusively on Paul now, and when Terry went to join him, he saw why. Paul was working on the master control panel for the lights, building what Terry had sent up the schematics for. It was something else to see live and in person.

"I only have a working knowledge of something this complex, so I was worried it wouldn't pan out." Terry leaned on the counter next to Evan and settled in to watch Paul work. "I'm glad to see you were able to make something of it."

"Oh, no, your designs were great." Paul smiled at him, no longer looking shy. "We had to adjust things here and there, but by and large we could build things exactly as you said. I think it's going to work out well, and it's going to make everything so much easier. We were both really excited when you sent it our way, and so was the council."

"We need to set up a time to meet with them." Terry rubbed his chin. "I forgot to ask Dale if he was going to set that up, or if we should. Though I don't know who to ask, so I guess we wait for him."

"The Christmas Town committee head will likely find you first." Arthur finished the last of his coffee before reaching for the thermos. "That would be my mother, Corrina Anderson. You meet her when you were up this summer?"

Evan ignored the question, too focused on Paul's work. Terry shook his head. "I only met people on the construction site and the six of you. Well, and I suppose a few people I ran into around town. I don't recall her name, though."

"You'd recall my mother if you met her. A word of advice: if there's something she tries to talk you into that you don't want, shut the conversation down and tell her she'll have to talk to Dale." Arthur regarded Evan thoughtfully. "Or let your partner here do the talking. I have a feeling the two of them together might be interesting. Kind of wish I could watch the showdown."

Terry wasn't sure he liked where this was going, but he didn't know what else to say. "We were about to go over to the library, because Evan wanted to check some of his model's designs against the actual building."

Paul lifted his head. "I had a question about that, out of curiosity. Didn't you see the library this summer, when you were here?"

This time Evan answered. "Terry and I weren't working together directly then, and we've made some significant structural and design changes since that time. We were working off my scale models, which while quite accurate, aren't the same as being on the ground and looking at the real thing. It was smart of Dale to send us up here together in advance of construction. I wasn't anticipating making this many changes, but they're simple edits when everything is on paper. Much more difficult while building is going on."

Arthur nodded. "Makes sense. Well, we don't want to keep you from your work, in that case."

It didn't take them long to get to the library, but before they went in, Evan thoroughly cased the exterior, murmuring new ideas. Terry was about to offer some suggestions as well when a woman's voice interrupted him.

"Yoo-hoo, hello there. Terry and Evan, is it?" The woman came over, bright smile in place as she extended a hand, her jacket flapping open. "Hi there. Corrina Anderson, chairperson of the Logan Christmas Town committee. Pleased to meet you both. Gabriel just started story time, but he wanted me to come out and say hi and answer any questions you might have."

Evan turned to her, shaking her hand absently. He was still staring at the roofline of the library and the line of deciduous trees against the south side. "Do you trim those fairly regularly?"

Corrina glanced at the trees. "I'm not sure. That usually falls to Arthur. I think they come by when the branches scrape the shingles."

Evan waggled his fingers at Terry, which had become their code for making notes. "I'd like to see them lifted a bit. They're a bit too raw as it is. I'm fine with the natural look, but if we lift the lower canopy, we can echo the shape of the roof and play with a light scheme more easily. I'd missed that in my first round with Dale, but I hadn't been focusing that in depth at the time, either."

Corrina rubbed her hands together. "Oh, this sounds wonderful, the work the two of you are doing.

You know, I have a lot of ideas about some of the improvements. Why don't the two of you come inside to the conference room, and I'll tell you about them?"

Terry could *feel* the managing hand coming down on him without her touching him. He opened his mouth to try to deflect, but Evan spoke first, still studying the roof.

"No thank you. Library interior reconstruction isn't until the fourth phase, and I only work with Terry at this part of the process. You can submit your ideas to Dale at the meeting next week, and we'll consider them then." He paused and turned to her. "Arthur said we might meet with the council before then. Do you think you could talk to them and see if they want to meet this week too, or wait until then? He said you might know."

Corrina looked slightly taken aback. "Yes, but I really think—"

"But he did say they'd probably find us too, so we can wait for that as well. I don't mind either way." He put a hand to his eyes to shut out the sun and frowned at the roofline. "Terry, how many lights did we have planned for the library?"

Terry had to tear his gaze away from the flustered Corrina. "Let me look it up."

"It's no trouble for me to accompany you," Corrina tried again, clearly not liking that she'd lost hold of this conversation.

Evan either missed the pointed edge to her tone, or chose to ignore it. "It's something of a trouble for me, so I'd rather you didn't. Thank you," he said when Terry passed him the notebook. "Oh, I see. Well, that's not going to work at all, is it. I don't know what I was thinking."

Terry let Evan absorb himself in his work and led the thin-lipped Corrina aside. "I'm really sorry. He's very particular about how he works. We'll be happy to hear your ideas at the meeting, though." He handed her his business card. "If you want to text me any details on that, I'd be so grateful."

"I will." She sighed in resignation as she pocketed the card. "I'll leave you to it then. I can see you have your hands full."

She left, and once Terry was sure she was absolutely out of earshot, he went back to Evan. "Did you mean to drive her off like that, or was that simply you being you?"

Evan turned to blink at him, fast enough to make himself unsteady. "I don't know what you mean."

Smiling, Terry righted his partner's arm and kept his hand at his elbow. "Don't worry about it. Let's get back to work."

IT WAS SO hard to hold back with Terry, but Evan was doing his best.

It helped that they were so busy with the prep for the start of construction, but in a way this made things worse, because Evan saw him constantly. They woke up together, had breakfast together, then worked together all day long. They ate all their meals together, and in the evenings they took walks around the lake, usually talking about the project, but sometimes they shared stories from their past. Terry told Evan about his parents, who both worked at the Mayo Clinic, though neither of them were doctors. His mother worked in administration, and his father worked in the accounting department. Evan shared stories about his parents as well: his mother who worked for the Department of Defense, and his father who was a physicist. Terry laughed when Evan told him he was the family embarrassment as a simple designer.

Terry did yoga on the deck every night, even though it was chilly. He said he preferred when it was chilly, that it helped him focus. Evan liked to watch him do yoga. He also enjoyed watching Terry work at the counter in the kitchen, which he used instead of the standing desk he apparently had at the office. So Evan quietly overnighted him a standing desk and a Wurf board, a bouncy inflatable mat to stand on.

The expression Terry made when it was all delivered was priceless. Terry was surprised, yes, but he also seemed happy. Very happy.

That day, it had been so hard not to kiss him.

Terry *wanted* Evan to kiss him, it was clear, which made matters worse for Evan. The trouble was, Evan knew he couldn't stop with a kiss again. Not for long. It was good they were nearly done with his part of the work for a while, because almost all he was good for was staring at Terry's ass while he stood at his desk and fidgeted on his board. Evan had to drink everything in now while he could.

"When will you start at the site again?" He asked this of Terry the day after Dale had returned and they'd gone to the city council meeting for the second time. They were in the cabin, where Terry was making the last of the edits to the plans. Evan was ass-gazing as usual.

"I think Dale wanted me there right away, so as soon as we finish these plans. But whenever you finish up with the shopkeepers, if you have anything you need me to adjust, let me know. You know I can do it on the fly."

This was the problem. Everything out of Terry's mouth, Evan could make sexual. "I...sure. I will."

Terry went back to drafting. "Is Charlotte coming up to help you?"

"Yes. At some point during the construction, she comes up and we start meeting with people to discuss the third phase. It won't start until after the holidays, but Dale wants the team to get ready."

"Well, you and I can look over anything you want in the evenings. That'll save some time later." Terry glanced over his shoulder at Evan. "Unless you don't want to work in the evenings."

No, Evan wanted to fuck Terry in the evenings. "Sure. You know I enjoy working with you."

Was that a shy smile? A hopeful smile? Evan couldn't tell. He never could, really. "Okay. I'll plan on it."

Dale wasn't any help with Evan's restraint, either. Once Terry started going to the construction site, Dale came to give Evan a ride into town—it turned out Charlotte wasn't coming until the first week of November, and Dale would be his "Evan whisperer," whatever that meant—and every day Dale asked how things were going between Evan and Terry. On the fourth day of construction, the fifteenth day of October, things weren't any different.

"You're still doing okay with Terry?"

"We're working well together."

"Not what I meant, Evan." Dale handed him a bakery bag. "Almost forgot. These are from the woman who's starting a bakery as soon as we hit the soft opening. She's operating out of her house at the moment, but I had her send over some samples for you. What do you think? Gourmet enough to compete with Glam Doll?"

Evan pulled out the donut, which wasn't as fancy as Glam Doll, but looked good. "Presentation needs work, both donut and packaging."

"I'll tell her to pull out the stops for her next sampling. How about the actual taste?"

Evan took a bite. His eyebrows lifted. "Very good. Excellent, even. She can't skimp on the packaging, though. People from the Cities will expect it. She can go for folksy, but she still has to have a brand."

"Most people here don't really know what a brand is. Not in terms of their own products. They feel like that's for fancy folks."

"It's not. I should meet with her. Am I meeting with her?"

"Of course. She's nervous, though." Dale glanced across the seat. "Also, between you and me, Sara's a member of our LGBTQIA family. Not out, but she's still in with us. So I take extra care of her."

"I will too, then." Evan took another bite of the donut. It was really good, and now that he thought of it, a little familiar. "She made the croissants at the cabin, didn't she?"

"Yes, but I made the wheat bread in the freezer."

"I know, I recognized it." They were in the town now, and people were waving at them as they drove by. Dale always smiled and waved back. "You seem very happy here."

"I am. I love our company, but my heart is here. My ultimate goal is to run Christmas Town myself, to make it my full-time job and let another director at Davidson Incorporated handle other projects."

The news startled Evan. "You mean you'll move here permanently?"

"As much as possible, yes. I'd come to the Cities to manage things on occasion, but this would be home base." He shrugged. "We're a long way from that, though. I plan to be more absent through this whole season, but it's only a start."

"Could you move Davidson Incorporated up here?"

"Too remote to do business."

"Not all of it. I mean, I could work from here. I don't ever come to the office anyway."

"Yes, but would you want to? That's the problem. I'm the only one who wants to live so far away."

Evan considered the prospect. "I'd do it if Terry were here too."

Now Dale smiled. "Then why aren't you making a move on him? You're driving him crazy, you know. He's waiting for it."

Evan was acutely aware of this. "I'm trying not to scare him."

"Are you worried he'll behave the same way Kevin did?"

Evan nodded. "Are you going to tell me I shouldn't worry?"

"No, you have good reason to. But I also think the situation is different. That was more of a one-night stand."

This, actually, was a conversation Evan needed to have. "How is this different? Because to me, I connected with Kevin and knew he was right for me. Part of me still feels that way. I feel connected to Terry too. I don't understand how I can feel this way about both of them. Though I suppose this is how it is for you. Or for Gabriel, who feels that way about you and Arthur."

"I'm polyamorous as well. I'm not dating anyone else at the moment, but I'm open to it. My situation isn't the same as yours, but yes, the feeling might be similar. Though I thought you'd given up on Kevin?"

"I have, but I still think about him. He wasn't a fling to me. I'll give him up if I have to choose, because Terry and I have a friendship too, and I don't want to lose it."

"That's what I mean about it being different. With Kevin, you had a hot flare, something easy to put out. With Terry you have a foundation. Do you honestly think he's going to vanish if you kiss him?"

"This is the thing. There's no way I can simply kiss him."

"Good, because I think if you stopped there, he'd be disappointed."

Evan thought about what Dale had said all that day and for the next several days, especially whenever he was with Terry. They continued to work well together, the same as they always had, but now Evan could only think about how much he wanted their relationship to go deeper, and how terrified he was of messing up his attempt to take it there. He tried to get ahold of Charlotte, but she was busy leading their team and several others as well, so he couldn't reach her. When Evan complained that he needed her, all she would say to him was, "You're doing fine on your own, honey. Keep up the good work."

He was decidedly *not* doing fine. He was caught in a

loop: getting up in the morning, having breakfast with Terry, pining over him all day while he worked with Dale or drafted design ideas from meetings with some of the local owners. Every night he had dinner with Terry. Sometimes in the evenings Terry would look at his designs with him, telling him where things were impossible from a practical standpoint or getting excited with him because something wasn't just feasible, it solved some other problem or inspired a whole new set of ideas. But no matter how many heavy glances passed between them, Evan always went to bed alone, without having so much as brushed his lips against Terry's hair.

On Halloween night, that changed.

Terry had spent the day overseeing construction as usual, but Frankie and Gabriel and the others roped Evan into helping with the Main Street trick-or-treating event. The local businesses hosted a parade for the children to collect candy, and afterward their parents were invited to shop while the kids played games in the new civic center, which would shortly become Santa's Workshop. Still a place for guests to gather and relax, but it would be themed to match the Christmas Town spirit. Evan was scheduled to oversee the decoration setup as soon as the Halloween festival was over. In the meantime, though, his task was to don a set of devil's horns and stand in front of one of the shops not yet finished in its remodel and whose new owner couldn't make it to the event and hand out candy.

He hadn't been eager for his task, especially since

the constant glancing up and down to distribute candy made him dizzy, but he soon forgot to be annoyed, because everyone—kids, parents, and shopkeepers—were so happy. Every single parent who came by thanked him not only for the candy but his work on the town, and several adults took his hands and expressed their gratitude with tears in their eyes. Evan was so overcome he didn't know what to say. Mostly he nodded and passed out the candy until it and the stream of people were gone. Then he went back to Frankie and Marcus's building, the law office and salon sharing a common wall, accessible inside by a shared door. Frankie was talking to someone, so Evan went to sit with Marcus, who was going over some paperwork. Marcus seemed to always be going over some paperwork.

He looked up at Evan when he came in, though, and smiled. "You looked like you had quite a crowd."

Evan sank into one of the black leather chairs facing Marcus's desk. "They all thanked me. They were very emotional."

Marcus closed the folder in front of him. "I'm not surprised. Logan had nearly winked out of existence even before the mill closed. To be honest, when that happened, Frankie and I were discussing whether or not we should leave. But now the town is coming back to life. The whole county is, and it's because of Christmas Town. We could never have had an event like this even a year ago. There were no downtown businesses for kids to trick or treat at. Next year there will be twice as many. It's not only jobs that have come back. It's a sense of civic pride."

"I didn't do that, though. Dale did."

"You made the designs, and they know. If Dale had been there, he would have been mobbed. He can't go into the café to grab a cup of coffee to go without it taking an hour."

Now Evan understood why he always had to go in and get the coffee. "Well, I'm glad they like the designs."

"The designs are incredible. You have to see what we came from, though. What you worked from was what Arthur and Paul started. Here—I think I have photos of the originals."

Marcus withdrew a binder full of photographs of Logan and the upgrades. He did indeed have the original, depressing and dilapidated empty fronts of Logan's downtown, as well as several shots of progress along the way. He also had all kinds of photos of the construction, which Evan explored as well.

"Are these from this summer?"

Marcus nodded. "I try to take photos whenever I can. This is Logan's history, and it should be documented."

It was quite a history unfolding. Dale would probably want the photos too, for Davidson Incorporated. Dale was in several of the photographs, directing construction.

Then Evan turned the page and saw Kevin.

Kevin. His heart skipped a beat, and he touched the page, outlining the figure.

Marcus smiled, chuckling. "I forgot about that. Terry was a wild man this summer, wasn't he?"

Evan glanced up at him, still dazed by the sight of the man who had wounded him. "Hmm? What about Terry?"

Marcus put his finger next to Evan's, also indicating the photo of Kevin. "This picture of Terry. He looked like he'd escaped from a medieval prison. I guess his hair wasn't long, but that beard. Frankie kept offering to trim it, but Terry got attached to it, I guess. He was so thin too. He's getting there again. He works too hard. Is he eating enough, do you know?"

The whole world spun around Evan, worse than any vertigo he'd ever experienced. His head threatened to split open, his stomach promising to show him what he'd eaten that day. "Wait...what do you mean, the picture of Terry? You're saying...you think this is Terry?"

"I *know* this is Terry. He stayed with us, remember?"

Evan wanted to sit down, except he was already sitting down. "This isn't a picture of a man named Kevin? You're sure?"

"I'm positive. This is Terry. Here, I think there's a better picture of him somewhere." Marcus flipped forward several pages, and sure enough, in the photo

Kevin waved at them close up. He was even wearing the shirt he'd worn the night Evan met him, the one with the name on it.

On closer inspection, Evan could see the resemblance to Terry. It truly did look like Terry with a thin face and a long, crazy beard.

For a tight, terrible moment the queasy feeling intensified. This was the truth Dale had been trying to tell him. What Terry had attempted to tell him as well.

What Evan's subconscious had kept burying deeper every time he looked into Terry's eyes and knew he was also seeing Kevin's.

Marcus squinted at the photo, then laughed. "You're right, look at that name tag. I forgot he did that. He ruined all his clothes he brought, which weren't many, so he went to the thrift store and bought a pile of cheap work shirts. One was a bowling shirt with some guy's name sewed on it. Arthur called him Kevin every time he wore it. Hey, are you all right?"

No, Evan wasn't all right. He stared at Kevin, who he had finally found again, letting it sink into his brain that he had in truth been with "Kevin" almost all along.

Chapter Eleven

T HE THOUGHTS KEPT circling in Evan's mind, swirling and dragging him slowly down the drain.

Kevin was Terry. Terry was Kevin.

Evan had already slept with Terry. He was holding back for nothing. This whole time he'd been dying to make love to Terry for the first time…and he already had.

Kevin hadn't run away from him. Terry had.

They both had.

On the one hand, the knowledge made so many things make sense. Why, though, had he been reluctant to let Terry tell him the truth—because this was clearly what Terry wanted him to know. It could be nothing else. If it wasn't, this *should* be what Terry told him. In a way, though, Evan had known all along.

So why had he been so unwilling to close that gap in his mind? Why did staring at that photo and knowing it was Terry make him feel anxious?

What if they're laughing at me?

The thought, once formed, was like lead in Evan's belly. *That* was why he'd feared this revelation. What *if* they were laughing? Dale said he knew Kevin—which meant he'd known it was Terry. Levi did too. What about Charlotte? Did everyone know?

They all knew. The truth that he'd been the last to figure out something which apparently everyone else had found to be obvious made him feel foolish and exposed. It was his elementary playground, his middle school homeroom, his lonely college lunchroom, his awkward staff meetings at every company until Davidson Incorporated. Now Evan feared his sense of belonging at this company was a lie, that he was the same awkward nobody he always was.

Everyone knows, everyone is laughing at you—

A heavy hand on his shoulder drew him back to reality. Marcus was kneeling in front of him, looking concerned. "What's wrong? Do you need me to call a doctor?"

Evan wanted to run, but he was too tired, and there was nowhere to go. "Did you know? Are you making fun of me too?"

"I wouldn't ever make fun of you. I don't know what you're talking about—does it have something to do with this photo of Terry?" Marcus squeezed Evan's biceps. "Maybe I should get Frankie."

Everything was falling apart. "Why did they lie to me?"

Marcus kept touching him, soothing him. "If I take

you to the back room in Frankie's salon, will you tell us the story, so we can help?"

Would he? Evan didn't exactly want to, and he didn't know how anyone could help, but he nodded because he didn't have any other option. He let Marcus lead him through the door into the salon, where it wasn't only Frankie but Gabriel, Arthur, Paul, and Kyle chatting.

Too many. "I don't want to tell this many people." Evan's gaze cut to Gabriel, and he thought of Dale, who had kept this from him. "Especially not *him.*"

Gabriel blinked, looking confused. "Sorry, what's going on?"

Evan spoke before Marcus could explain. "You're Dale's partner. You're probably laughing at me too."

Now Arthur was prickly. "I don't know what you're talking about, but I do know Gabriel wouldn't laugh at anyone."

Gabriel put a hand on Arthur's shoulder and gentled him. "It's true, I wouldn't laugh. But more to the point, Dale doesn't usually share work details with me. I don't know much about you, Evan, except what I've gathered from talking with you. I'm not sure why you're upset or what you think is happening, but we'd like to help you. If you don't want me to help, though, I won't be offended. I can leave the room."

Arthur started to argue with Gabriel about whether or not he needed to leave, and Gabriel argued back. Paul looked worried, Frankie asked Marcus quietly what was going on, and Kyle came up to Evan, appearing concerned. Except Evan had already had enough. He'd just tell them the truth, drive them away, and get it over with.

"I've been looking for four months for a man named Kevin who I met and slept with in Logan during the first phase of Christmas Town."

Everyone in the room hushed, turning to give him their focus.

Evan kept his gaze on the floor. "He was sweet and funny and wonderful and good in bed, and I fell in love for the first time with him. But he vanished in the middle of the night. All I knew was that he'd worked on the construction for the project and that he was connected to Terry in some way."

Arthur snapped his fingers. "Right, we were all looking for the guy, remember? But nobody could find the right Kevin."

"Be quiet and let Evan tell his story," Gabriel said.

Evan continued. "I tried to find Kevin, but the only lead I got was that Terry knew him. When I asked Terry about Kevin, at first he told me Kevin never wanted to see me, which upset me for several days, and then Terry came to apologize.

"As I worked with Terry on the setup for the second phase of renovation, I started to fall in love with him too, and I thought maybe he liked me as well. But I was afraid of him acting like Kevin. Then we moved up here together, and it seemed even more like he liked me, but I was still afraid, because we were living in the place where things went badly. But today I saw this photo, which I knew was Kevin and Marcus insisted was Terry. Now that I look at it more closely, I can see it is Terry. Terry is Kevin. I've been looking for him this whole time, and he's been right in front of me. Everyone but me knew, though I think I knew for a long time but didn't want to admit it. Probably you guys all knew. Probably everyone has been laughing at how I couldn't figure it out."

Evan fully expected them to do that, except no one so much as cracked a smile. No one regarded him as if he were a child, either. In fact, Gabriel was the first one to speak, and he seemed...angry.

"I didn't have any idea about this, Evan, and I can assure you, if I had, I would have called a stop to it immediately." He flattened his lips and folded his arms over his chest. "Which is likely why I wasn't told, and which, frankly, makes me furious. For you especially, Evan, but for myself as well. Trust me when I tell you Dale is getting an earful the next time I talk to him."

Arthur rubbed his beard. "I don't think anybody meant anything cruel by it, but I agree with Gabriel. Whatever game they're playing, it's gone too far."

Kyle kept shaking his head. "I can't understand *why*. Why would Terry give a false name? Then why would he perpetuate the lie?"

Frankie frowned at Evan. "You really didn't recognize him when you saw him at work in Minneapolis? I know he looks very different without the beard, but surely…"

"I'm not good with faces. I'm not good with *people*." Evan sighed and fixed his gaze on the floor. "My memory of Kevin was hazy. I'd idealized him more than I wanted to admit. It wasn't until I saw the photo that I truly understood."

"That doesn't explain the false name," Marcus pointed out.

Yes, that was true. Why had that happened? "I…don't think he ever said he was Kevin, actually. I read his shirt and started calling him Kevin. He simply didn't tell me I was wrong."

Paul nodded, stroking his beard. "If you were hitting on him and he wasn't interested, that's a common bar tactic. Don't correct their mistakes, let them dig their own grave."

It was? Evan had no idea.

Kyle frowned. "But to *never* correct him? That's just odd."

Evan kept replaying the evening, trying to remember if Terry had attempted to explain then. "We argued a lot. Then…then we were at the cabin, and I was seducing him. There wasn't a good time, I guess. Maybe he could have in the morning, but he'd left by then."

Frankie snapped his fingers and turned to his husband. "That last night he was here! Remember how he showed up at four thirty, bedraggled and shaken? He wouldn't tell us what had happened. We'd assumed some of the guys had shown him too much of a good time and he was recovering from a hangover. But that wasn't it. He'd been running from Evan."

Marcus nodded. "We didn't know Evan then, so it wasn't as if we could put two and two together when Dale had us hunting for Kevin." He turned to Evan. "I'm very sorry."

Evan was still reeling from the idea that they were on his side, *all* of them. "So you don't think I'm stupid for not figuring it out?"

Arthur rounded on him. "Stupid? Why would you be stupid? You didn't do anything. All you did was have a good time after a long session of work and then try to pick up a guy. Not your fault the guy bailed on you."

Evan had the ridiculous urge to defend Terry. "I'm a strange guy, though. I'm bad at picking people up. Charlotte had to coach me, and she says herself she's a big scary lesbian. Maybe I came off as awkward scary lesbian."

Gabriel was still pissed. "Did he go to bed with you willingly?"

Evan didn't hesitate. "Yes. He was quite willing, no question."

"Then it doesn't matter how you came off. He found it attractive. If he freaked out about it later, that's *his* issue, not yours. Leaving you the way he did is *his* rude behavior, and *he* needs to apologize to you. He should have done it long ago. He also should have told you about Kevin immediately."

As the shock of the revelation wore off and his friends' support bolstered him, Evan forced himself to examine the situation with more logic and to acknowledge all the facts. "He *has* attempted to tell me, but I wouldn't let him. I think part of me knew what he was trying to say on some level, maybe. Or perhaps it was simply that I was nervous about having feelings for both Kevin and Evan." He remembered Gabriel was poly and hurried to explain. "I wouldn't mind seeing them both, but I knew Terry wasn't interested in a polyamorous relationship. Except now I feel ridiculous because I was worried about cheating on a man with himself."

Gabriel's lips kept getting thinner. Arthur shook his head and winced. "Dale, you dumb shit, you're not getting laid for a month."

Marcus tapped his cheek. "I want to examine that point, though. Why did Dale help hide the truth? Also, Evan, you said *everyone*. Do you mean that other people also know?"

Evan considered this. "Levi knows, but I'm not sure about Charlotte."

"This just keeps getting stranger," Paul said.

Gabriel looked *very* angry, and Evan felt he should say something in Dale's defense. "I'm pretty sure Dale wanted to tell me, but for some reason he couldn't."

Gabriel's smile could have cut glass. "I'm quite interested to hear what that reason is. I'm certain he and

I have much to discuss."

Marcus shook his head, still thoughtful. "We're missing something here. Something quite important."

Kyle snorted. "I bet I know what it is."

Evan turned to him, as did everyone else. "You do? Will you tell me?"

"Of course I'll tell you. But can I ask you a few questions first? It'll help me confirm if I'm right or not."

This was exciting, actually, to have so many friends trying to help him. "Ask me anything."

"They'll be a little personal. That okay?"

"I don't mind. You're my friends." Evan hesitated, then glanced at the group of them, all focused on him. "Right?"

They agreed readily, but though Kyle nodded too, he also smiled a knowing smile. "Okay, so that ties into my first question. Evan, were you ever tested for any developmental disabilities? Or more specifically, social ones?"

The question surprised Evan, but he didn't mind it. "Yes, a long time ago, when I was still in school. They tested me for several things. Most of them were inconclusive, though several tests said I had mild Asperger's syndrome. My parents got angry about that. But why do you ask?"

"Because I'd already guessed you were on the spectrum. Up here anyone with any kind of developmental, physical, or mental disability gets lumped into the same programs, so Linda Kay has always been good friends with all the kids who are 'other' in that way, and since her friends are usually my friends, I've gotten to know plenty of kids with those same disabilities as well. We also sometimes get adults, even young adults, who have disabilities but no caretakers at the residential care center where I work. So I guess you could say you seemed familiar to me. But given what you said about your parents, I'm thinking you've had a hard time making friends. Am I right?"

"Yes. I've never had any until Dale and Charlotte."

Kyle smiled. "Well, you have plenty of friends now. There's nothing wrong with you or Linda Kay, and there's nothing wrong with Dale or Terry or me or Gabriel. You're different, is all. You're different than Linda Kay, but in some ways the two of you can relate better because you're both different than the rest of us who are all pretty much the same. She really likes you, you know. If you weren't gay, she'd be trying to date you."

Evan felt flattered. "Well, tell her if I wasn't already in love and she were a man, I would accept her invitation to a date."

"See? You understand Linda Kay. A lot of people don't. And I think Dale understands this too. I think he was wrong to do what he did, though I don't know the whole story, so maybe I would agree with him if I knew everything. But I do think he knows you're like Linda Kay, that you're on your own level and that the world doesn't always understand how amazing you are, and he wants to protect you. I do that to Linda Kay a lot, and when I do it too much, she gets mad at me. She tells me I'm being overprotective, and sometimes I am. I suspect Dale is being overprotective. But what we don't know is whether or not he's being overprotective of you or of Terry. Because from what I know of Terry…well, he's not different in the same way, but I could see Dale trying to shelter him a little too."

Now Evan was confused. "Why would he need to protect Terry from me? I wouldn't hurt him."

Kyle held up a finger. "Ah, but see? That's the problem, isn't it? Linda Kay and I have this argument all the time. She doesn't always mean to inspire the reaction she has with people, and yet sometimes she does."

"Yes, but if Dale's concerned about Evan scaring Terry, he needs to come out and say so, then help him do better," Gabriel said.

It was as if a sun was rising slowly in Evan's mind. "No, Dale has been coaching me. He told me I should move forward with Terry, to not worry about Kevin. And he honestly did try to tell me about Kevin several times." Evan frowned, thinking hard. "I can't decide if he's protecting Terry too or not, though."

"Well, what should Evan do?" Paul asked.

Kyle touched Evan's hand. "Do you still want him, Evan? Even after all of this?"

Evan nodded. "I do. Maybe even more. It was a

shock at first, but now that they're one person and you've helped me figure out he probably didn't do it to make fun of me, it's like I get to have both of them."

"Well, there you go." Marcus brushed his hands together. "You said he wanted to tell you before. Give him a chance to step up."

A thousand butterflies took flight in Evans stomach at once. "You mean, *now?* Go talk to him now?"

Marcus laughed. "What, you wanted to drag this nonsense out longer?"

Well, yes, a little bit. Evan sighed. "You're right. I suppose I need to. I'm afraid of it going badly, is all. What if I mess up the conversation?" He hugged himself tightly. "He promised me he wouldn't run, but what if he does anyway? What if he doesn't want a relationship with me?"

"Then you have us," Paul said, and the others agreed.

Evan's chest felt tight as he glanced around the room at their kind, eager faces. "No matter what happens with Terry, when the design work for Christmas Town is over, I think I might like to stay in Logan, if that's okay."

"Of course it's okay." Kyle's expression was bright. "You're really thinking of coming to live here? For good?"

Evan nodded. "The one concern I have is sex, because it's too far for escorts. If things work out with Terry and he wants to stay as well, that problem will be solved, but otherwise that's my only reservation. I like the people here, and the food, and the quiet. I can work remotely and go to the Cities when it's important, if someone will give me a ride. I have friends here, and a community. I like that."

"Well, Logan will welcome you with open arms." Arthur patted Evan on the back. "Don't worry about the sex. Let's think positively that you can catch yourself the man in front of you."

The task ahead of Evan loomed large, and he searched the faces of his friends for support. "I don't think I can catch him without help."

All six of them grinned at once, and Marcus answered for them. "Don't worry. You're going to have all the help you need."

THE CONSTRUCTION WAS going well, but it was taking so long. Or rather, it was taking about as long as Terry had expected it to, but he wished his days would end sooner so he could potentially have more energy and might possibly, maybe, work up the nerve to get somewhere with Evan. Every night had him stumbling into the cabin dead on his feet, grateful for the food in the oven or Crock-Pot and the smile Evan had for him…but they never progressed any further than that. It was just as well, he told himself, since he didn't have the stamina for much else. He wasn't sure where the food came from or how the cabin was cleaned—there seemed to be a quiet army of townspeople who took on the task, hired by Dale. Sometimes he'd catch them dropping off a casserole or leaving with a cleaning bucket, but mostly it was as if magical elves had made things happen like a dream.

On Halloween night, however, when Terry arrived at the cabin, it was dark and quiet, and it didn't smell of anything but the furnace. The women who kept the house up had been through to do dishes, and they'd put food in the fridge, but Evan hadn't put anything out for dinner, and he wasn't home.

Odd. Terry called Dale. "Is Evan with you?"

"No, I'm on my way back from Duluth. Fetching supplies. I think he went to the Main Street Trick-or-Treating Festival with the guys. Maybe text him?"

"I did, but he didn't answer." Not entirely unusual though, to be honest. "Maybe I'll try Frankie."

"They might be at dinner or something. I called Gabriel earlier, but he didn't answer or even return a text."

That was odd. "All at dinner, huh?" Why hadn't they invited him? Probably because they assumed he'd be at work, which he had been. He sighed. "I'll wait, then, and see if he shows up." And eat alone.

"I'll let you know if I hear anything."

"Okay."

He hung up and heated up some leftover lasagna, which was good, but somehow not as great as when Evan set it out for him. Once he finished, Terry texted

Evan a third time, but still received no response. He told himself he'd call Frankie after he did the dishes, but while he was putting the last plate in the cupboard, the door opened. It was Evan.

"Oh, there you are." Terry set down his towel and walked toward Evan. "I called, but you didn't answer. I was worried, though Dale said you were with the others, so I tried not to. Worry, I mean." Geez, now he just sounded like an idiot.

Was he imagining it, or was Evan giving him an odd look? "I was with Frankie and Marcus at their house with everyone. We had dinner after the trick-or-treating event. I handed out candy from an empty storefront." He hung his coat up on the pegs by the door and took off his boots. There wasn't snow, but it was cold. "I have a few design note changes for that store."

"I'd love to see them. Unless you're too tired. You sound like you had a busy day." He did his best to focus on that and not how much fun Evan had had without him, with other people. It wasn't Evan's fault Terry had to work so late.

"I enjoyed myself. I like Logan a great deal." Evan finished hanging his coat, but he kept his hands on it as he spoke. "I think I'd like to live here."

The way he said it made Terry pause. "You mean it, don't you? That wasn't just an idle thought."

Evan nodded. "I'd like to buy this cabin. Perhaps rent it at first to make sure. But I'd like to stay here.

Permanently."

Terry was becoming more and more upset he'd missed this dinner. "That's...that's a big change. Are you certain that's a good idea?"

"Reasonably." Evan came into the kitchen, looking around. "Oh. Lasagna? Was it good?"

Fuck the lasagna. "Evan—I want to talk about this idea of moving to Logan."

Evan turned to face him carefully. He still had that strange expression on his face. "Yes. Let's discuss that, and other things."

Why did that sound so ominous? "What other things?" The man couldn't be breaking up with him. They'd never started going out.

Evan took a step closer. Was he sweating? Yes. He was sweating. "I'd like to hear, Terry, what it was you've been trying to tell me. I'm ready."

Oh. Shit.

Terry backed away. "I—I don't think this is the time to discuss that."

Evan's brow lifted in surprise, then lowered into a frown. "Why not? You've been trying to tell me since we came up to Logan."

That was true, Terry had. So why was the prospect of confession freaking him out so much? Now *he* was the one sweating. "I've changed my mind. There's no need to tell you anything."

Forget odd, now Evan looked...disappointed? "You're sure about that?"

No, Terry wasn't, and yet, he knew he didn't want to dredge that up right now. At the very least he needed to warm up to something like that. "I'm sure." He forced a smile. "I'd like to hear about this idea you had about moving to Logan, though."

Never had Terry seen someone's expression shutter as fast as Evan's did. "Why? You don't need to move here."

It was a slap in the face, and Terry reeled from it. "I—I know that, but...but I like...working with you."

"We can work remotely." Evan headed toward the stairs. "I'm going to go to bed. It was a big day."

Terry couldn't take it. He followed Evan, catching his wrist as he started across the room. "It's not only about projects."

Evan didn't face him. "I don't know what you mean."

This cold version of Evan was awful. Terry wanted his Evan back. "I mean I like working with you for more than just projects. I like being with you, Evan. I like *you*." His hands shook and his voice trembled, but he pressed on. "I told you I promised not to run off, but you've barely touched me since then. Now you're telling me you want to move away." A thought occurred to him, and he blushed. "Have—have you been waiting for me to make a move? Is that why you're angry?"

For a moment Evan's shoulders were stiff, and Terry feared he would shout. Then Evan relaxed, and he sighed. "No, it's not about that."

"Then what is it? Please, don't be like this."

Evan faced Terry, still unsmiling, but he wasn't quite as cold. "I'm not sure this will work."

Terry couldn't believe this. "You're giving up?"

Evan averted his gaze. "I'd rather have you as a friend than nothing."

That was tough on its own, but Terry might have been able to accept it.

Except then Evan added, "So I'm thinking of trying to make things work with Kevin after all."

"*What?*"

Evan's gaze glinted, and if this wasn't so serious a subject Terry would have thought it was mischief. "I said I was thinking of trying to make things work with Kevin. Don't worry, I won't expect you to help me find him. That would be awkward."

Terry kept shaking his head, as if that would clear this nonsense. "Evan, you don't need to—"

"It's fine. Like I said, I have feelings for both of you."

This was ridiculous. *I'm right here.* Except even when Terry opened his mouth to tell him, he couldn't.

So he lashed out instead. "How do you think you're going to find him, exactly?"

"I've got a few leads. There's a Kevin on a dating app who looks familiar. I might send him a message."

What? "Let me see this."

Why did Evan look *smug?* "I don't need to show

you anything."

Panic clawed at Terry, at the idea of Evan with some random stranger he thought was Kevin. Would he believe it? *No. You can't have him.* "Why can't you make it work with me instead?"

The way Evan's gaze sharpened made Terry's breath catch. "Because if you can't be honest with me, I can't build a relationship with you."

This was a nightmare. "I thought you only had flings. I thought you didn't *do* relationships." *I thought what you had with me was special.*

"Meeting Kevin changed my mind about that."

"And what did *I* change?"

Terry's anger deflated at the hurt in Evan's expression. "You made me believe you might be someone I could build something with too. But if you can't be honest with me, I can't—"

"*I'm Kevin.*"

The words were out of Terry's mouth before he could panic and stop them. He froze, trembled, and tried to back away.

Evan caught his arm. "Say that again, please."

He didn't seem surprised, or upset. He must not have heard him. Terry's stomach roiled at the thought of having to repeat his confession, but he couldn't, he *couldn't* let him go…

"I'm Kevin," he whispered again.

Evan let go of Kevin's arm, sliding down to twine their fingers together. "I know."

Terry had averted his gaze, but now he stared at Evan in disbelief. "You—what?"

Evan wasn't smug *exactly*, but it was close. "I know you're Kevin."

What in the hell. "Then why did you put me though all that?"

"Because it was important you tell me. Now you did, and I'm glad. Why didn't you tell me, though?"

"You wouldn't let me." Terry's head was spinning. "When did you find out? How long have you known?"

"Today. Marcus showed me a photo of you from this summer and said it was you."

"Oh." He rubbed his arm self-consciously. Evan still held his hand.

Evan laced their fingers tighter. "Why were you so nervous to tell me?"

Terry felt awkward all over again. He had no idea confession would only be the first wave of discomfort. "I didn't want to wreck what we have."

"But we had something else as well. I was *looking* for you."

"You were looking for Kevin."

"Are you telling me you're not Kevin?"

Terry shook his head. "I'm not even close."

Evan frowned. "But you're literally the same person."

Now Terry was getting nervous. "I'm not. That was a fluke, a one-night thing. I was that way because you didn't know who I was, because I was angry at you for not knowing I was the architect, except then you were really interesting, and then…" He ran a hand through his hair. "You don't know all the hangups I have. I'm messed up in so many ways. I'm not Kevin. I've heard how you talk about him, what you think he's like. I can't be that."

Evan seemed uncertain now as well too. "I don't think I ever said such things. I'm fine with starting where we are."

Terry felt out of body, as if he wanted to run and reach for Evan all at once. "You'll be disappointed in me. I'm sure of it."

He didn't know what he hoped for, or what he expected, but it certainly wasn't for Evan's expression to shutter as he turned away. "Fine. You've made it clear you aren't interested, so I won't—"

Terry didn't remember consciously moving. One minute he was standing in front of Evan, and the next he'd pressed Evan to the wall, pinning his arms and trapping his legs with his own. His breathing was quick and shallow, and his lips were an inch from Evan's.

Evan's pupils were dilated, his lips wet. "I thought you were turning me away."

"I don't know what I'm doing. I'm a mess. You should stay away from me. But I don't want you to. I need this." He shook as he let go of Evan and stared him down. "I need *you*, Evan."

Evan stared right back at him, but he didn't touch him. "Terry, you don't understand. If I kiss you, if I make love to you, I can't hold back."

This man was going to drive Terry crazy. *Absolutely crazy*. "That's fine. I don't care. Just don't turn away from me like this, *please*."

"I don't mean that I wouldn't stop if you told me to, but I think I would be very aggressive. My feelings for you are strong."

How could he say things like that so calmly? Also, why was he still not touching Terry? "That's fine. Seriously. Aggression sounds perfect."

Evan looked doubtful. "But I can barely tell whether or not you want this. I worry you might run away the same as you did the last time."

Smart man, because the itch to flee was already building in Terry. He tamped it down. "I won't run."

"How do I know what to trust, though? I'm serious when I say I want to preserve our work relationship and our friendship. Perhaps we should leave things as they are."

"*Evan.*"

Evan cast his gaze to the ceiling. Then he let out a breath and looked Terry squarely in the eye. "Very well then. We can go forward, but I'm going to insist you be the one to act first."

Terry startled. "You…want me to kiss you?"

"If it's not too much trouble." When Terry hesitated, Evan took gentle hold of his hands. "You're right, it's probably a bad—"

Terry pressed his lips to Evan's.

It was an awkward, untutored kiss, as if he'd never done such a thing before, and he was embarrassed, but it was all he could manage with how nervous he was. When he drew back, he was still shaking, and he couldn't look Evan in the eye.

Evan stroked his hair. "Why do I make you so nervous?"

Terry tried to laugh, but it didn't work well. *It's not you, it's me. It's everything.* He curled his fingers against Evan's chest. "Just don't talk about walking away from me."

Evan frowned. "I didn't mean to blackmail you."

Terry did smile then. "You weren't, exactly. But that's what I like about you, that you're so blunt."

Evan seemed dubious. "Yes, but what if I push you too hard?"

"You act like I'm a virgin and haven't ever had sex."

"Well, you're acting a little bit like one, to be honest."

Terry shut his eyes. Leave it to Evan hit the vein Terry didn't want him to tap. "I'm not a virgin, but I…have hangups about relationships, like I said." He licked his lips, not wanting to say anything more, but he knew he had to. "I also sometimes freak out when partners get too kinky too fast, even though I really enjoy it. I don't communicate in bed well. I prefer to walk away."

"Ah."

Something about the way Evan said the word worried Terry. He opened his eyes, searching Evan's face. "What do you mean, *ah*?"

"We have a problem, given what you've told me about yourself. You know me enough to understand I don't always know when people are telling me with body language they want something, yes? I need them to use words."

He wasn't wrong. *And yet.* "I still want this, Evan. Don't you?"

A hand in Terry's hair. "Yes. But I need you to talk to me. To *tell me things.*"

"Then I'll tell you. I'll tell you everything, but I need you to be patient with me."

"It's just that I don't understand how you were so ready before and now you're not."

"Well, the short answer is that I'm a mess." Terry inhaled a deep breath of Evan. "The longer answer is that before I was sure when I told you that you would send me away."

"But now you don't want me to send you away?"

Terry nodded.

Evan's fingers felt so good in Terry's hair. "I don't suppose it helps if I tell you I promise I won't do that?"

"Unfortunately, no."

Terry worried Evan would be upset by this, but he took it in stride. "Very well. I am going to make you set the rules, though. What do we do from here? What happens tonight?"

The ideas formed as they fell out of Terry's mouth. "A...timer. Set a timer. We can talk about what we'll do, then do those things only, for a set time." He blushed scarlet. "Unless that's stupid?"

"No, that sounds very practical. If you can state in clear terms what *slowly* means for you, then agree on a set time with me, I would be happy to have sex with you as many times as you'd like. In a slow fashion. What do you think?"

Terry thought he was feeling a little dizzy. "I...yes. That...that sounds fine."

Evan smiled at Terry, spun him around, switching their positions so it was Terry who was pinned against the wall. Evan's smile took on a slightly devilish hue.

"Shall we get started now?"

Chapter Twelve

TERRY HELD UP his hands, but his palms merely landed in the center of Evan's chest. His warm chest. "W-wait."

"Of course I'll wait. We haven't decided how long we'll have sex for, and you haven't told me how slowly you'd like to go."

Shit. Terry needed to put distance between them, but he could feel his systems shutting down.

Evan let go of him and took a step away. "Will this conversation be easier if I stand farther from you?"

Immensely. Though now Terry felt like he should be *properly* honest with Evan. About this, at least. "It will, but the thing is, I don't like to talk about this at all. I get…embarrassed." He sighed and averted his gaze.

"I don't think you need to be embarrassed. Let's keep talking. How far is okay to go tonight? How about I make suggestions, and you nod or shake your head? That way you don't have to talk, and even if you're embarrassed, all you have to do is nod or shake. Sound good? Practice with that question."

Terry nodded without meeting Evan's gaze.

Evan sounded pleased. "Great. So how about kissing? I assume kissing is fine?"

Terry nodded again.

"Can it be a passionate kiss, with a lot of tongue?"

More nodding.

"How about touching you at the same time? Maybe arms and upper body? And nipples?"

Terry hesitated. Then nodded—and blushed.

"Great. Can we do it naked?"

Terry shook his head. Violently.

Evan sighed. "All right. What about if we have our shirts off?"

Terry thought about saying no, then remembered what Evan could do to his nipples. It was impossible to answer.

"I promise, I'll only do what we agree to." Evan's voice was gentle, and when Terry dared a glance at him, he looked...kind. "Now that I know how important that is to you, I won't do anything more than what we discuss. Ever."

The way Evan said it, Terry believed him. Without question. "O-okay. Shirts off is fine. But...but that has to be it. And only the kisses and touching."

"Can I kiss you on more than your mouth? Anywhere on your upper body?"

Terry shivered...and nodded.

Evan smiled. "Great. How long?"

Terry blinked. "What?"

"How long should we make out for? An hour?"

Terry's knees buckled. "You want to kiss me for an hour?"

"I could kiss you for three, but that seemed like it might be too long for you."

Dear Lord. "I think an hour might be too long for me. Half would be better."

Evan looked dejected, but he didn't press. "All right. Maybe next time." He glanced at the stairs, then back at Terry. "I think this would be more comfortable lying down. Would it be okay if we went to my room, or would you rather go to yours? Or would you prefer we do this on the couch?"

Terry was glad Evan had stopped touching him, or he'd have no prayer of logical thought. He almost said couch, because the idea of going back to Evan's bed still left him in a panic, but he also knew if they went to the couch, he'd look at it every day after and get hard. Of course, the same thing would be true of his bed.

Hell, he was panicking anyway.

Evan brushed a hand briefly over his shoulder. "Remember what I promised."

Terry let out a breath. "Sorry."

"It's okay. Would you rather do it here?"

Terry shook his head. "Y-your bed."

His whole body trembled as Evan led him up the stairs, and his teeth chattered as Evan took off their shirts.

"Sorry," he whispered as Evan lowered him to the sheets. Sheets that smelled like Evan. "Sorry I'm such a mess. Do you really want to be with someone this out of control?"

"Yes," Evan said, then kissed him.

Initially the kiss was almost sweet, lips teasing while Evan's hands roved over Terry's shoulder, down his side, shifting his arms so they rested above his head. Evan sucked gently on his bottom lip, stealing his tongue inside.

Slowly, though. As if he had all the time in the world. As if he could do it all night.

An hour. And Terry had given them only half. Terry groaned and opened his mouth to protest, to change his mind.

Evan deepened the kiss, and Terry forgot how to speak.

Lips. Tongue. The gentle scrape of teeth. Skin against skin, Evan's fingers so reverent as he stroked Terry's arms, shoulders, the slope of his neck, the planes of his chest. Terry gasped into his mouth, arching into his touch.

When Evan's lips left his, mapping his jaw, trailing along his beard and down the undergrowth of his neck, Terry cried out softly, melting into the sheets.

"Your beard is getting longer." Evan ran his fingers through it as he kissed his way along Terry's throat, working his way down to his collarbone.

Speaking felt like fighting his way through treacle.

"I…get lazy when I'm working a site. Sorry. I'll…trim it tomorrow."

"It's fine. I suppose this is how Kevin was born. Probably it will keep you warmer up here."

Evan's thumbs had found Terry's nipples and were working lazy circles around them. Terry shut his eyes and took deep breaths to keep from getting lost. "*Evan.*"

He didn't stop, but he slowed a little. "Too much?"

Terry shook his head, but he shivered too. "I just…sorry. I react a lot."

"I know. I like it." When Terry tensed at this comment, Evan stopped kneading and smoothed his hands over Terry's pectorals. "Do some people like it too much?"

Terry's eyes fluttered open, and he stared at Evan, who was hovering over him, looking so patient. Terry cut his gaze away, guiltily. "It's my fault. I send mixed signals."

"What do you mean?"

Evan was still touching him, but the mood had cooled enough that Terry could form thoughts and respond somewhat. "I get caught up, and I like what people are doing to me." He blushed, feeling awkward confessing this, but Evan was oddly easy to talk to. "I let them do more than I should. It feels okay in the moment, but later I regret it. Then they get angry because I'm freaked out, and they have a good reason. I'm too inconsistent."

Evan frowned. "But you just said the real issue is you're not able to accurately speak to your needs in the heat of passion. No one ever bothered to find that out?"

Terry faltered. "I—no, because I was always…" He trailed off, not sure what else to say.

Evan carded fingers through Terry's hair, his thumb resting on Terry's forehead. "Now I know. I'm glad you told me. That's not a mixed signal. I understand your situation clearly. Would you like to continue? We don't have much of our half hour left."

Terry startled. "You can't count all this talking as part of the half hour. It's not fair."

Evan smiled darkly as he pressed a kiss to Terry's neck. "Did you want to keep talking, or should I kiss you?"

Terry flushed. "You haven't even kissed below my neck yet."

"I'll take care of that now."

Evan closed his mouth over Terry's nipple.

Terry cried out, his hands latching on to Evan's hair, his head tipping back as he arched helplessly into the sensations Evan gave him. When Evan took Terry's other nipple between his fingers, Terry trembled, his vision going white behind his eyelids. Terry slid away, lost to Evan's touch, to the sensations he evoked. He moved in concert to Evan's ministrations, arranging his body however his lover asked—he was Evan's to command, completely.

He was deep in a kiss, tongue tangled in Evan's mouth, his nipples twisted in Evan's fingers, his arms twined and lax around Evan's neck, when somewhere in the distance an alarm sounded. Terry blinked, confused and bereft as Evan pulled away to fumble with his phone—and didn't resume the kiss.

"That's half an hour." He ran a hand over Terry's limp arm and smiled. "That was wonderful. I hope we can do it again."

Terry couldn't believe this. "Evan, please, it's fine—"

Evan was already halfway out of the room. He stopped in the doorway, held carefully on to the frame, and turned to Terry. "Take your time. I'm going downstairs to work on the models."

Once Evan was gone, Terry stared at the darkened doorway, sexual frustration rising from him in waves. Seriously, the man was going to abandon him like this because a timer went off? All this want and need, this helplessness, this feeling of being ready to do anything…he was just going to abandon him because a half hour had passed?

Yes. Because that's what you asked him to do.

The thought echoed in Terry's head as he lay there, as the desire and shameless readiness to do whatever his partner ask faded and he was left only with himself, the part of him that usually, in these moments, was uncomfortable, ashamed, and afraid. Not this time. This time he was simply shocked.

Then, as that wore off…he was moved.

Finding his shirt, Terry climbed out of the bed and got dressed, then went downstairs, all the way to the model room, where Evan was working naked. Evan looked up as Terry entered, and started to reach for his boxers, but Terry didn't give him time to grab them. Terry clutched his face, kissing him firmly on the mouth.

"Thank you," he said as he pulled away.

Evan blinked, then smiled, pushing his glasses back into place. "Do you regret anything?"

Terry shook his head. "I'd like to do it again, please."

"How about tomorrow night, after dinner?"

Joy filled Terry, chasing away the last of his clouds. "Yes, please." But he squared his shoulders and added, "For an hour this time. And I'd like to be naked."

Evan's smile was dark with satisfaction. "Oh, good."

THE FIRST FEW days of November were interesting for Evan. He and Terry continued their habit of dinner together and then working, but now they added a conversation about how much sex they were having and for how long and under what conditions. He found the process intriguing but a little baffling. Terry seemed eager but also highly nervous, both before and after. During the time they set aside for making love—usually an hour—he was more than relaxed, so lost in his own world. Evan had also learned Terry relaxed a great deal if he gave Evan a massage before they got started. It was like winning the lottery.

Bit by bit, Terry told Evan stories about his past, about old lovers, about his fears and sense of inadequacy. Evan shared his own tales as well, and slowly they grew closer. Yet Evan still felt as if there was something between them they needed to tear down, some fear of Terry's Evan couldn't surpass. He'd been so certain Terry confessing he was Kevin would eradicate everything, but if anything, it created new obstacles.

Terry was so bright and cheerful to everyone out in the world. Everyone in Logan and the whole team on the Christmas Town project loved him, but now that Evan knew Terry intimately, he could see the nervousness and insecurity lurking beneath those smiles. He worried, quietly, constantly. It was a strange kind of anxiety, not so much about what people thought, but about things in general. It drove the perfection for his work, but it also kept him from getting too close to people. It made him distracted at home, sent him pacing the edge of the lake or out onto the deck to do yoga. Terry worked long hours, Evan realized, because it was the only way he could calm down.

Sex calmed him somewhat too, but every instinct Evan had told him he had to walk carefully there, that he was forging through landmines he barely understood.

He could have called to talk to Dale, and would once he came up to Logan, but Evan wanted to talk to someone in person about this, and the one he chose to discuss the situation with was Arthur.

Arthur had come to see Evan and Terry at the cabin, inviting them to the shop to see the final version of the light control panel before it was installed and the snow cannons Dale had finally approved. Terry hadn't been able to come along, too busy with construction, so Arthur and Evan went to the fixit shop alone. On the way, Evan brought up what Terry had said about his trouble with bedpartners.

"I don't want to take advantage of him. Obviously I never would intentionally, but I'm not sure how to get to a point where we can both relax. Where he feels safe and I don't worry that he'll run away again."

Arthur rested an arm on the back of the bench seat of the truck and stared thoughtfully out the windshield. "That setup you two have going where you agree to times and activities is good, but from what you've described, Terry needs space to accept you more than anything else."

"So what should I do?"

"What you're doing. Keep laying everything out beforehand, and never, ever break your word. Even if he begs you during sex to switch things up, you don't. It's like he's that Jekyll and Hyde guy. You have to listen to the cool and collected one, let him drive the bus, even if the party version is promising a better time. Because you'll be facing the other version soon enough. Though I bet you get to the point where they even out before too long—where you're setting some pretty kinky boundaries and high limits with Terry before you have sex with Kinky Kevin. You're building up trust right now, which will take time. Follow your instincts, and keep talking everything out."

"I want to talk to Dale, because I think he might know more."

"He should be back up here soon enough, and I'll make sure we have a date shortly after he arrives. I'll bring it up then. But obviously call him up anytime if you want information sooner."

What was this about Arthur and Dale having a date? This was news to Evan. "I thought it was only Gabriel who had a relationship with Dale. You do too?"

"Oh, Dale and I have a different sort of arrangement."

That sounded interesting, but it was also clear Arthur wasn't going to tell him anything else. "Is Gabriel still angry at Dale?"

"No, Gabriel went down for a weekend in Minneapolis, and they sorted everything out. I think there were also theater tickets involved, though, which never hurts." Arthur clapped Evan's thigh with his hand. "Don't worry about your man. From where I sit, you're doing a fine job. I'm sure things will turn out right in the end."

Evan couldn't help but feel a bit proud. "Thank you."

"Say, Frankie's been after me to ask. What are your plans for Thanksgiving, since it's coming up? Are you going home for the holiday? Back to the cities?"

Thanksgiving? Evan shook his head. "I hadn't thought much about it. I usually don't do anything."

Arthur looked scandalized. "We can't have that. Frankie's family is heading out of town, so he's going to host this year. My mother is a little put out, but Gabriel and Dale and I are going to his place. I'm not sure about Paul and Kyle—the Parks family lays out quite a spread. They might try to hit both meals, since I think the Parks meal is earlier in the day. You should come over. We'll have a great time. Invite Terry too, if he's not going anywhere."

Normally the idea of so many people would put Evan off, but *those* people would be all right. "I'll ask him. Thank you."

Evan didn't ask Terry right away. The light panel display was great, but once Evan saw it placed, he wanted to disguise it a little more, and the three of them, Arthur, Paul, and Evan, spent the day redesigning the hut on the square where the panel would live so it was both unobtrusive and accessible. Evan took several pictures and a video so he could show Terry when he got home, and they reviewed them together as they ate a stew someone had brought over.

It occurred to Evan he would need to learn to

cook, if he stayed in Logan. He also thought a lot about how much Terry was starting to look like he had when Evan had mistaken him for Kevin. His beard wasn't quite as long and thick, but it was close enough the resemblance was clear. Evan wondered how he had ever thought there were two men at all.

As usual, after dinner, Evan made love to Terry. He checked in with him while they washed dishes, finding out what his lover was comfortable with that day, but before that, he talked with him about his day. All the exteriors were finished on downtown Logan, and now they were putting the final touches on the interiors of the businesses. Some of them were already open, including the sweet shop Evan had helped advise a better design scheme for. The temperature had dropped enough that they'd started the snow machines, mostly to test at this point, but the roofs of several businesses had picturesque snow on top, as did several trees on the square. As of tomorrow, the exterior lights would be working as well.

"If you're free, I could use your advice on a few of the shops we're trying to finish." Terry passed Evan a plate from the dishwater. They had a dishwasher, but they'd found they liked to wash dishes by hand together, for the conversation. "We never got to the interiors as much as I'd like. Originally I'd planned to talk with the shop owners with Levi, but he's not due to come up until next week. I thought maybe if it was the two of us…?"

"I'd be happy to."

Terry's shoulders sagged in relief. "Thanks. That's going to help so much. I've done what I can, but I'm more about where to put the walls, as you know."

"I don't mind." Evan ran a hand down Terry's back. "What would you like to do tonight?"

Though Terry shivered and a blush stained his cheeks, he didn't hesitate or worry around the issue the way he used to. "I was thinking. I'm feeling pretty relaxed. I'd like to take the time frame out of the equation."

Evan nearly dropped the glass he was holding. "Oh?"

Terry's cheeks grew pinker. "Yes. Also, you always make it about me. What is it you want to do to me? Or what do you want me to do to you?"

"I don't know if that's a good idea. I want to do a lot of things to you, and they're pretty intense."

"That's what I want tonight, though. I want you to do a lot of intense things to me."

Evan gave up and set the glass down, shutting his eyes. He was dizzy and he wasn't even looking away. "Well. You'll tell me if it's too much, right?"

"Yes. But I want to know."

"I'd like to tie your hands behind your back, then fuck your mouth. Very slowly." He reached over to brush Terry's fingertips on the edge of the sink. "With you blindfolded and naked. To be honest, I'd like your ankles tied too, and your wrists clipped to them."

Terry had to hold on to the sink, and he stared out the window into the night. "That's…quite a step up from what we've been doing."

"Yes. You asked, though. I can come up with something gentler."

He started to pull away, but Terry gripped his hand, stopping him. "Would you fuck me after? Untie my feet but leave my hands and eyes, bend me over…something, then fuck me? With your tongue, with your fingers, with your cock, anything?" His face was red, and he clutched Evan's hand tight. "Let me be shameless. Let me be lost to it. Talk dirty to me while you do it. Point out to me how shameless I am. Please."

Evan could imagine what Terry described all too well. He felt like he should redirect this into something slower, but instead he asked for clarification. "I'll want to spank you in that position. How do you feel about that?"

"It sounds perfect. Please do it. Not so that I can't sit the next day, or that I'm hurt, but I want it. God, I want it right now at the sink, all of it."

Evan forced himself to stay calm. This was what he'd been waiting for, but was it really a good idea? "How will you feel in the morning, when all of this is over?"

Terry's smile was wan. "I don't know. But I want this, Evan. I promise."

Evan let go of Terry's hand and drew his head in

closer, pressing a kiss to his temple. "Finish the dishes so I can make love to you."

It wasn't that Evan wasn't eager to give Terry what he asked for—on the contrary, he was *quite* ready to deliver those requests. He couldn't help worrying about what things would look like once the haze wore off. Usually they did well, but this was quite a step up.

Follow his instincts, Arthur had said.

"I have one request," Evan said as they went up the stairs. "When we're done, instead of you leaving to go to your room, will you stay in my bed with me so we can keep talking?"

Terry let out a shaky breath, but he nodded. "Okay."

Evan still wasn't convinced. "Are you still sure about this? Because I never meant for us to go this far this fast."

Terry nodded. "It's fine. I want to. And we already…I want to. I swear."

He touched Terry's cheek. "You're very important to me."

Some of the darkness evaporated from Terry's face, and he leaned into Evan. "Please make love to me, Evan."

"Then take off your clothes and kneel on the carpet, so I can get you ready for what you asked for."

Evan went to the walk-in closet to take the supplies he needed out of the drawer, and when he came back into the bedroom, Terry was already undressed and kneeling on the floor, his breathing slower, his vision unfocused as he tracked Evan's movements. It was too late now to ask further questions or add any conditions or parts to the game—once Terry reached this state, it was only Evan who would or could slow anything down.

The thought of anyone else touching Terry ever again made Evan's vision go red. He threaded his fingers through Terry's hair. *He's mine.*

Terry shut his eyes and leaned into the touch, though he didn't break his pose. He was waiting to be tied up. Evan wouldn't deny him his pleasure.

Evan had learned long ago how to properly tie someone up. One of his escorts had taken him to a series of classes, and after that whenever they got together, Evan employed bondage in their sex acts. He already knew bondage with Terry was pleasant, from their night when Terry had posed as Kevin, but this would be his first night with Terry as himself. He took great care to tie Terry's wrists tightly but comfortably, making him admit what hurt and what didn't so he could gauge the right tension. He tied his feet too, then bound his arms and legs together. When he came around to Terry's face again, he could see his lover had slipped somewhere deeper into his pleasure.

Evan stroked his cheeks. "How does it feel?"

Terry blinked, and when he spoke he sounded slurred. "So good."

"Maybe sometime we can have a whole afternoon

where you do nothing but demeaning things for me. We'll plan them in advance, and you can be as depraved as you like. Afterward we can design something together, the two of us, to put us back on equal footing. Then go out to eat in town, and no one will know what we've done. Except you, because your backside will be sore. Though perhaps you can wear something in your ass to remind you and extend the game."

Terry was quaking so hard he would have fallen over but for Evan's hand on him. "*Evan.*"

"I'm going to blindfold you now, and then it's time for you to suck my cock."

Terry sucked Evan's cock enthusiastically, and he looked so good doing it with the black blindfold on, bobbing back and forth on the long, erect flesh. Evan kept stroking his hair, murmuring encouragement. "There you go. Make some noise, please—hum, because the vibration feels nice. There you go. Suck it like a good slut. That's right. You're only here for this cock, Terry, so suck it well."

A few times he pulled out and teased the tip around Terry's lips, encouraging him to keep his mouth open in a wide O. "Do you want to have your face slapped with a cock?" He teased the stiff flesh against both sides of Terry's cheeks as he groaned. "Maybe next time. Let me trace your lips for now. Mmm. That looks nice. Now suck it again. There you go. You need to make me come, so work hard. Take it deep. Yes, like that. Again. Oh…yes. I'm going to come in your throat. Then I'll take off your blindfold and give you what you asked for over the ottoman downstairs."

Terry did as he was told, and when Evan came, Terry swallowed until he couldn't catch up and the cum ran down his chin. Evan wiped it with a rag, then took off the blindfold and helped Terry to his feet once he untied the bonds and made sure he had proper circulation.

"Let's go downstairs."

Naked now too, Evan led Terry to the living room, carrying a basket of supplies. At the ottoman, Terry knelt and tipped up his ass, his hands still bound and tucked at the small of his back.

Evan snuck a pillow under Terry's belly to push that beautiful backside higher. "You're incredible."

Terry spread his legs wider, pulling the pucker of his hole open. "I want to be slutty."

"You are. You're ready to be played with." Evan dipped into a jar of lube and smoothed it onto Terry's eager hole. "I won't keep this pretty hole waiting. I'll fuck it open for you."

Terry met Evan's fingers, clenching around them. "I want to be raw—" He buried his face in the ottoman. "I just…need…"

"Do you need it rough, Terry?"

"*Please.*"

Everything about this night was dangerous. They hadn't quite agreed to that, had they? Evan pushed his thumb inside Terry and pressed deep. "Raw like this?

Rough like this?"

Terry tried to thrust back, but he couldn't. "More. *More.*"

Evan moved his body between Terry's thighs. "Beg."

"Please, Evan. Please fuck me raw and rough. Pull me…open and…" He shuddered and sagged, running out of words.

Evan whispered dirty things against Terry's spine, kissing it reverently.

"I can't get that image of you naked in an apron out of my mind." He nipped lightly at Terry's cheek, three fingers of one hand inside him as he began to slide in the index of his other. "I'd love to see you in it while you worked in the kitchen. I'd have you bend over so I could see this view." He kissed the apex of his crack as Terry whimpered. "I'd fuck you against the counter. Over the sink."

"The railing of the deck," Terry whispered.

Evan licked the edges of Terry's hole. "Whatever you want. We can discuss it tomorrow. But if you still want it then, I'll do whatever you want."

Terry buried his face in the ottoman, wriggling and gasping. "Please—please do the rest."

"Fuck you?" He couldn't, not quite yet.

"And spank me. *Please.*"

Evan pushed deeper inside Terry, twisting his fingers. "Beg for me some more, like a little whore."

Terry begged, pleading, spreading his legs wide and

holding his ass high as Evan told him to. He was wanton, shameless, desperate—and beautiful.

When Evan brought down the first blow, Terry cried out and shivered. By the third he was moaning, and by the fifth, so was Evan. Terry's skin pinked so easily—the marks would stay for hours, possibly until the morning.

"Fuck me like this." Terry kept his face pressed down. "Keep spanking me. Hold me down. Tell me...*nggh*. Make me let go. Let me feel it."

Evan did. He let go of Terry long enough to put on a condom, then thrust inside. He managed to keep slapping him for a while, but after a few minutes, he stopped, gathering Terry to him and lifting him off the ottoman, finding his cock with one hand and a nipple with the other.

"You feel it. You know you do. Come for me, Terry. Let go. Be a mess for me. Know how dirty you were for me, and let me see more." He sucked on Terry's earlobe. "Then come to bed with me and wake up beside me. Don't be ashamed in the morning. Just stay."

Terry came, gasping and shuddering, ejaculating all over the ottoman. Evan followed after, and then they collapsed together onto the sofa, trembling.

"Don't drift away from me," Evan murmured.

Terry shook his head as if it were very heavy. "I'll...try not to."

They did go to bed together after Evan cleaned up

the furniture, Terry almost falling asleep on the stairs, losing consciousness as soon as he hit the pillow. Evan, however, slept fitfully, because he knew what was coming. It happened at four in the morning, when the bed stirred and he sat up to find Terry already awake, staring at the ceiling.

Evan rolled onto his side to face him. "It was too much."

Terry shook his head, not looking at him. "No. It wasn't. Give me a minute, though." He shut his eyes. "You probably figured it out, but this is how all my relationships ended. I can't get over this part of myself. I'm working on it. I just…" He turned to Evan, his expression bleak. "I really want it to work this time."

"We can go slower. We *should* go slower. I shouldn't have let you talk me into that."

Terry took Evan's hand. "I don't want to go slower, though. You're right. I need to let you make me talk. Before and after. I feel like I have so much to tell you. I keep thinking I should be embarrassed, but you never seem to mind."

"I want to hear all of it. You don't have any reason to be embarrassed."

Terry leaned closer, pressing his lips to Evan's shoulder. "I…I have a lot of feelings for you, Evan."

Evan put his arms around Terry. "I have a lot of feelings for you too."

And the biggest one, Evan knew, was love.

Chapter Thirteen

T HE SOFT OPENING for Christmas Town was set for two weeks before Thanksgiving, which meant the weekend before that the full team from Davidson Incorporated came up from the Cities to set up the final details for the launch. To try to reserve as many of the hotel rooms and cabins for potential guests, employees were crammed in everywhere: on residents' couches and in their spare rooms, in unrented apartments, and in the case of Levi, with Terry and Evan.

"I won't be here long." Levi set down his suitcase in the entryway and unlaced his shoes. "You know I go home as often as I can, and Dale promised I could get back to my family as soon as things were square here. Besides, someone has to run management."

Terry's eyes went wide. "Wow—are you serious? You're in charge while Dale is gone? Congratulations. That's great."

Levi adjusted his tie with a lascivious grin. "Not only that, but he's indicated if this goes well, I'm at the top of his list to be the manager once Christmas Town is a permanent thing. And you know he intends to live up here pretty much full-time and run it himself. Which means I'm about to get one hell of a promotion, because I will make damn sure this goes well. Laurel is going to be over the moon. She's going to brag to everyone at Thanksgiving."

Terry was happy for Levi—his friend had been waiting for something like this for so long. He'd miss him on the team, though. "We'll be happy to have you here as long as you stay. There are three bedrooms, so make yourself at home."

"I'll take the couch. I think Charlotte is staying here too. She won't be up for a few more days, though." Levi waggled his eyebrows at Terry. "Unless *your* bedroom is empty because you're sleeping elsewhere?"

Terry averted his gaze. "No comment."

Levi laughed. "That means you *are* getting busy with your favorite designer. About time. Did he finally figure out you and Kevin are the same person, or did you have to tell him?" When Terry blushed and looked at the ceiling, Levi took a step closer to him, his smile fading. "You're kidding. He still doesn't know? You're sleeping with him and he doesn't know?"

"No, he knows. He…figured it out."

Levi's shoulders relaxed. "Thank God for that. Why do you look so guilty then?"

Terry waved his hands helplessly. "Because it's getting serious. You know how I get when things are serious. We were going slow, and it was working, but now we're stepping things up, and…"

Levi sighed as he sat beside Terry. "You, my man, have some serious issues."

Terry worried his fingers. "Tell me about it. I don't want to ruin a good thing."

"And yet I bet that's exactly what you're fixing to do. Look—he's as weird as you. You're two odd peas in a pod. Relax and enjoy it. What the hell is so hard about that?"

Nothing at all. And yet simply thinking about it made Terry want to panic. "I don't know. There's something wrong with me."

"You must have asked for something kinky. You fold on every relationship when you let people in far enough to see your kink, and when you do, you kick them out because you can't accept yourself. But it sounds like Evan is trying to help you around that barrier."

"*Yes,* and that's why I don't want to screw it up."

Levi snorted. "You're looking *for* another way to screw it up. It's what you do. *Stop doing that.*"

What Levi said echoed with Terry that night as Evan led him to bed. Terry did give Levi his room, since at this point, yes, he was basically sleeping full-time with Evan. Did Terry fold on his relationships because he didn't want people to know his kink? Except it had to be obvious what his kink was, once they slept with him, right?

What a mess.

A hand on Terry's shoulder drew him out of his reverie before Evan rolled him over. "Are you all right? What are you thinking about so hard?"

Terry studied his lover's face in the dark. Should he tell him his fears? Would Evan be understanding or offended? If he bared his heart and let Evan in, he was admitting to himself this was more than just a fling, that Evan wasn't yet another relationship he'd walk away from. That this time he'd let someone in all the way. But if he confessed how flawed and fucked up he was and Evan rejected him...

Evan stroked his face. "You look so sad."

"I don't want this to stop," Terry admitted.

Evan smiled, his thumb caressing Terry's jaw. "I don't want it to stop either."

For now, those declarations would have to be enough.

The chaos of Christmas Town's opening distracted him for the next week—he didn't have much to do as the architect any longer, but he helped Evan put the finishing touches on all the interior designs of the shops. Or rather, he played social interpreter when Evan's bluntness or general awkwardness didn't mesh well with the out-of-town shopkeepers. Anyone from Logan had already worked with Evan and knew his quirks, but several of the businesses were seasonal only and run by individuals imported to Christmas Town for the duration of the event. Normally Charlotte ran interference for Evan, and she was now living with them as well, but she was busy doing her own work managing the teams on site.

Terry got to know Charlotte more, and she was quite a force of nature. She got along with Evan in a way that made Terry a little envious at times. She seemed to like Terry, however, and approved of their relationship. Though she did pull Terry aside at one point and make him promise not to hurt Evan.

This only gave Terry more to feel guilty about.

Levi came and went, staying with them doing the week but returning home on the weekends. He went back to Minneapolis three days before Thanksgiving with plans to stay for the rest of the season. On the way out the door he clapped Terry on the back and told him to relax and not to worry.

Terry continued to worry.

He had agreed to go to Frankie's house for Thanksgiving with Evan and the others. Charlotte came too, to Terry's surprise, and they were a full house: Frankie, Marcus, Gabriel, Arthur, Dale, Kyle, Paul, Terry, Evan, and Charlotte. There was so much food, more than Terry had ever seen on a Thanksgiving table: a smoked turkey made by Arthur and Marcus, and a table groaning with side dishes prepared by Frankie, Gabriel, Kyle, Dale, and Paul. Terry, Evan, and Charlotte brought the wine, and they ate, drank, and laughed together, sharing stories and getting to know one another better.

"Do you usually have Thanksgiving with your family?" Frankie asked Terry.

Terry shrugged as he set down his wineglass. "It depends. My parents are in Rochester, but my siblings are in Colorado and Arizona, so it's not always a big event. I'm working a lot, so I don't always get back either."

"Do you go back for Christmas?" Kyle asked.

"Sometimes. We're not a big gathering kind of family."

Gabriel leaned over to glance at Evan. "What about you? Do you get together with your family at holidays?"

"No. My parents are usually traveling. We call each other to catch up on Christmas."

The cool way Evan gave that reply made Terry sad. "We should do something for the holiday, then."

This made Evan smile. "I'd like that."

Arthur grinned. "We have a Three Bears' Christmas every year. Except it's kind of four bears now."

Dale arched an eyebrow. "I don't think I qualify as a bear."

"Three bears and an otter? Anyway, we have a get-together before we go off to our families the weekend before the official holiday. If you're still around, you're welcome to come."

"And you could pick any of our families to tag along to for the official holiday," Kyle added. "To be honest, they'll probably fight for you."

Gabriel raised his eyebrows at Terry and Evan. "Do you think you'll be here that long?"

Terry stammered. "I—I really don't know. Dale hasn't said how long he wants us here."

Dale reached across the table for another roll. "Stay as long as you like. You can leave anytime or continue to work on the third phase from here."

Terry turned to him. "We—what?"

Dale was unperturbed. "What I just said. You can do whatever you like. You're doing an excellent job. You got the second phase up and running with plenty of time to spare, plus you improved it by leaps and bounds by staying in residence. I'd be more than happy to fund your stay here to complete the project."

Terry couldn't believe what he was hearing. "That's going to take months."

"Exactly. You two seem to work better together and on site. If you change your mind, you can go back to the Cities. It's entirely up to you."

Terry sank back in his chair, stunned.

Evan spooned more green bean casserole and mashed potatoes onto his plate. "I'd like to stay here. I want the cabin, though."

"You can have the cabin." Dale motioned to Evan. "Pass me the cranberry sauce, would you?"

Charlotte handed it to him with a sparkle in her eye. "You're staying up here as much as possible from now on, yes? Still need a team manager back at the office?"

Dale grinned at her. "Of course. Counting on you."

Terry mostly drank wine after that, but when Evan brought him a slice of pie and cup of coffee in the living room, Terry said, "Do you really mean to stay here permanently?"

"For now, yes." Evan sat beside him and gazed intently at his plate, which had a slice each of pumpkin, pecan, and chocolate mousse pie. "These look amazing."

"But won't you miss the Cities? And how will you get around?"

"I didn't get out much in the Cities, so I don't think I'll miss much." Evan glanced at Terry. "I was hoping you would stay too. Then you could drive me."

Terry became busy forking into his pie. "I have a lease on my apartment."

"Dale would pay it."

Terry knew that. It was a weak excuse. Why was he making excuses, anyway? *I don't know. What's wrong with me?* "Logan is very remote."

"It has more because of Christmas Town, though. And if the two of us worked hard on designing the next phase, they'd get even more development."

Terry sighed. "I…I have to think about it."

"I'll have to convince you, then." He brushed fingers over Terry's knee. "I'll start tonight."

Terry blushed. "Charlotte is still staying with us."

"I'll ask her to stay with Frankie and Marcus. Their houseguests went home for the holiday. I think she's leaving tomorrow too."

Terry tried to protest, but Evan kept teasing his fingers against Terry's, and eventually Terry stopped fighting. He was nervous all the way back to the cabin, though.

Evan wasn't. He looked out the window, pleased with the thick snowfall they'd received the day before. "We'll get a lot of visitors tomorrow, and this will look very nice. I think they're going to pump out some new snow over the top of the dirty snow downtown, but other than that, everything is set for the grand opening." He took Terry's hand. "Are you ready?"

No, Terry wasn't ready. He was nervous, and he had no idea why, so he didn't know how to calm down. He tried reaching for random excuses. "Everything has gone by so fast. I feel like we just got here."

"I really like it here. It's quiet, and everyone is nice. Well, most people are nice. Enough of them are. I like having friends. I've never had friends like this. And I like our cabin that we made together. I like working with you. I like living with you, Terry."

They were at the cabin now, its lights glinting quietly in the snow. It looked just as they'd designed it to. A place to relax and feel comfortable.

Why can't you be the one relaxing and feeling comfortable here?

Why can't you stay with Evan and live happily ever after instead of relegating him to being another fling?

Why are you always running away from happiness?

Evan took Terry's hand as they climbed the stairs, and Terry didn't fight him. Inside the door, they hung up their coats and removed their boots, and then Evan turned to face Terry.

"Tell me what you want to do tonight."

Terry stared at him, trying to decide what answer to give. Evan asked him this every day, but tonight it felt charged. It wasn't just that Evan was hoping Terry would say he'd stay in Logan with him. It was that Terry knew the only way he could go that far was if he confessed everything. All the truths about himself. All the neuroses he had. Maybe if he did that he wouldn't feel so agitated—perhaps that was the way to end all this noise in his head.

Terry let out a shaky breath. "I want to tell you things tonight."

Evan looked surprised, but he smiled. "Okay." He stroked Terry's hair. "Can I make love to you while you tell me?"

Terry nodded, shutting his eyes. "That would help, actually."

Evan massaged his neck, his shoulder. "Let's go upstairs."

Except once they were upstairs, once Terry undressed, Evan didn't lead him to the bed. He took him to the bathroom. Terry's stomach did a flip. He knew what was coming.

Evan ran a hand down Terry's naked back as they faced the shower door. "You're usually so much more relaxed if we start in the water. What will you let me do to you in the shower?"

Terry shut his eyes as he gathered his courage, then opened them again. "Whatever you want. Tonight I want you to do whatever you want."

Evan's hand skimmed Terry's side. "You know you have to tell me, Terry. I want quite a bit with you, most of it wicked."

Time to start unmasking. "I know, and I want all of it too." He caught Evan's hand and brought it to his nipple. "That's one of the things I want to tell you. I know we keep playing this game where I tell you what I want, but the truth is, I really do want all of it. If we lived here together, I'd play any game you wanted. Honestly, *anything*. Once I got over my guilt afterward, I'd do anything." He shut his eyes, shuddering. "I get nervous when I feel like people start to see it about me. I'm ashamed of it sometimes. Okay, most of the time. But it's still true."

Evan had started tugging gently on Terry's nipple, and now he kissed Terry's neck tenderly as well. "I knew all those things about you already. You told me."

Terry blushed, trying to duck his head, but all he did was lean into Evan. "But you don't understand *how much*."

Evan licked Terry's neck and reached around with his free hand to stroke Terry's cock. "Would you like to show me?" When Terry nodded, Evan sucked on Terry's shoulder. "Tell me what you don't want me to make you do."

Terry tipped his head back and thrust into Evan's hand. "Nothing. I want to do anything you tell me."

"I'll stop if you ask me."

"I won't tell you to stop."

"Then I'll watch you carefully to make sure you're okay."

EVAN WASN'T SURE if Terry had meant to lead them into a repeat of their first night on purpose, but somehow that's where they'd gone, and he had no objections. They'd been upping the stakes on their sexual adventures for some time, with Evan cajoling Terry, saying Charlotte and Levi could probably hear him, taunting him and feeding his shame kink. There was almost nothing left but this, for them to play out their first encounter…and hopefully for Terry to finally come clean in the end and admit he wanted this as much as Evan did.

Now here they were in the shower, where they'd started. Would Terry truly share his secrets? All of them, even the one Evan kept hoping for? Would everything be okay between them once he did?

Evan hoped so. In the meantime, there was only one thing for Evan to tell Terry to do.

"Stand against the wall, spread your legs, and push the tip of the wand inside you."

Terry didn't object, didn't make any fuss. He simply

obeyed, giving Evan a beautiful view of the black wand sliding between Terry's furry cheeks. The wand wasn't on, but Terry held it there as instructed, waiting.

Evan came up behind him, stroking his back, his shoulders. "What else?"

Terry was perfectly relaxed, no more blushes, no more hesitation. "All of it, please."

"Tell me what you desire. Let me hear it."

Buttocks clenched around the wand, Terry rolled his shoulders back and began to speak. "I want to kneel on the floor while you work the wand in me, to lean over a stool in here so you can use all kinds of toys in me, toys that I can't see. I want you to spank me in the water. Rim me in the water, make me cry out. I want to come undone right here. Then take me to bed and do it again, until I'm completely wrecked."

"What about the rest of your fantasies? Do you want me to tease you about others seeing you?"

Terry leaned against him. "Yes. I don't want you to ever actually do it, though, shame me in front of people. I'm serious that you could bring someone into our bedroom, but that's different."

Evan kissed his hair. "I don't know if I can share you. I'm awfully possessive of you. I can certainly tease you, though."

Terry clutched at his arm. "I have more to tell you. But I want to tell you after."

"You can tell me anything you want, anytime."

Terry squeezed him again, nodded.

Evan patted Terry's backside, then pulled out the wand with a gentle twist. "Now kneel on the floor for me, facing the door."

He started the shower while Terry did this, being careful to make sure it only hit Terry's feet and legs, not anywhere near his face. Evan was also mindful of his balance, since he didn't have his glasses on— nothing would ruin the moment like falling over. Then he knelt with the wand in his hand, sent out a burst of water to give it lubrication, and slid the wand inside.

Terry shuddered, and Evan soothed him with a stroke of his hand as he worked the wand in and out. "You're lovely. But tell me how this feels. How you feel. I want to hear everything."

"I feel...turned on. Humiliated, but turned on."

"I don't really know why you're humiliated, but you like that, don't you? Feeling humiliated. *That* turns you on, doesn't it?" Evan fucked him gently with the wand as Terry groaned and went limp for him. "It's such a fine line for you, though. Letting someone in to know what humiliates you. Finding out yourself what humiliates you." Evan licked Terry's arm and pushed the wand a little deeper. "I know what you need, Terry, here and everywhere. Maybe we're both a little bit of a mess, but I want to be a mess with you. I'll take care of you. You're safe with me. You can let go with me."

Terry's arms shook. "I want to do that, but...I'm scared."

"Why?"

"I don't know. I really don't know. It's like I want it, but I can't have it." He shuddered and buried his face in his arms. "Please, don't stop making love to me."

"Very well, but there's a condition." Evan turned off the wand and moved Terry to the stool, producing a dildo instead. It was long and twisted, and Terry shuddered as the tip slid inside him. Despite Terry's eagerness, however, Evan only allowed the toy to tease at Terry's opening. "If you want this to fuck you, if you want me to give you want you asked for, you have to keep your promise to me when we finish. I want you to tell me everything."

The hesitation in Terry's body told Evan his lover had already been thinking of backing down. Terry nodded, though, and let out a breath. "I will."

"It's important to me." Evan's fingers danced down Terry's spine. "I want us to be open with each other."

"I do too." Terry glanced over his shoulder at Evan, steel-blue eyes nervous, but shining. "I promise."

"All right." Evan pushed the dildo in deeper, almost halfway. "Open your eyes and imagine you're looking out at a crowd watching you."

Terry's shoulders relaxed. "Yes."

"Strangers who want to watch a guy take a dildo in his ass. You have to tell them your name and how this feels. Articulately, or I'll stop. If you tell them how happy you are they're here to see your humiliating performance, I'll fuck you with it harder and deeper. If you stop talking, I'll stop fucking."

Terry whimpered. "This is a sick game."

"Are you saying you don't want to do it?"

"Of course not."

Terry pushed up higher on his knees. "Let's go."

Terry performed beautifully. He cried out helplessly, telling his imaginary crowd exactly what Evan told him to say. "My name is Terry Reid, and I'm getting fucked by this dildo—*ngh*—and it feels so good. *Ha—ha—oh God*—it goes so deep I swear it's in my belly. It freaks me out a little. But—*oh shit*—I love this."

"I'd love to make it go faster, Terry. Tell them you're a slut."

"I'm a big slut—*fuck, fuck, fuck*—I'm kneeling with my ass up begging for this—*shiiiit*—I want this, I need this—*God, God, shit*—I'm a whore for this, I want you to watch—*oh God, Evan, I can't, I can't*—"

Terry's babbling became an incoherent stream after that, only letting up when Evan withdrew the dildo, at which point he cried out in helpless frustration.

Evan stroked his back while he prepared the next toy. "Shh. You said you wanted all kinds of toys in you. Hold still and take it for me."

Terry gasped as it went in, trying to turn around.

"It's *cold*." He moaned. "And…rigid, and full of…round…and…long…what the hell is it?"

It was a metal anal joystick, but since Terry had asked not to know, Evan didn't tell him. "Let it give you pleasure. It doesn't matter what it is, does it?" When Terry quivered, Evan added, "Just imagine, though, that there's a crowd of people watching it go inside you. Taking notes. Wouldn't you enjoy that? Open wider for them, Terry, so they can get a better view."

Terry did. Shaking, clearly almost overcome with shame, he did it. He did everything Evan asked, every lewd thing, played every wicked game with every toy he produced, until Evan was out of toys and it was his hand against Terry's backside, giving him the spanking he'd promised.

When they finished, Evan dried the weak-kneed Terry off and led him to the bed, where he put him on his back and fucked him gently, kissing his spent body as he built them both to a climax.

"I love you," he whispered to Terry as he pushed his knees higher. "Not just for this. For everything."

Terry clutched at him. "I...I...oh, Evan..."

Even before they came, Evan achieved his promise: he wrecked his lover, utterly. Which was something of a problem, because yet again Terry was going to drift away from Evan without giving him the promises, the words he wanted to hear.

Evan nudged Terry as he drifted out of his sex haze. "Are you doing okay? Not feeling like running into the night?"

Terry didn't look like he could run to the edge of the bed. "I'm good. Thank you. It was wonderful."

"So you'll stay with me, then, and live in Logan?"

Tension returned to Terry as if someone had poured it back into him. "I didn't say that."

Evan told himself not to be disappointed. That was a big jump, certainly. "You'll come and see me often? Every weekend? Sometimes working up here when you can?"

More tension. "I…I mean…maybe."

Uncertainty hollowed Evan's stomach. What was happening? Hadn't they connected? *Don't push him*, Arthur's voice warned from the back of his mind, but Evan couldn't listen to it.

"Terry, don't you love me too?"

It wasn't how he wanted to hear the words, but in that moment he wasn't particular. He needed them however he could get them. Three little words, balm for his aching heart.

They were not, however, the three words he heard.

Terry sat up in bed, hugged his knees to his chest and said, "I don't know."

Chapter Fourteen

I DON'T KNOW.

Terry's own words rang in his ears as Evan stared at him disbelief.

"What do you mean, you don't know? It's not a difficult question. You do, or you don't."

The room swam in Terry's vision. His breathing became tight. "I don't know."

He threw on whatever clothes he could find, grabbed his wallet and keys, and bolted for the stairs.

Evan followed, not wearing any clothes whatsoever. "Where are you going? *Where are you going?*"

Terry didn't have a clue. "I need to take a drive and clear my head."

"What—why? You're going now? In the middle of our conversation?"

Absolutely. Terry said nothing.

Evan wouldn't stop talking. "I'm coming with you."

Terry whirled around, and in Evan's effort to step

back he lost his balance and nearly fell over. Terry righted him, but the contact was too much for him to take, and he quickly let go. "*No.* I need to think, and I need to be alone to do it."

"What is there to think about? All I did was ask you a question. Do you love me or not?"

There wasn't any wind in the cabin, and yet it was if there were gale force winds screaming in Terry's mind. *I. Don't. Know.* He turned away and continued for the door.

Evan followed. "Where are you going? *Terry!*"

Terry ignored Evan—tried to, anyway, stepping into his unlaced boots and going out the door. His head throbbed. It had been hours since he'd had a drop of alcohol, but he felt as sick as if he'd downed all the bottles of wine himself. He had to get out of here. If he got away from Evan, this feeling of panic would leave too.

"Terry, stop!"

He turned, then had to grip the front of the SUV as he saw Evan following him wearing nothing but boots and a coat. Evan stumbled into the railing on the stairs.

Terry couldn't believe this. "It's only twenty-two degrees out. Get inside, for heaven's sake. You'll die of exposure."

"*You can't leave.*" Evan lost his footing again on the sidewalk and listed into a bush before pushing himself back to his feet. "You told me you wouldn't run. You promised you wouldn't."

Terry had said that, hadn't he? "I'll come back." Except even as he said the words, he felt the lie in them. Run, yes, that's what he *had* to do. Escape. Flee. To leave this feeling and not look back.

Evan saw right through him. "You won't come back. You'll leave me the way you did before. But I don't understand, Terry—I reacted *well*. I like you as Kevin and you as Terry. I like you in all your ways. I like the part of you that you're afraid to show people. I like you even though you're an idiot who wants to run from your problems. I just like you. I love you, Terry. Even if you don't want to tell me you love me back."

Terry's heart seized with terror. "I have to go."

As he got into the car, Evan tried to follow but fell into a snowbank.

It was the first time Terry didn't stop to rescue him.

EVAN WATCHED TERRY'S taillights vanish and felt the walls of his mind threatening to close in on him. Chasing Terry was impossible, and without that option, all Evan could do was go into the cabin, crawl into his bed, and hide. Part of him didn't even want to bother with that. He'd stay in this snowbank. The bite of the cold had already started to fade, after all.

No. I'm not letting him get away this time.

He couldn't chase Terry, couldn't drive a car even if he had one, but he knew people who could. Lots of people. After stumbling back up the stairs and into the house, Evan shed his coat and boots, wrapped himself in a blanket, and found his phone. He had so many more people in his contacts than simply Charlotte and Dale now. Marcus. Frankie. Paul. Kyle. Gabriel. Arthur. People from town, shopkeepers he'd helped. Patty from the café. Sara the baker. Arthur's mother.

They would help him get Terry back.

He hovered over Dale's name, Charlotte's too, then settled on Arthur. His friend answered on the third ring.

"Hey, Evan, what's up—?"

"I need help. Terry's gone." He couldn't keep the panic out of his voice. "Terry left me. He's gone."

"Whoa. You mean he left tonight? What happened? Everything seemed fine at—"

"I told him I loved him and asked if he loved me too. He got upset."

"Ah, shit."

There wasn't any way Evan could keep himself under control. "I didn't mean to push him. He was almost telling me, I was sure of it, but he was taking forever, and I was impatient." Evan's throat started to narrow. "Arthur, he drove off. I don't know where he went. I don't know if he's coming back."

"It's okay, buddy. We've got this, all right? You just stay calm."

"I can't stay calm. I messed it up. I drove him away. I didn't want to, but I drove him away—"

"Hush. Hush. I want you to take deep breaths,

okay? There you go. Keep breathing like that. I want to hear those exhales. I'm going to put the phone down for a minute while I talk to the other people here, and then I'll be back. You with me?"

Evan nodded, still breathing heavily. "Yes."

It felt like forever before Arthur came back, but while he was away Evan did as he'd been instructed, breathing deeply and keeping as calm as he could. Eventually, Arthur returned.

"Okay. Paul and Daryl, Kyle's dad, are out looking for the SUV, and Kyle is heading to you. Dale wants to know if you want Charlotte to come over. He's already called Marcus and Frankie, and she's up. She wants to come see you, but he can tell her to wait."

Evan didn't want to be alone. He wanted Terry though, not Charlotte. "What if he goes to Minneapolis?"

"We're going to try to find him, but I want people there for you. Let me send you Charlotte and Kyle. Who else would make you feel better?"

Terry. But he couldn't have Terry. Evan ached. He shut his eyes. "I tried not to upset him."

"I know. I don't think this is about you, Evan. Tell me who I can send you."

Evan tried to think. "Frankie?"

"He'll come with Charlotte. The rest of us will hunt down Terry if we can. No matter what though, I want you to know we're all here for you."

Evan wrapped himself tighter in the blanket.

"Okay."

"Dale wants to talk to you."

There was a pause and a fumbling of the phone, and then Dale was there. "Evan, I'm so sorry. This is all my fault."

That didn't make any sense. "I'm the one who pushed him."

"*I'm* the one who didn't make the two of you clear the air right away about Kevin. I didn't give you enough background on each other. I thought this was the best way for the both of you, but now I feel like I should have stayed out of it. Or been more involved. I don't know, I feel like I could have done *something*."

Evan didn't know about any of that. What did it matter now? "I just want Terry to come back."

"I'll bring him back. I'll find him, and I'll talk to him."

The thing was, Evan wasn't sure Dale could deliver on that promise.

When he hung up from Dale, Evan curled on the couch in a ball, staring at the lights of the living room as his vision unfocused. The darkness caught up with him then, pulling him into his thoughts, into the heaviness. He heard the knock on the door distantly, but it was too much work to lift his head and call out for whoever it was to come in. All he knew was Terry wouldn't have knocked. The door opened and closed, boots scuffled at the door, but Evan didn't care.

Then a familiar, slightly lisping female voice said,

"It's pretty in here."

Linda Kay. Evan lifted his head as she came around the couch to smile at him, though her smile faded, her eyes widening as she looked at him. "Lord almighty, Kyle, he's naked."

Kyle appeared then, concerned, though he relaxed as soon as he saw Evan. "Linda Kay, he's got a blanket on."

"Well, he's naked under the blanket." She shook a finger at Evan. "I'm gonna go find you some pants, mister. This isn't decent."

She shuffled off, muttering about naked men, and Kyle sat down on the coffee table in front of Evan. "Hey. I hear you've had quite an evening."

Evan didn't answer. He didn't feel like talking now.

Kyle didn't seem to mind this. "Paul and my dad are driving around looking for him, and we called in a favor to the sheriff. We'll find him. The others are looking too. I'm sorry, though, that this happened. I know how hard you were working to have the conversation properly."

A tug in Evan's stomach made him draw the blanket tighter to his body. "I tried. But I drove him away. I couldn't control myself, and I drove him away."

Kyle leaned in close to Evan. "You didn't drive him away."

"He's gone. He left because of what I said."

Linda Kay came clumping down the stairs bearing a pair of Terry's pants and one of his shirts. "Put these on, cowboy."

Evan clutched at the clothes, aching because they smelled like Terry. He thought about refusing, but then he decided no, he would put them on and ache harder, to have Terry surround him this way in case it was the only way he could have him. He went into the bathroom and put them on. When he came out, Charlotte was talking to Kyle and Frankie in the kitchen.

Linda was standing in front of the stove, and five mugs were on the counter. She smiled at Evan. "I'm making everyone tea."

Tea sounded good. "Thank you."

Charlotte stopped talking to the others and came over to Evan. She gave him a big hug, lingering in the embrace. "Don't go into your dark place, okay? Let us help you."

Frankie followed her over and squeezed Evan's arm. "Yes, please, let us help."

Evan wanted to go to the dark place. He longed to go to his room, pull his covers over his head, and drown in the smell of Terry's clothes. His kitchen was full of people though, and he was a little afraid Linda Kay might start a fire. "I don't think there's anything anyone can do. If he wants to be gone, I can't stop him." The ache tugged at him. "I just really thought he wanted to be with me. I was as careful as I could be, but it wasn't enough."

Charlotte's face twisted in anger. "I'm going to punch that little shit when we catch him."

Evan shook his head. "No. I love him. You can't punch him."

"Did you tell him you loved him?" This question came from Frankie as he helped Linda Kay put tea bags into the mugs.

"Yes." Evan could recall each of the three times he'd said it. "Very clearly. But he never told me he loved me back. That was the problem. That's why we fought, why he panicked and ran." He let out a sorrowful breath. "Maybe that's it right there. Maybe he doesn't love me."

Charlotte looked angry again, but Kyle remained calm, gently nudging Linda Kay out of the way as he poured the boiling water and passed out the mugs, carrying Linda Kay's with his own to the living room. "I'm pretty sure he does. I got a good view of how he looked at you tonight."

"Then I must have messed it up."

"You didn't mess it up," Charlotte insisted.

"I agree." Frankie sat on the ottoman, crossing his ankles and tucking his legs to the side. "Even if you explained something clumsily, Terry's reaction makes me strongly suspect this is something he has to work through for himself, about himself."

"Then what do I do when you find him?"

Frankie's expression was sad. "You talk to him again, when he's cooled down. We all talk to him. But mostly we have to wait for him to let go of whatever is keeping him from connecting with you."

Now Evan despaired worse than before. "But there's nothing I can do to make that happen."

Kyle's laugh was bitter. "Believe me. I've been where you are."

Frankie blushed. "And I've been in Terry's shoes, with everyone else telling me to open my eyes. This is the trouble, Evan—we can't open other people's hearts and minds for them. They have to decide to do it themselves."

Evan hated this answer. It made him want to tuck himself away. But there were too many people here who wouldn't let him hide, so he sat and drank his tea instead. Listened to Linda Kay and Kyle bicker, to Frankie's kind voice as he kept Evan distracted.

Evan remained present. It left him feeling exhausted, but it felt...good too.

When Gabriel and Dale showed up, Evan stood, hoping to see Terry behind them, but it was only the two of them. Dale hugged Evan and sat beside him on the couch.

"We still haven't found him, but we haven't stopped looking."

"Then why are you here?"

Dale glanced at Gabriel, who nodded back before Dale spoke again. "Because we've searched everywhere in town, all the roads, and we're pretty sure he headed south. Someone saw him on the road heading toward the interstate."

Evan stared down at his hands. "So he's heading to

Minneapolis, like I thought."

"Arthur is heading that way, and Paul and Daryl are already well after him. The sheriff called the state troopers too. We'll get a hold of him."

Evan thought of what Kyle had told him about letting Terry go. Heart heavy, he shook his head. "No. Let him go."

Dale put a hand on Evan's shoulder. "Evan, I promise, I'll fix this—"

Evan looked at Kyle, Frankie. "You can't fix this. Only Terry can. It won't help if you force him back here."

Dale seemed frustrated, but his shoulders sank in defeat. "I'd still like to have the trooper stop him to make sure he's okay."

"I think that's a mistake too. He wasn't drunk. He wasn't in any danger of going off the road. He was upset, but he knew what he wanted: to get away. The same way I did, until you guys stopped me. The way I tried to stop him, but he wouldn't let me. He has to let us stop him, Dale. He has to come back to me, on his own, or it's not real." Evan sighed, a tear escaping, but only one. He would cry later. "I only want him to come to me if it's real."

Dale squeezed Evan's arm. "Very well, but I need to talk to him for my own benefit."

Evan shrugged, swallowing hard. "That's fine." *I wish I could do that.*

They sat like that for another hour, and Evan was

proud of how he held it together right up until Arthur and the others came in the door, and Evan had to acknowledge Terry was officially gone. That he really had run away, had broken his promise.

He understood why, but it hurt. It hurt so much.

When Dale stood to greet Gabriel and Arthur, someone else took his place beside Evan. At first he thought it was Charlotte, but when he looked up, he saw it was Linda Kay. She smiled at him, put her arm around his shoulders, and pulled his head against her chest.

"You look like you could use a good cry, mister. Go on ahead. I won't tell anybody."

Shutting his eyes, Evan drew a deep breath and took her up on her offer.

Chapter Fifteen

TERRY WAS RESTLESS.

He didn't have a project, because he was supposed to be in Logan. His condo had been set up for a long-term absence, and it was awkward to undo everything. He'd cancelled his laundry and cleaning services, and for reasons he couldn't explain he didn't restart them, though that meant his place quickly became a disaster and he didn't have anything clean to wear.

He didn't sleep at all. A few hours here and there, but mostly he paced his apartment and went through notes of old projects. He was going mad, though, because he didn't have any work to do.

He lived with his furniture covered and most of his necessities missing, boxed up, or still in Logan. One of those things, as it happened, was his beard trimmer, which meant when he finally gave in and went into the office to find something to occupy his time, the security guard almost sent him away.

"Sorry, Mr. Reid. I barely recognized you."

Most of the staff was surprised to see him. Levi wasn't, and he was angry. He'd moved into Dale's office, and he parked Terry into the chair he'd sat in a million times, except this wasn't the gentle shepherding he received from the owner of Davidson Incorporated. This was Levi Daniels, mad as hell.

"You mind explaining what in the devil's name you're doing?" Levi put his hands on his hips, spreading the lapels of his unbuttoned suit coat wide.

Terry couldn't for the life of him meet Levi's gaze. "I thought I should come in to work. I know I don't have an official project, but I figured—"

"I'm not talking about any damn project, and you know it." He threw up his hands and paced to the window, his body a vessel of barely contained fury. "Goddamn it, Terry. Davidson made me swear to leave you alone, but the hell I can keep that promise. Things were going well with Evan the last time I was up there, and from all reports I got, they were great up until the minute you left that Thanksgiving dinner. You finally found somebody as neurotic as you, and he loved you for it. What the hell did you run for this time?"

This time. Guilt bubbled up, but Terry tempered it with outrage. "Look, sometimes thing just don't work—"

"Oh cry off, you know this guy was perfect for you."

"I don't. He didn't know me when he saw me

again. It took a photo months later for him to figure it out. He should have recognized—"

"I can barely recognize you right now. Try again." Levi glared at him. "You know his whole story now too. He's not a regular apple in the drawer, and it's more than he has trouble remembering faces. He did manage to fall in love with you twice, though. You'd think that would count for something, but no. You just ran. *Twice*."

Terry's chest was tight. There was nowhere in the room to put his gaze. "I...it's..."

"It's what? Complicated? I don't understand? Go ahead. Pick an excuse. Lay one out for me. Just be ready for me to shoot them all down. Because maybe I don't know Evan as well as you do, but I know you plenty. You're scared. You don't want him to see, or he's already seen too much. Probably both. You can't take it, so you're throwing something incredible away. That's your choice, and you have every right. Be honest about it, however. Don't think you can sit in front of me and make up crap about it being anybody's doing but yours. You want to break his heart, you own it."

Talk about hearts. Terry's felt like lead. "I don't want to upset Evan, but I can't...I *can't*..."

Levi crossed the room to sit on the edge of Dale's desk, leaning over Terry. His anger bled out, now his expression full of concern. "What in the world is stopping you from letting him in?"

The panic Terry thought he'd left in Logan was

back again, as loud and terrifying as ever. He couldn't even surrender to it, because there was nothing to do with the feeling except despair. "I don't know." Terry could barely speak in a whisper, and he couldn't meet Levi's gaze. "Something's wrong with me. I know that, but I can't fix it. I can't name it, and I can't fix it, I…*I don't understand*, Levi. I don't know what to do with this. With *me*."

He expected another lecture, but instead Levi put a hand on his shoulder. "Will you do something for me?"

God, the thought of doing anything at all made Terry want to weep, he was so exhausted. "Maybe?"

"I want you to go to my house and take a nap in my den." Levi withdrew his keys from his pocket and extricated the house key. "I'll disarm the alarm with my phone so you don't have to worry about that. Let yourself in, pour yourself some expensive scotch, and sleep. We'll talk more about this once you've rested. Can you do that?"

Sleep. God, but Terry hoped it would actually happen. "I can try."

He went to Levi's house, hoping the change of venue—and the scotch—would help him along. At first Terry wasn't sure it would work, because mostly he felt out of place in Levi and Laurel's elegant surroundings. A few sips of alcohol helped that, and the soft leather of the couch and warmth of the microfiber blanket soon had Terry lost, at long last, to slumber.

When he woke, Levi sat in the recliner across from

him. His friend looked starkly different than usual, however, wearing faded jeans and an old sweater. The only thing that seemed remotely like Levi were the expensive athletic shoes on his feet.

Then the man across from him smiled, and Terry corrected his assumption. Not Levi, but his twin. "Hello, George," he said as he sat up.

George winked and crossed his ankle over his knee. "Well done. Was it the clothes that gave me away?"

"Your smile."

"You're getting good. We're going to have to start inviting you to Thanksgiving, if you can tell us apart that easily." George tilted his head to the side, studying Terry carefully. "Levi asked me to come talk to you. He says you're having some trouble." When Terry opened his mouth to deny this, George added, "In fact, his exact words were that you had sabotaged the best thing that had ever happened to you and were melting into a hot mess, and would I please come screw your head on straight."

Terry let his head fall against the back of the couch and stared at the ceiling. "I don't want to talk about this."

"I understand. And yet from the sounds of things, you need to talk to *someone* about this. Levi reached out to me because I'm a licensed social worker and do counseling, but I understand if you'd rather not talk to me. I can help you find someone you *would* feel comfortable with. I'd be happy to."

All Terry wanted to do was insist he didn't need help, but he was so busy fending off that panic. He didn't mean to, but he began to voice his feelings out loud. "I don't understand why I feel so nervous. I don't know what I'm afraid of."

"Sometimes we're not afraid of anything. Sometimes we're simply anxious because it's the way we are."

Hearing George say that made Terry want to scream, or cry, or both. "So what, I just have to live with this feeling? I run from everything, I work too hard, I can't—" He shut his eyes and swallowed hard as his voice broke.

"Not at all. You need some assistance, though, I think, walking through this."

Terry laughed bitterly. "People keep trying. Even when I don't push them away or run from their help, it doesn't work."

"Hon, I'm talking about professional help. You need a therapist. Haven't you figured it out yet? You have anxiety. Clinical anxiety."

Terry frowned at George. "I don't, really, I—"

George raised an eyebrow and lifted his hand as he ticked off his facts. "You work yourself to exhaustion to distract yourself from your nervous thoughts. You reject deep personal relationships to avoid situations that make you nervous. You have difficulty sleeping. These are just the things Levi and you have told me. Are you going to sit there and pretend there isn't more you simply haven't shared yet?"

Terry was almost too stunned to respond. "I...yes, that's all true, but..."

"Anxiety is a condition, Terry. It's part of who you are, but it's something you need to manage and be aware of. Levi does what he can—our mother has severe anxiety, so he's used to it. From what I gather, your employer supports you too. However, you need to be conscious of your situation as well. *You* need to be an active part of your own care. You need to believe you can be whole and safe just as you are."

There was no containing the thickness in Terry's throat, not anymore. "How can I do that when all I feel is panic?"

"With slow, careful steps through counseling. Quite probably with medication as well, but the counseling is important. It's as simple as what we're doing right now. You and I, talking, practicing finding calm spaces for you. Believing you can claim that safety. Will you do that, Terry? Will you try?"

Terry's head was spinning. *Anxiety. Therapy. Medication.* "I need to think about it."

George didn't seem upset by this response at all. "That's fine. I'm in Minneapolis through the holidays." He passed Terry a card. "Call me when you're ready to talk. We can set up sessions, or I can help you find someone else."

Terry pocketed the card and left Levi's house, though once he was home he didn't go up to his apartment. He wandered the streets aimlessly, letting his mind spin out.

It was cold, but not as cold as it had been in Logan. Out of habit, Terry checked the weather app and saw it was almost ten degrees colder there and snowing. He wondered what everyone there was doing, how the preparations for the festival were coming.

He wondered if Evan was okay.

Terry returned to his apartment, the listlessness building in him again now that he'd begun thinking about Evan. He didn't want to break Evan's heart. He hadn't meant to run, either, he just…had. It had been a stupid impulse. *What the hell did you run from this time?* That's what Levi had asked, or yelled, really. *This time.* Because there had been so many times. In so many ways, Terry's entire life had been one distraction after another, mindless flings to keep his panic at bay. Every time, though, the distractions fell apart in his hand, and he had to escape again.

Sometimes we're not afraid of anything. Sometimes we're simply anxious because it's the way we are.

Could it be that easy?

Levi was right, he had to stop this. He kept hurting people. So many lovers, so many friends.

So many excuses why the relationships didn't work out. So many jobs.

So much of his life.

Could he really get that back if he let George help him?

Could he get Evan back?

The panic didn't feel as if it had as tight of a hold on him now, though. His hands trembled as he pulled George's card out of the drawer he'd stowed it in, but it wasn't only fear inside him now.

It was hope.

"Terry." George's voice, so like Levi's, was warm and soothing. "How can I help you?"

The fear lapped at Terry, but he pushed it away, thinking of Evan and everyone in Logan. *I want that back.* "I was hoping I could get an appointment."

He did get one—several, in fact. George made time for him that day and the day after that, and the following week he helped Terry get in to see a psychiatrist, who prescribed him some simple antidepressants and antianxiety medication. Terry was reluctant to take the meds at first, but George insisted he give them a try...and the thing was, they worked. It took about a week before he noticed much, but once they got into his system, Terry felt a lot calmer. He couldn't believe how much different his ability to face his thoughts and even the world was.

"The panic is still there," he told George in a session at Levi's house, "but I feel like I can control it so much easier. I can focus on my work better as well. I'm keeping up with my housekeeping a little more too. It's...it's like a miracle."

"I'm glad it's doing so much for you." George smiled. "Now, I want you to be prepared for things to not always be so full of sunshine. You're still going to struggle. That's why you need to keep up with therapy. We need to find someone for you once I leave the Cities. Have you gone through that list of names?"

"About that." Terry rubbed his thigh self-consciously. "I'm hoping I can be looking for some names in a different city. Before that happens, though, I need to do some repair work. I'm not sure how do that, however."

"This is the boyfriend in Logan?" George raised an eyebrow. "Are you finally ready to talk about that?"

Terry nodded. "I am."

He told George everything, about how he met Evan, how Evan had mistaken him for Kevin, and how Terry had run. He confessed how he'd kept running, how he'd been afraid, and how when he'd had happiness in his hands, he'd ruined it before it could bloom.

"That's the thing I still don't understand." Terry shook his head, staring at his lap. "Why did I do that? Why did I sabotage myself? Why was I so afraid of being happy? Why am I having so much trouble apologizing and going back to him?"

"Sometimes fear is more comfortable than the alternative, because it's familiar. But you've been doing better with that, choosing to face your problems. What do you think it would take to be ready to face Evan?"

Terry didn't know. "I want to apologize to him. Tell him I love him. I don't know how."

"Saying simply that would be enough, you know."

"It doesn't *feel* like enough."

"Then why don't you write out your feelings until you can find what you want to say."

That's what Terry did. He went home and wrote things out in the back of a Moleskine, opened a new one and wrote more, and more, and more, until his thoughts were clear.

"I want to apologize," he told George at their next session, "not only to Evan, but to all the people I've hurt in my relationships. I want to apologize to Levi, who's had to bear so much at work and in my personal life. I want to apologize to my former lovers. To my family. I think it'll make me feel better."

"And Evan, and your friends in Logan?"

"Yes. I want to apologize to the others first, because I want to teach myself that it will be okay. I taught myself that nothing mattered, that I could keep disposing of relationships and people, and I believed each time I destroyed those connections they wouldn't take me back." He shut his eyes and drew a deep breath. "I don't know if Evan will forgive me. I might have ruined things beyond repair. I want to practice with a few other apologies first, so I'm ready if he doesn't want me any longer."

The twinkle in George's eyes gave Terry hope. "I approve of this plan, so long as you don't take too much time before you go to Evan. It's fine to work up your courage to face him, but don't forget there's good odds he's in Logan waiting for you to reach out."

Terry did remember.

On December 11, he started making his apology phone calls. They were rougher than he'd anticipated.

Some of his exes wouldn't talk to him, and even when they did, it was awkward. Talking to his family was almost worse. Despite that, however, it felt good to apologize, to own up to his mistakes.

Every time he said the words *I'm sorry*, he felt so much better.

He wanted to say the words to Evan and the others too.

Terry knew how he wanted to apologize to them now—he'd say the words, but he wanted to *show* Evan and all of Logan how he felt.

He worked like a fiend in his condo, though he was slower than he'd normally be on projects like this. Thanks to his medication, he slept every night. That wasn't a bad thing, because he didn't feel agitated and jittery while he worked. He put all his sorrow, all his regret, all his love into his project. He ordered all his food delivered to him, and he found a courier service that would bring him Glam Doll donuts, which he ate in honor of Evan.

He worked naked too. Evan was right. You could think a lot better that way.

He could see quite clearly what he wanted to create, and he executed his vision. His only trouble was that he kept having to fetch supplies from the office because his were in Logan.

Everything important to him was in Logan. He couldn't wait to go back.

On December 22, he was finally finished.

On December 23, he headed back to Logan.

THE WEEKEND BEFORE Christmas was always the Winter Wonderland festival in Logan.

In the days leading up to the event, Evan kept busy assisting shopkeepers with decoration repair and adjustments, but sometimes he helped serve hot cider and cocoa at Sara's bakery or sold sleigh ride tickets in the booth next to Santa's workshop. There was always something happening, and by rights, Evan should have been easily distracted.

From the moment he woke up until he went to bed, however, Evan missed Terry. For the first time he didn't handle his insomnia by getting up and playing with his models or finding someone to have sex. He lay in the bed that still smelled like Terry, remembering the sound of his voice, the feel of his hair, his skin, his body in Evan's arms.

On Saturday the twenty-third there were no more tickets to sell for the sleigh rides, since they'd been sold out long ago, but Dale did have him selling bags of hot chestnuts from the ticket booth instead, and Charlotte stayed to help him.

"You don't need to babysit me. I'm fine." He smiled at a family as he passed them their bag of chestnuts.

"You're not fine."

Evan wasn't going to argue. He was too tired. "When are you going back to the Cities? I heard Dale tell you everything was good here."

"You think I'm leaving you here alone at Christmas?"

"I'm hardly alone."

"Let me rephrase. You think you're leaving *me* alone at Christmas?" She stole a bag of chestnuts and peered inside. "How *do* you eat these things, anyway?"

"Haven't you been listening to me explain to everyone I pass them out to?"

"Honestly, no."

"They're heated and scored at the top. You crack them open and eat the meat inside. Break them with your hand."

Charlotte did as he said and sniffed the meat. "They smell great. Do they taste good too?"

"I don't know. But if you ask Dale about them, he'll tell you how armies lived on them and why they went extinct in North America."

"I think I'll just eat one." She popped one in her mouth. "Not bad." When she held one out to him and he didn't eat it, she stroked his hair with the back of her hand. "Smile for me someday again, will you, honey?"

Evan shrugged. "I smile."

"Not with your eyes, you don't."

"I miss him, Charlotte. That's not going to go away overnight."

She pursed her lips. "I can't get over that he hasn't called or anything. That *you* haven't called him. You have to fight for your man, Evan."

"I've done all I'm going to do. It's up to him now."

"What if he never does anything?"

"Then I have to move on." Evan swallowed against the lump in his throat and looked out over the Logan square, a thin smile managing to make its way onto his lips. "But I have friends here, lots of them, and I have the town too. I have somewhere I belong, and people I belong with."

"So you're really going to stay?"

"No matter what."

She shook her head, but she smiled too. "You've come a long way, Evan. Who knew Christmas Town would be the place you finally found yourself?"

"Dale keeps saying Logan is a magical place. I think I understand why now."

"*Evan!*"

He blinked and leaned out of the hut. "Linda Kay?"

She pushed her way through the crowd, out of breath, holding the hand of a blushing man who also had Down's syndrome. "Evan. Evan, you have to come and see this, because you are *not* going to believe it."

Evan glanced at Charlotte, but she just shooed him. "Well, go on and see. I'll hold down the chestnut fort."

Evan tugged on his mittens and pulled up his hood as he followed Linda Kay through the crush and down the street. "What's going on?"

"There's this crazy guy in front of the café, and he put up a rogue light display. I was going to tell him to take it down, but Kyle said to get you instead. I guess he wants you to take him down since he's ruining your design."

Evan didn't want to take anybody down. "What do you mean, a crazy guy? And why does he have a light display?"

"I don't know who it is, but he's got a big beard. Looks like a hippie."

Evan's heart skipped a beat. "A brown beard, and it's really messy?"

"Yes. He's wearing something strange too."

Don't get your hopes up. There's no real reason that would be him, and anyway, even if it was, wouldn't he come to see you? Why would he create a disturbance in front of the café?

Yet Evan couldn't turn off the hope that it was Terry he was hurrying down Main Street to see. When he rounded the corner and parted the crowd by the Christmas trees in front of the café, he held his breath as he saw a man in a red flannel jacket and a stocking cap crouched beside…well, a rogue light display. Linda Kay was right. It was quite a mess.

Evan stepped forward, heart beating too quickly. "Excuse me, sir, but what—?"

He caught his breath as the man rose and turned

around.

Kevin. It was Kevin.

It was Terry, as Kevin. He was even wearing the shirt with his name on it. A different one, but there was no mistaking the name on the lapel.

Terry tugged at his stocking cap self-consciously. "Hi."

Evan could barely breathe. "H-hi."

Terry rubbed at his cheek with reddened fingers, then gestured at his display. "You got here before I was finished."

Paul waved a hand at him. "Don't worry. We've got this. You say your piece."

Evan didn't understand what Paul and Arthur were working on, or why Terry was here. He was simply glad Terry had come back. "Please tell me what you have to say."

While Arthur and Paul continued to shift wire and pieces of foam, Terry stood in front of the strange sculpture and faced Evan.

Taking a deep breath, Terry folded his hands in front of himself and bowed his head. "I'm sorry."

Evan blinked, then let out a breath, beginning to hope this might be going the way he wanted it to. "It's okay."

"No, it isn't. I broke my promise to you. I ran out, just like I said I wouldn't, the way I always do. I wouldn't admit my feelings to you, or to myself. I hurt you. I'm very sorry."

Terry looked so miserable. He lifted his head and met Evan's gaze. "I've been working on a lot of things, and I've gotten some help. I'm going to keep getting help. I'm sorry I wrecked things between us. I didn't mean to. I didn't *want* to."

Evan ached for Terry. "You didn't wreck anything."

"I *did*, and I'm sorry. I want to fix it if I can. If you can tell me how, I will."

Now Evan smiled. "But you already did. All you had to do was show up."

Terry stared at him blankly. "That's it?"

Evan nodded. "That's it." He stepped forward and touched Terry's hair, stroked his beard. "I told you I love you, Terry."

The last of Terry's sorrow bled away, his soft smile making something warm begin to unfurl inside Evan. "I don't know why you want someone as screwed up as I am—"

"I do," Evan said quickly.

"—but I'm grateful you do. Because I want you too. I'm sorry I hurt you, and I'll try not to do it again, but I probably will. I'll apologize again then too. I want to be with you, though, Evan. I want to stay wherever it is you want to stay, and I want to work with you on whatever project you're working on. Also, for the record, while we work, I'm fine with whatever office attire you declare appropriate."

Evan laughed, and he almost had to wipe away a

tear. "I knew you'd come around to my way of thinking."

"I have. In every way. Also, there's something I forgot to tell you. You've told me so many times, and I've been an idiot and haven't told you back. So I'm telling you now." He glanced over his shoulder, and Arthur gave him a thumbs-up.

Paul flipped a switch, and the ugly mess of wires and bulbs and foam transformed into a beautiful display of lights, and in the middle, white letters spelled, *I love you, Evan.*

Evan covered his mouth with his hands, and this time he couldn't stop the tears.

Terry came up to him and kissed his cheek, gently displacing his hands to kiss his mouth. "I love you, Evan. Can you forgive me?"

"I forgave you the second I saw you'd come back." Evan leaned into him, staring over his shoulder at the display. It was very pretty, but... "This really needs some design work."

"I know. I did my best, but I've gotten so used to leaning on you. You've ruined me."

Smiling, Evan leaned into Terry's ear and whispered, "How about I take you back to the cabin and ruin you a little more?"

With a sigh like a man coming home, Terry wrapped his arms around Evan's body and kissed his neck. "I thought you'd never ask."

Not ready to leave Logan?

Many characters you met here have stories.

The Minnesota Christmas Series

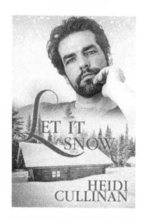

Let It Snow (*also available in German*)

Frankie's malfunctioning GPS sent him to Logan, and a blizzard ensures he won't be leaving anytime soon.

Being rescued by three sexy lumberjacks is a nice fantasy, but the biggest of the bears seems cranky…and ready to gobble Frankie right up. Once a high-powered lawyer, Marcus has no interest in a sassy city twink who might as well have stepped directly out of his past. Yet as the snow falls, the deeper they fall in love. Though all they want for Christmas is each other, the gift of forever may be too much to ask.

Featured Characters: Frankie, Marcus, Arthur, Paul

Sleigh Ride (*also available in German*)

Arthur wants nothing to do with romance, and he certainly doesn't want to play Santa in his mother's library fundraising scheme. He knows full well she really wants to hook him up with the town's lanky, prissy librarian. It's clear Gabriel doesn't want him, either—as a Santa, as a boyfriend, as anyone at all. As their arguments strike sparks, two men who insist they don't date wind up doing an awful lot of dating. The sleigh they're trying not to board could jingle them all the way to happily ever after.

Featured Characters: Arthur, Gabriel, Frankie, Marcus, Paul, Corrina

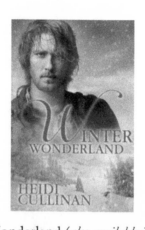

Winter Wonderland (*also available in German*)

Paul can't find a gay man within a fifty-mile radius who wants more than casual sex. No one, that is, except too-young, too-twinky Kyle, who sends him suggestive texts and leaves X-rated snow sculptures on his front porch. Kyle's loved Paul since forever, and this Christmas, since they're both working on the Winter Wonderland festival, he might finally get his chance for a holiday romance. But Paul comes with baggage. When his family's anti-LGBT crusade spills beyond managing Paul's love life, Kyle and Paul must fight for *everyone's* happily ever after, including their own.

Featured Characters: Paul, Kyle, Arthur, Gabriel, Frankie, Marcus, Linda Kay, Dale

Santa Baby

A one-night threesome becomes more when Dale Davidson joins already coupled Arthur Anderson and Gabriel Higgins, which is complicated enough in their sleepy northern Minnesota town. When Dale's abusive ex draws him into a dark web, the whole community must put aside their preconceptions of relationships, come together, and help bring their Santa home.

Featured Characters: Dale, Gabriel, Arthur, Paul, Kyle, Marcus, Frankie, Corrina

More adventures in Logan, Minnesota, coming soon

About the Author

Heidi Cullinan has always enjoyed a good love story, provided it has a happy ending. Proud to be from the first Midwestern state with full marriage equality, Heidi is a vocal advocate for LGBT rights. She writes positive-outcome romances for LGBT characters struggling against insurmountable odds because she believes there's no such thing as too much happy ever after. When Heidi isn't writing, she enjoys cooking, reading, playing with her cats, and watching anime, with or without her family. Find out more about Heidi at heidicullinan.com.

Did you enjoy this book?

If you did, please consider leaving a review online or recommending it to a friend. There's absolutely nothing that helps an author more than a reader's enthusiasm. Your word of mouth is greatly appreciated and helps me sell more books, which helps me write more books.

Other books by Heidi Cullinan

There's a lot happening with my books right now! Sign up for my release-announcement-only newsletter on my website to be sure you don't miss a single release or rerelease.

www.heidicullinan.com/newssignup

Want the inside scoop on upcoming releases, automatic delivery of all my titles in your preferred format, with option for signed paperbacks shipped worldwide? Consider joining my Patreon.

www.patreon.com/heidicullinan

THE ROOSEVELT SERIES
Carry the Ocean (also available in French)
Shelter the Sea
Unleash the Earth (coming soon)
Shatter the Sky (coming soon)

LOVE LESSONS SERIES
Love Lessons (also available in German, French coming soon)
Frozen Heart
Fever Pitch (also available in German)
Lonely Hearts (also available in German)
Short Stay
Rebel Heart (coming soon)

THE DANCING SERIES
Dance With Me (also available in French, Italian coming soon)
Enjoy the Dance
Burn the Floor (coming soon)

THE SPECIAL DELIVERY SERIES
Special Delivery
Hooch and Cake
Double Blind
The Twelve Days of Randy
Tough Love

CLOCKWORK LOVE SERIES
Clockwork Heart
Clockwork Pirate (coming soon)
Clockwork Princess (coming soon)

TUCKER SPRINGS SERIES
Second Hand (written with Marie Sexton) (available in French)
Dirty Laundry (available in French)
(more titles in this series *by other authors)*

SINGLE TITLES
Antisocial
Nowhere Ranch (available in Italian)
Family Man (written with Marie Sexton)
A Private Gentleman
The Devil Will Do
Hero
Miles and the Magic Flute

NONFICTION

Your A Game: Winning Promo for Genre Fiction
(written with Damon Suede)

*Many titles are also available in audio and more are in
production. Check the listings wherever you purchase audiobooks
to see which titles are available.*

CPSIA information can be obtained
at www.ICGtesting.com
Printed in the USA
BVHW030340300420
578924BV00001B/72

9 781945 116285